With his toe Hanmer draws a quick line across the ground. The soil splits as if unzipped and Hanmer pulls up a gray tuber, bulging and heavy. He puts it to his lips and sucks at it a moment. Then he hands it to Clay, who stares, uncertain. Is this a test? 'Eat,' Hanmer says. 'It's permitted.' Though his hunger is gone, Clay sucks at the tuber. Some drops of a gritty juice enter his mouth. Instantly flames shoot through his skull and his soul withers.

'What world is this?'

'The world. Our world.'

'My world?'

'It was. It can be.'

'What era is this?'

'A good one.'

'Am I dead?'

Hanmer chuckles. 'Death is dead.'

'How did I get here?'

'Caught in the time-flux like the rest.'

'Swept into my own future? How far into the future?'

'Does it matter?' Hanmer asks, looking bored.

ROBERT SILVERBERG

Son of Man

VGSF

VGSF is an imprint of Victor Gollancz Ltd
14 Henrietta Street, London WC2E 8QJ

First published in Great Britain 1979
by Panther Books, Granada Publishing Limited.

First VGSF edition 1991

A catalogue record for this book is
available from the British Library

ISBN 0-575-04688-0

Printed and bound in Great Britain
by Cox & Wyman Ltd, Reading

for
Bill Rotsler
Paul Turner

fellow voyagers

Immediately after the tribulation of those days shall the sun be darkened, and the moon shall not give her light, and the stars shall fall from heaven, and the powers of the heavens shall be shaken:

And then shall appear the sign of the Son of man in heaven: and then shall all the tribes of the earth mourn, and they shall see the Son of man coming in the clouds of heaven with power and great glory.

– Matthew 24: 29–30

Shrink not from blasphemy – 'twill pass for wit.
– Byron, *English Bards and Scotch Reviewers*

We know what we are, but know not what we may be.
– *Hamlet*, IV, v, 43

I

He wakes. Beneath him the black earth is cool and moist. He lies on his back in a field of scarlet grass; a soft gust of wind comes by, ruffling the blades, and they melt into a stream of blood. The sky is iron-blue, an intensely transparent color that briefly sets up a desperate clamor in his skull. He finds the sun: low in the heavens, larger than it ought to be, looking somewhat pale and vulnerable, perhaps flattened at top and bottom. Pearly mists rise from the land and swirl sunward, making vortices of blue and green and red lacings as they climb. A cushion of silence presses against him. He feels lost. He sees no cities, no scars of man's presence anywhere in this meadow, on those hills, beyond that valley. Slowly he lifts himself to his feet and stands facing the sun.

His body is bare. He touches it, discovering his skin. With quiet curiosity he examines his hand, spread out below his chin against the dark hairy mat on his chest. How strange the fingers are: ridged at the joints, lightly tufted with hair on the flat places, two knuckles skinned a bit, the nails in need of a trimming. It is as though he has never seen his hand before. He lets the hand slip slowly down his body, pausing to tap the fingertips into the drum of hard muscle at his belly, then to study the faint puckered line of his appendectomy. The hand goes lower and he finds his genitals. Frowning, he cups his testicles, lifting them slightly, perhaps weighing them. He touches his penis, first the shaft, then the rim of soft pink flesh at the head, finally the head itself. It seems odd to have such an intricate device attached to his body. He inspects his legs. There is a broad bruise, purple and yellow, on his left thigh. Hair grows on his insteps. His toes are unfamiliar to him. He wriggles them. He digs them into the soil. He flexes his knees. He shrugs his shoulders. He plants his feet far apart. He makes water. He looks straight at the sun, and it is a surprisingly long

7

time before his eyes begin to throb. When he looks away, he sees the sun behind his eyeballs, embedded in the front of his brain, and he feels less lonely for having it in there.

'Hello!' he calls. 'Hey! You! Me! Us! Who?'

Where is Wichita? Where is Toronto? Where is Dubuque? Where is Syosset? Where is São Paulo? Where is La Jolla? Where is Bridgeport? Where is McMurdo Sound? Where is Ellenville? Where is Mankato? Where is Morpeth? Where is Georgetown? Where is St Louis? Where is Mobile? Where is Walla Walla? Where is Galveston? Where is Brooklyn? Where is Copenhagen?

'Hello? Hey? You? Me? Us? Who!'

To his left are five rounded hills covered by black glossy vegetation. To his right the field of scarlet grass expands into a choking plain that streams toward the horizon. In front of him the ground dips gently to form a valley that is something more than a ravine but something less than a canyon. He recognizes no trees. Their shapes are unfamiliar; many have swollen, greasy brown trunks, limbless and plump, from which cascades of fleshy leaves dangle like festoons of shiny white and yellow beads. Behind him, smothered in long and inexplicable shadows, lies a maze of formless hummocks and pits, over which grow rank, sandy-colored little plants with woody stems.

He goes forward into the valley.

Now he sees his first sign of animal life. Out of a stubby tree he startles a sort of bird that catapults straight into the air, hovers, circles back more calmly to take stock of him. They survey one another. The bird is hawk-sized, dark-bodied, with a pinched ungenerous face, cool green eyes, thin lips closely clamped. Its fire-hued wings are ribbed and gauzy and from its hindquarters there trails a wedge-shaped filmy tail, edged with pink ribbony filaments streaming in the wind. Passing over him, the bird dungs him with a dozen shining green pellets that land artfully to enclose him in a geometrical figure. Hesitantly he stoops to touch the nearest pellet. It sizzles; he hears it hissing; but when he puts his finger to it he feels neither texture nor warmth. He flicks it aside. The bird caws at him.

'I am Hanmer's,' says the bird.

'Why are you hostile? How have I harmed you?'

'I am not hostile. I take no responsibilities. I place no blames.'

'You bombed me.'

'It established a relationship,' says the bird, and flies off. 'I am Hanmer's,' it calls again, from a distance. He studies the creature until it is gone. The sun slowly moves toward the hills. The sky seems slick and lacquered now. His tongue is papery. He continues toward the valley. He becomes aware that a creek flows through the valley, green water, burnished sun-shimmered surface, trembling shrubs sprouting on the bank. He goes to it, thinking that the sharp sensation of water against his skin will awaken him, for now he is weary of this dream; it has somehow taken on an ugly and implausible tone.

He kneels beside the creek. It is unexpectedly deep. Within its rushing crystal depths he sees fishes, swept tempestuously along, driven by an irresistible current. They are slender creatures with large, wistful gray eyes, deep-cut toothy mouths, sleek flattened fins. Victims. He smiles at them. Cautiously he puts his left arm into the flow up to the elbow. The moment of contact is electric and stunning. He pulls his arm back and claps his hands over his face, and weeps as an uncontrollable surge of fiery sadness cuts through him. He mourns man and all his works. In his mind there churns an image of the world of man in gaudy complexity: buildings and vehicles and roads and shops and lawns and oily puddles and crumpled papers and blinking signs. He sees men and women in close-fitting clothing, with tight shoes and fabric binding their breasts and loins. That world is lost and he mourns it. He hears the roar of rockets and the screech of brakes. He hears the throb of music. He admires sunlight's glint on lofty windows. He mourns. Cold tears sting his cheeks and trickle across his lips. Are the old blossoms gone? Are the old weeds gone? Are the old cities gone? Friends and family? Stress and strain? Cathedral bells, the redness of wine on the tongue, candles, turnips, cats, cactus? With a little defeated sigh he tumbles forward and lets himself fall into the creek. He is carried swiftly downstream.

For some minutes he refuses to offer resistance. Then,

quickly, he extends his body and seizes a submerged boulder. Clinging to it, he crawls downward until his face rests just above the pebbled bottom of the stream, and he hangs there a long moment, acclimating himself to his altered surroundings. When his breath is finally exhausted he erupts surfaceward and scrambles onto the bank. He lies face-down a short while. He stands. He touches himself.

The tingling waters have changed him slightly. His body hair is gone and his skin is smooth and pale and new, like the hide of an infant whale. His left thigh no longer is bruised. His knuckles are whole. He cannot find the scar of his appendectomy. His penis looks strange to him, and after a moment's contemplation he realizes in awe that he has been decircumcised. Hastily he pushes a thumb into his navel; it is still there. He laughs. Now he realizes that night has come while he was in the water. The sun's last limb slips from view, and instantly darkness spreads out over the sky. There is no moon. The stars pop into view, announcing themselves with high pinging tones, singing, I am blue, I am red, I am golden, I am white. Where is Orion? Where is the Dipper? Where is the Goat?

The shrubs of the valley emit a coarse leathery glow. The soil stirs and quivers and splits at the surface, and from a thousand tiny craters glide nightcrawling creatures, long and liquid and silvery, emerging from hidden burrows and slithering amiably toward the meadow. They part as they approach him, leaving him as an island in the midst of their gleaming myriads. He hears furry whispering sounds from them but detects no meaning.

There is a feathery flap and two flying creatures descend, unlike the other one; these have heavy, drooping, baggy black bodies ringed by tufts of coarse fur, and angular wings mounted on a jutting knobby breastbone. They are as big as geese. Methodically they pursue the nightcrawlers, sucking them up in flexible puckering bills and shortly excreting them, apparently unharmed. Their appetites are insatiable. He draws back, offended, when they give him a sour glare.

Something bulky and dark clatters across the stream and

disappears before he can see it properly. From the sky comes raucous laughter. The scent of elegant creamy flowers drifts from the creek, decays into saltiness, and departs. The air grows chill. He huddles. A light rain comes. He studies the troublesome constellations and finds them altogether strange. In the distance music unfolds from the night. The tones swell and diminish and increase again in an easy trembling throb, and he finds he can seize them and shape melodies to suit himself: he carves a lively tootling horn-call, a dirge, a minuet. Small animals scramble by. Have toads perished? Are mice extinct? Where are lemurs? Where are moles? Yet he knows he can come to love these new beasts. The boundless fertility of evolution, revealing itself to him in bright bursts of abundance, makes him joyful, and he turns the music into a hymn of praise. Whatever is, is good. Out of the plasticity of the raw tones he manufactures the drums and trumpets of a Te Deum. Against this in sudden bleak counterpoint come thumping footsteps, and he is no longer alone, for three large creatures emerge and approach. The dream is somber now. What things are these, so bestial, so foul, so malevolent? Upright, bipedal, great splayed toes, huge shaggy hams, sagging bellies, massive chests. Taller than he is. The stink of decay precedes them. Cruel faces, nevertheless almost human, glistening eyes, hooked noses, wide gummy mouths, thin gray beards sticky with muck. They shuffle awkwardly along, knees flexed, bodies canted forward at the waist, colossal upright goats modeled loosely after men. Wherever they tread, bristly weeds spring up instantly, giving off fishy odors. Their skins are paperwhite and wrinkled, hanging loosely from the powerful muscles and the thick underflesh; little tufted blisters pockmark them everywhere. As they clump forward they nod, snort, snuffle, and exchange blurred murmured comments. They pay no attention to him. He watches them pass by. What are these dismal things? He fears that they are the supreme race of the era, the dominant species, the successors to man, perhaps even the descendants of man, and the thought so squeezes and grinds him that he drops to the ground, rolling over and over in agony, crushing the gliding nightcrawlers that still stream past. He hammers his palms against the earth. He clutches the malign weeds that have newly sprouted, and rips them from the soil. He presses his forehead against a flat rock. He vomits, yielding nothing. He clasps his hands in terror to his loins. Have these beings inherited the world? He imagines a congregation of them kneeling on their own turds. He visualizes them grunting outside the Taj Mahal in the full moon. He sees them clambering over the Pyramids, dropping spittle on Raphaels and Veroneses, fracturing Mozart with their snorts and belches. He sobs. He bites the earth. He prays for morning. In his anguish his sex stiffens, and he seizes it, and, gasping, spills his seed. He lies on his back and searches for the moon, but there is still no moon, and the stars are unfamiliar. The music returns. He has lost the power to shape it. He hears the clang and clatter of metal rods and the shriek of strained membranes. Desperately, grimly, he sings against it, shouting into the darkness, covering the raucous noise with a lamination of ordered sound, and in this way he passes the night, sleepless, uncomforted.

2

Streaks of arriving light stain the sky. The darkness is vanquished by pink and gray and blue. He stretches and greets the morning, finding himself hungry and thirsty. Going down to the creek, he bends into it, splashes cold water in his face, scrubs his eyes and teeth, and, embarrassed, wipes the dried sticky sperm from his thighs. Then he gulps until his thirst is gone. Food? He reaches down and, with a deftness that astonishes him, plucks a thrashing fish from the creek. Its smooth sides are deep blue, with red filaments plainly pulsing within. Raw? Well, yes, how else? But at least not alive. He will pound its head on a rock first.

'No, please. Don't do that,' a soft voice says.

He is prepared to believe that the fish is begging for its life.

But a purple shadow falls on him; he is not alone. Turning, he sees a slim, slight figure behind him. The source of the voice. 'I am Hanmer,' says the newcomer. 'The fish – please – throw it back. It isn't necessary.' A gentle smile. Is that a smile? Is that a mouth? He feels it is best to obey Hanmer. He flings the fish into the water. With a derisive swish of its tail it shoots away. He turns again to Hanmer and says, 'I didn't want to eat it. But I'm very hungry, and I'm lost.'

'Give me your hunger,' says Hanmer.

Hanmer is not human, but the kinship is apparent. He is as big as a tall boy, and his body, though slender, does not seem fragile. His head is large but his neck is sturdy and his shoulders are wide. There is no hair anywhere on him. His skin is golden-green and has the seamless, durable quality of a supple plastic. His eyes are scarlet globes behind quick transparent lids. His nose is merely a ridge; his nostrils are latched slits; his mouth is a thin-lipped horizontal slash that does not open wide enough to reveal its interior. He has a great many fingers and not many toes. His arms and legs are jointed at elbows and knees, but the joints appear to be universal ones, giving him immense freedom of motion. Hanmer's sex is a puzzle. Something about his bearing seems indisputably male, and he has no breasts nor any other visible feminine characteristics. But where a male member might be, he has only a curious inward-folding vertical pocket, vaguely like the vaginal slit but not really comparable. Beneath, instead of two dangling balls, there is a single small, firm, round swelling, possibly equivalent to the scrotum, as if it had remained evolution's goal to keep the gonads outside the body cavity but a more efficient container for them had been designed. There can be little doubt that Hanmer's ancestors, in some remote era, were men. But can he be called a man also? Son of man, perhaps. 'Come to me,' Hanmer says. He stretches out his hands. There are delicate webs between the fingers. 'How are you called, stranger?'

It is necessary to think a moment. 'I was Clay,' he tells Hanmer. The sound of his name spills to the ground and bounces. Clay. Clay. I was Clay. Clay I was when I was Clay. Hanmer looks pleased. 'Come, then, Clay,' he says gently. 'I'll take your hunger.' Hesitantly Clay gives his hands to Hanmer. He is drawn close. Their bodies touch. Clay feels needles in his eyes and black fluid spurting into his veins. He becomes fiercely conscious of the maze of red tubes in his belly. He can hear the ticking of his glands. In a moment Hanmer releases him and he is wholly without hunger; it is incomprehensible to him that he could have considered devouring a fish only moments ago. Hanmer laughs. 'Is it better now?'

'Better. Much.'

With his toe Hanmer draws a quick line across the ground. The soil splits as if unzipped and Hanmer pulls up a gray tuber, bulging and heavy. He puts it to his lips and sucks at it a moment. Then he hands it to Clay, who stares, uncertain. Is this a test? 'Eat,' Hanmer says. 'It's permitted.' Though his hunger is gone, Clay sucks at the tuber. Some drops of a gritty juice enter his mouth. Instantly flames shoot through his skull and his soul withers. Hanmer darts forward, catching him just before he falls, and embraces him again; Clay feels the effects of the juice instantly ebbing. 'Forgive me,' says Hanmer. 'I didn't realize. You must be terribly early.'

'What?'

'One of the earliest, I suppose. Caught in the time-flux like the rest. We love you. We bid you be welcome. Do we seem fearfully strange? Are you lonely? Do you grieve? Will you teach us things? Will you give yourself to us? Will you delight us?'

'What world is this?'

'The world. Our world.'

'My world?'

'It was. It can be.'

'What era is this?'

'A good one.'

'Am I dead?'

Hanmer chuckles. 'Death is dead.'

'How did I get here?'

'Caught in the time-flux like the rest.'

'Swept into my own future? How far into the future?'

'Does it matter?' Hanmer asks, looking bored. 'Come, Clay,

dissolve with me, and let's begin our travels.' He reaches for Clay's hand again. Clay shrinks back. 'Wait,' he murmurs. The morning is quite bright now. The sky is that painful blue again; the sun is a gong. He shivers. He puts his face close to Hanmer's and says, 'Are there any others like me here?'

'No.'

'Are you human?'

'Of course.'

'But changed by time?'

'Oh, no,' says Hanmer. '*You* are changed by time. I live here. You visit us.'

'I speak of evolution.'

Hanmer pouts. 'May we dissolve now? We have so much to see—'

Clay tugs at a tuft of the foul weeds of the night before. 'At least tell me about these. Three creatures came by, and these grew where—'

'Yes.'

'What were they? Visitors from another planet?'

'Humans,' sighs Hanmer.

'Those also? Different forms?'

'Before us. After you. Caught in the time-flux, all.'

'How could we have evolved into *them*? Not even in a billion years would humanity change so greatly. And then change back? You're closer to me than they are. Where's the pattern? Where's the track? Hanmer, I can't understand!'

'Wait until you see the others,' says Hanmer, and begins to dissolve. A pale gray cloud springs from his skin and envelops him, and within it he grows misty, fading placidly away. Bright orange sparks shoot through the cloud. Hanmer, still visible, appears ecstatic. Clay is able to see a rigid fleshy tube slide out of the pocket at Hanmer's loins: yes, he is male after all, showing his sex in this moment of pleasure. 'You said you'd take me!' Clay cries. Hanmer nods and smiles. The internal structure of his body is apparent now, a network of nerves and veins, illuminated by some inner fire and glowing red and green and yellow. The cloud expands and suddenly Clay too is within it. There is a sweet hissing sound: his own tissues and fibers boiling away. Hanmer has vanished. Clay spins, extends, attenuates; he perceives his own throbbing organs, an exquisite mixture of textures and tones, this one green and oily, that one red and sticky, here a gray spongy mass, there a coil of dark blue, everything so ripe, so lush, in the last moments before dissolution. A sense of adventure and excitement possesses him. He is drifting upward and outward, flowing over the face of the land, taking on infinite size and surrendering all mass; he covers acres now, whole counties, entire realms. Hanmer is beside him. They expand together. Sunlight strikes him along the vast upper surface of his new body, making molecules dance and leap in prickly gaiety, pinging and popping as they bounce around. Clay is aware of the shuttling electrons climbing the energy ladder. Pip! Pop! Peep! He soars. He glides. He visualizes himself as a great gray carpet skimming through the air. Instead of a tasseled fringe he has a hundred eyes, and in the center of everything the hard knotted mass of the brain glows and hums and directs.

He sees last night's scenes: the valley, the meadow, the hills, the creek. Then the field of vision changes as they go higher, and he takes in a tumbled, scarred countryside of rivers and cliffs, of eroded teeth jutting from the earth, of gulfs, of lakes, of headlands. Figures move below. Here are the three goaty ones, farting and mumbling beneath a sprawling rubbery tree. Here are six more of Hanmer's kind, merrily coupling at the edge of a golden pond. Here are nightcrawlers slumbering in the soil. Here is a savage thing with monstrous choppers in place of teeth. Here is something buried shoulders-deep in the ground, radiating solemn, passionate thoughts. Here comes a platoon of winged creatures, birds or bats or even reptiles, flying in tight formation, darkening the sky, now catching an up-draft, piercing Clay's body from underside to top like a million stinging bullets and vanishing in the cloudless heights. Here are saturnine intelligences browsing in the mud of dark pools. Here are scattered blocks of stone, perhaps ancient ruins. Clay sees no whole buildings. He sees no roads. The world bears no human imprint of consequence. It is springtime everywhere; things bulge with life. Hanmer, billowing like a stormcloud, laughs and cries out, 'Yes! You accept it!' Clay accepts it.

He tests his body. He makes it fluoresce and sees violet shadows dance below him. He creates steely ribs and an ivory backbone. He weaves a new nervous system out of bristles of vacuum. He invents an organ sensitive to colors beyond ultraviolet, and happily topples off the spectrum's deep end. He becomes a vast sexual organ and rapes the stratosphere, leaving contrails of luminous semen. And Hanmer, beside him constantly, calls out, 'Yes,' and 'Yes,' and 'Yes' again. Clay now covers several continents. He accelerates his pace, seeking his own termination, and after some brief effort finds it and links with himself so that he now is a cloudy serpent encircling the world. 'See?' Hanmer cries. 'It is your world, is it not? The familiar planet?' But Clay is not sure. The continents have shifted. He sees what he believes to be the Americas, but they have undergone changes, for the tail of South America is gone and so is the Isthmus of Panama, and west of what should have been Chile is an enormous cancerous extension, possibly a displaced Antarctica. Oceans drown both poles. Coastlines are new. He cannot find Europe. A tremendous inland sea winks up out of what he suspects is Asia; a sunblink glances off it, transforming it into a giant mocking eye. Weeping, he scatters gobbets of lava along the equator. A domed shield bulges serenely where Africa might have been. A chain of radiant islands glitters across thousands of miles of altered ocean. Now he is frightened. He thinks of Athens, Cairo, Tangier, Melbourne, Poughkeepsie, Istanbul, and Stockholm. In his grief he grows chilled, and, freezing, splits into a shower of icy particles, which small buzzing insects instantly seek, darting up from swamps and marshes; they begin to gobble him, but Hanmer cries out to them, sending them stunned to the ground, and then Clay feels himself being collected and restored. 'What happened?' Hanmer asks, and Clay replies, 'I remembered.' 'Don't,' says Hanmer. Again they soar. They spin and leap and break through into the realm of darkness girdling the world, so that the planet itself is nothing more than a little spherical impurity in the soft fluttering mantle of his body. He watches it turning. So slowly! Has the day lengthened? Is this my world at all? Hanmer nudges him and they transform themselves into rivers of energy millions of miles long and go boiling out into space. He is inflamed with tenderness, love, the hunger for union with the cosmos. 'Our neighbor worlds,' says Hanmer. 'Our friends. See?' Clay sees. He knows now that he has not been whisked to a planet of some other star. This is plainly Venus, this cloudy ball here. And this red pocked thing is Mars, although he is puzzled by the green weedy sea that laps the rusty plains. He cannot find Mercury. Again and again he slides into that inner orbit, hunting for the tiny rolling globe, but it is not there. Has it fallen into the sun? He dares not ask, for fear that Hanmer will say that it has. Clay cannot bear to lose a planet now. 'Come,' says Hanmer. 'Outward.'

The asteroids have vanished. A wise move: who needs such debris? But Jupiter is there, wondrously unchanged, even to the Great Red Spot. Clay exults. The bands of color also remain, bright stripes of rich yellow, brown, and orange, separated by darker streaks. 'Yes?' Clay asks, and Hanmer says it can be done, so they plunge planetward, swirling and floating in Jupiter's atmosphere. Foggy crystals engulf them. Their attenuated bodies entwine with molecules of ammonia and methane. Down they go, down, to cliffs of ice rising above bleak greasy seas, to turbulent geysers and boiling lakes. Clay spreads himself flat across a snowy continent and lies panting, loving the sensuous impact of the atmosphere's many tons upon his back. He becomes a mallet and probes the great planet's craggy core, striking it happily, with a bong and a bong and a bong and a whong, and waves of sound rise up in jagged creamy blurts. He spends himself in ecstasy. But then, immediately afterward, there is compensating loss: brilliant Saturn is ringless. 'An accident,' Hanmer confesses. 'An error. It was long ago.' Clay will not be consoled. He threatens to fracture again and patter down to Saturn's tawny surface in a cloud of snowflakes. Hanmer, sympathetic, hoops himself and surrounds the planet, whirling, gliding up and down the spectrum, flashing gilded lights, turning now edge-on, now at a sumptuous angle. 'No,' Clay says. 'I'm grateful, but it won't work,' and on they go toward Uranus, toward Neptune, toward frosty Pluto. 'It was not our doing,' Hanmer insists. 'But we never realized anyone would care so much.' Pluto is a bore. Hovering, Clay watches five of Hanmer's cousins trekking across a black wasteland, going from nowhere to nowhere. He looks questioningly outward. Procyon? Rigel? Betelgeuse? 'Another time,' Hanmer murmurs.

They return to Earth.

Like matched jewels they plummet through the atmosphere. They land. He is in his mortal body again. He lies in a manicured field of short fleshy blue-green plants; above him looms a giant triangular monolith, forked at the peak, and through the fork races a bubbling river that hurtles hundreds or perhaps thousands of feet down the huge slab's onyx face into a neatly circular basin. He is trembling. His journey has drained him. When he can, he sits up, presses his palms to his cheeks, draws some deep breaths, blinks. The worlds swing in stubborn circles inside his skull. His joy over Jupiter wars with the grief for Saturn's rings. And Mercury. And the beloved old continents, the friendly map. Stabbed by time's needles. The air is mild and transparent, and he hears distant music. Hanmer stands at the edge of the basin, contemplating the waterfall.

Or is it Hanmer? When he turns, Clay sees differences. On the smooth waxen chest two breasts have emerged. They are small, like those of a girl newly come into her womanhood, but beyond any question they are female. Tiny pink nipples tip them. Hanmer's hips have widened. The vertical pocket at the base of the belly has narrowed to a slit, of which only the upper cleft is visible. The scrotal hemisphere below has vanished. This is not Hanmer. This is a woman of Hanmer's species.

'I am Hanmer,' she says to Clay.

'Hanmer was male.'

'Hanmer is male. I am Hanmer.' She walks toward Clay. Her stride is not Hanmer's: in place of his free-wheeling loose-jointed jauntiness there is a more restrained motion, equally fluid but not as flexible. She says, 'My body has changed, but I am Hanmer. I love you. May we celebrate our journey together? It is the custom.'

'Is the other Hanmer gone forever?'

'Nothing goes forever. Everything returns.'

Mercury. Saturn's rings. Istanbul. Rome.

Clay freezes. He is silent for a million years.

'Will you celebrate with me?'

'How?'

'A joining of bodies.'

'Sex,' Clay says. 'It's not obsolete, then?'

Hanmer laughs prettily. She eases herself in one quick sprawl to the ground. The fleshy plants sigh and quiver and sway. Eyelets open in their tips and spurts of jeweled fluid leap into the air. A balmy fragrance spreads. An aphrodisiac: Clay is abruptly aware of the rigidity of his member. Hanmer flexes her knees. She parts her thighs and he studies the waiting gate between. 'Yes,' she whispers. Lost in amazement, he covers her body with his. His hands slip down to grasp her cool flat silken buttocks. Hanmer is flushed; her transparent eyelids have gone milky, so that the scarlet glow of her eyes is dimmed; when he slides a hand up and caresses her breasts, he feels the nipples hardening, and he is dazed with wonder at the changelessness of certain things. Mankind tours the solar system in a moment, birds talk, plants collaborate in human pleasures, the continents are jumbled, the universe is a storm of marvelous colors and dazzling scents; and yet in all the gold and crimson and purple miracle of this altered world, pricks still cry out for cunts and cunts cry out for pricks. It does not seem fitting. Yet with a small smothered cry he goes into her and begins to move, a swift piston in the moist chamber, and it is so unstrange to him that he briefly loses the sense of loss that had been with him since his awakening. He comes with such haste that it shatters him, but she merely sings a fragile series of semitones and he uncomes just as quickly, and is disembarrassed, and they continue. She offers him a spasm of disciplined intensity. Her swivel-kneed legs twine about him. Her pelvis churns. She gasps. She whispers. She chants. He chooses his moment and unleashes his lightning a second time, touching off a storm of sensation in her, during which the texture of her skin undergoes a series of changes, becoming now rough and bristly, now liquid-smooth, now stiffened into high-crested waves, at last returning to its original state. In the moment after final ecstasy he remembers the moon. The moon! Where was it when he and Hanmer sped through the cosmos? There is no moon. The moon is no more. How could he have forgotten to look for the moon?

They disengage and roll apart. He feels exhilarated but also faintly depressed. The beast from the past has soiled the sprite of the future with his salty flow. Caliban topping Ariel. When they join bodies here, do they mark completion with such a torrent of fluid? He is prehistoric. Moments pass before he dares to look at Hanmer. But she is smiling at him. She rises, gently draws him to his feet, and leads him to the basin beneath the waterfall. They bathe. The water is knife-cold. Hanmer's many fingers fly gaily over his body; she is so wholly feminine that he can barely summon a memory of the lean and muscular male with whom he began his journey. She is coquettish, playful, archly possessive.

She says, 'You couple with great enthusiasm.'

A sudden shower of radiance falls from the sun, which is almost directly overhead. A line of unfamiliar colors marches across the peak of a lofty mountain to the – west? He reaches for her, and she eludes him, and runs laughing through a thorny thicket; the plants claw halfheartedly at her but cannot touch her. When he follows, they shred him. He staggers forth bloodied and finds her waiting for him beside a stubby, squat tree no taller than herself. The latches of her nostrils flutter; her eyelids open and close repeatedly; her little breasts heave. Briefly he sees her with flowing green hair and a dense black pubic mat, but the moment passes and she is as sleek as before. Five creatures call his name hoarsely from branches of the tree. They have huge mouths and scrawny necks and puffy wings, and, so far as he can tell, no bodies at all. 'Clay! Clay! Clay! Clay! Clay!' Hanmer dismisses them; they hop to the ground and scurry away. She comes to him and kisses each scratch, and it heals. Austerely she examines the parts of his body, handling everything, learning his anatomy as though she may have to build something just like him one day. The intimacy of the inspection disturbs him. At length she is satisfied. She unzips the ground and draws a tuber from it, as the other Hanmer had done yesterday. Trustingly he takes it and sucks the juice. Blue fur sprouts on his skin. His genitals grow so monstrous that he sags to the ground under the pull of their weight. His toes unite. The moon, he thinks bitterly. Hanmer crouches over him and lowers herself, impaling herself on his rod. The moon. The moon. Mercury. The moon. He barely notices the orgasmic jolt.

The effects of the tuber's juice diminish. He lies belly-down, eyes closed. Stroking Hanmer, he finds that the scrotal bulge again has grown at the juncture of her thighs. Hanmer is male again. Clay looks: yes, it is so. Flat chest, wide shoulders, narrow hips. Everything returns. Too soon, sometimes.

Night is coming. He searches for the moon.

'Do you have cities?' he asks. 'Books? Houses? Poetry? Do you ever wear clothing? Do you die?'

'When we need to,' Hanmer says.

3

In the darkness they sit side by side, saying little. Clay watches the procession of the stars. Their brilliance often seems unbearable. Now and again he thinks of embracing Hanmer once more, and has to remind himself of Hanmer's unmetamorphosis. Perhaps that female Hanmer will return eventually; her turn upon the stage seems all too brief to him.

To the existing Hanmer he says, 'Am I monstrously barbaric? Am I coarse? Am I gross?'

'No. No. No.'

'But I'm a dawn-man. I'm a fumbling early attempt. I have an appendix. I urinate. I defecate. I get hungry. I sweat. I stink. I'm a million years inferior to you. Five million? Fifty million? No clue?'

'We admire you for what you are,' Hanmer assures him.

'We do not criticize you for what you could not have become. Of course, we may modify our estimate as we come to know you better. We reserve the right to detest you.'

There is a very long silence. Shooting stars split the night.

Later Clay says, 'Not that I mean to apologize. We did our best. We gave the world Shakespeare, after all. And – you know of Shakespeare ?'

'No.'

'Homer ?'

'No.'

'Beethoven ?'

'No.'

'Einstein.'

'No.'

'Leonardo da Vinci.'

'No.'

'Mozart!'

'No.'

'Galileo!'

'No.'

'Newton!'

'No.'

'Michelangelo. Mohammed. Marx. Darwin.'

'No. No. No. No.'

'Plato ? Aristotle ? Jesus ?'

'No, no, no.'

Clay says, 'Do you remember the moon that this planet once had ?'

'I have heard of the moon, yes. But none of these other things.'

'Everything we did is lost, then ? Nothing survives. We are extinct.'

'You are wrong. Your race survives.'

'Where ?'

'In us.'

'No,' Clay says. 'If everything we have done is dead, our race is dead. Goethe. Charlemagne. Socrates. Hitler. Attila. Caruso. We fought against the darkness and the darkness swallowed us anyway. We are extinct.'

'If you are extinct,' Hanmer says, 'then we are not human.'

'You are not human.'

'We are human.'

'Human, but not men. Sons of men, maybe. There's a qualitative gap. Too great a lapse of continuity. You've forgotten Shakespeare. You race through the heavens.'

'You must remember,' Hanmer says, 'that your period occupies an extremely narrow segment of the band of time. Information crammed into a narrow bandwidth becomes blurred and distorted. Is it surprising that your heroes are forgotten? What seems like a powerful signal to you is merely a momentary squirt of noise to us. We perceive a much broader band.'

'You speak to me of bandwidths?' Clay asks, astounded. 'You lose Shakespeare and keep technical jargon?'

'I sought a metaphor only.'

'How is it you speak my language?'

'Friend, you speak *my* language,' says Hanmer. 'There is only one language, and everything speaks it.'

'There are many languages.'

'One.'

'Ci sono molte lingue.'

'Only one, which all things comprehend.'

'Muchas lenguas! Sprache! Langue! Språk! Nyelv! The confusion of tongues. *Enchanté de faire votre connaissance. Welcher Ort is das? Per favore, potrebbe dirigermi al telefono. Finns det någon här, som talar engelska? El tren acaba de salir.'*

'When mind touches mind,' Hanmer says, 'communication is immediate and absolute. Why did you need so many ways of speaking with one another?'

'It is one of the pleasures of savages,' says Clay bitterly. He wrestles with the idea that everyone and everything are forgotten. By our deeds we define ourselves, he thinks. By the continuity of our culture we signify that we are human. And all continuities are broken. We have lost our immortality. We could grow three heads and thirty feet, and our skins become blue scales, and so long as Homer and Michelangelo and Sophocles live, mankind lives. And they are gone. If we were

24

globes of green fire, or red crusts on a rock, or shining bundles of wire, and still we remembered who we had been, we would still be men. He says, 'When you and I flew through space before, how did we do it?'

'We dissolved. We went up.'

'How?'

'By dissolving. By going up.'

'That's no answer.'

'I can't give you a better one.'

'It's just something you do naturally? Like breathing? Like walking?'

'Yes.'

'So you've become gods,' Clay says. 'All possibilities are open to you. You zoom off to Pluto when you need to. You change sexes on whim. You live forever, or as close to forever as you like. If you want music, you can outdo Bach, each of you. You can reason like Newton, paint like El Greco, write like Shakespeare, except you don't bother to do it. You live every moment in a symphony of colors and forms and textures. Gods. You've come to be gods.' Clay laughs. 'We tried for that. I mean, we knew how to fly, we could get to the planets, we tamed electricity, we made sound come out of the air, we drove out sickness, we split atoms. For what we were, we were pretty good. For when we were. Twenty thousand years before my time men wore animal skins and lived in caves, and in my time men went walking on the moon. You've lived twenty thousand years all by yourself, haven't you? At least. And has there been any real change in the world in that whole time? No. You can't change once you're a god, because you've attained everything. Do you know, Hanmer, that we used to wonder whether it was proper to keep striving upward? You've lost the Greeks, so maybe you don't know about *hybris*. Overweening pride. If a man climbs too high, the gods will strike him down, for certain things are reserved only for the gods. We worried about *hybris* a lot. We asked ourselves, are we getting too god-like? Will we be smitten? The plague, the fire, the tempest, the famine?'

'Did you really have such a concept?' Hanmer asks, genuine

curiosity in his voice. 'That it is evil to attempt too much?'

'We did.'

'A stinking myth conceived by cowards?'

'A noble concept invented by the deepest minds of our race.'

'No,' Hanmer says. 'Who would defend such an idea? Who could refuse the mandate of human destiny?'

'We lived,' Clay says, 'in the tension between the striving and the fear of climbing too high. And we kept climbing, though choked with fear. And we became gods. We became you, Hanmer! You see our punishment, though? For our *hybris* we were forgotten.'

He is pleased with the intricacy of his argument. He awaits Hanmer's reply, but no reply comes. Gradually he realizes that Hanmer is gone. Bored with my chatter? Will he come back? Everything returns. Clay will wait out the night without moving from this place. He tries to sleep, but finds himself wholly awake. He has not slept since his first awakening here. He can see little in the starry blackness. But there are sounds. The tone of a snapping string twangs in the air. Then there comes a sound like that of some vast mass shifting its period of vibration. Then he hears six hollow stone columns rising and thumping the ground. A thin high whine. A rich black boom. A sprinkle of pearly globes. A sappy gurgle. A scraping of wings. A splash. A clink. A hiss. Where is the orchestra? No one is near him. He is certain that he is contained in a dark cone of solitude. The music dies away, leaving only a few vagrant scents. He can feel a mist drifting in and engulfing him. He wonders how much contagion there is in Hanmer's miracles, and experiments with transforming his own sex; lying belly-up on a slick slaty slab, he attempts to grow breasts. Rigid with concentration, seeking to make mounds of flesh rise on his chest, he fails; he wonders if it might be more effective to begin by creating the inner glandular structure of mammaries, and tries to imagine what that structure might be like, and fails; he asks himself if it might not be impossible to take on female glands without first ridding himself of his male organs, and briefly he contemplates willing them out of existence, but he hesitates, and fails. He writes the sex-changing experiment off as unsuccessful. Next, thinking of touring the seacoasts of Saturn, he tries to dissolve and soar. Though he writhes and sweats and grunts, he remains hopelessly material; but then he surprises himself when, in a moment of relaxation between efforts, he does indeed bring forth the pale gray cloud of dissolution. He encourages it. He yields to it. He believes that he is getting there, and tentatively flickers his periphery, trying to rise. Something surely is happening, but it does not seem to be quite the same thing as before. A greasy green glow envelops him and he hears ragged sputtering sounds. And he is pinned to the ground. He gives way to fear and goes sliding halfway down the spectrum before he can regain some control. Was man meant to do such things? Is he not venturing into forbidden territory? No! No! No! He deliquesces. He dissolves. He flaps like a sheet in the wind, nearly taking off, unable somehow to commit that final severing of the terrestrial bond. He is so close, though. Lights swirl in the sky: orange, yellow, red. He is fiercely eager to succeed, and for a moment he thinks he *has* succeeded, for he has the sensations of ripping loose and bounding into the firmament, and cymbals clash and lightnings flash, and there is a terrible wrenching pull and some potent event occurs.

He realizes that he has gone nowhere. Instead he seems to have drawn something to him.

It sits beside him on the slaty slab. It is a smooth pink oval spheroid, jellylike but firm, within a rectangular cage of some heavy silvery metal. Cage and spheroid are interwoven, the bars passing through the body at several points. A single gleaming spherical wheel supports the floor of the cage. The spheroid speaks to him in a prickly gurgle. Clay cannot understand a thing. 'I thought there's only one language,' he says. 'What are you telling me?' The spheroid speaks again, evidently repeating its statement, enunciating more precisely, but Clay still cannot comprehend. 'My name is Clay,' he says, forcing a smile. 'I don't know how I came to be here. I don't know how you came to be here either, but I may have summoned you accidentally.' After a pause the spheroid replies unintelligibly. 'I'm sorry,' Clay says. 'I'm primitive. I'm ignorant.' Suddenly the spheroid turns deep green. Its surface ripples and trembles. A string of glossy eyes appears and vanishes. Clay feels cold fingers sliding through his forehead and stroking the lobes of his furrowed brain. In one broad blurting flow he receives the soul of the spheroid and understands it to be saying: *I am a civilized human being, a native of the planet Earth, who has been ripped from his proper environment by inexplicable forces and carried to this place. I am lonely and unhappy. I would return to my matrix-group. I beg you, give me all assistance, in the name of humanity!*

The spheroid subsides against the bars of its cage, obviously exhausted. Its shape sags into asymmetry and its color changes to pale yellow.

'I think I follow your meaning,' Clay says. 'But how can I help you? I'm a victim of the time-flux myself. I'm a man of the dawn of the race. I share your loneliness and unhappiness; I'm as lost as you are.'

The spheroid flickers feebly orange.

'Can you understand what I say?' Clay asks. There is no response. Clay concludes that this creature, which claims to be human though it is so wholly alien in form, must come from still farther down the curve of time, out of Hanmer's race's own future. The logic of evolution tells him that. Hanmer, at least, has arms and legs and a head and eyes and genitals. So, too, had the goatish man-beasts whose era lay somewhere between Clay's and Hanmer's. But this, with all limbs gone, all humanity tucked into some internal packet, surely is an ultimate version of the pattern. Clay feels faintly guilty, believing he has dragged the spheroid from its matrix-group in the course of his bungled attempt at soaring, but also he feels a tremor of pride that he could have done such a thing, however unintentionally. And it is a delight to meet someone even more displaced and confused than himself. 'Can we possibly communicate?' he asks. 'Can we reach across this barrier? Look: I'll come closer. I'm opening my mind as wide as I can. You have to forgive me my deficiencies. I come from the Vertebrate Age. Closer to Pithecanthropus than I am to you, I bet. Talk to me. *Donde está el teléfono?*' The spheroid returns to something like

28

its original pink hue. Wearily it offers Clay a vision: a city of broad plazas and shining towers, in whose lovely streets move throngs of pink spheroids, each in its own glittering cage. Fountains send cascades of water to the skies. Lights of many colors twirl and bob. The spheroids meet, exchange greetings, occasionally extend protoplasmoid blobs through the bars of their cages in a kind of handshake. Night arrives. There is the moon! Have they rebuilt it, pocks and all? He surveys the beloved scarry face. Gliding like a camera's eye, he passes into a garden. Here are roses. Here are yellow tulips. Here are narcissi and jonquils and heavy-headed blue hyacinths. There is a tree with familiar leaves, there another, there another. Oak. Maple. Birch. These are antiquarians, then, these jiggling giant mounds of bland meat, and they have rebuilt old Earth for their pleasure. The vision wavers and crumbles as an impenetrable curtain of regret descends. Clay realizes he has drawn an improper conclusion. Are the spheroids not beings of the incalculably remote future? Are they, then, the short-term descendants of man? The vision returns. The spheroid seems more animated, telling him he is on the right track. Yes. What are they, the mankind of five, ten, twenty thousand years after Clay's own day, a time when oaks, tulips, hyacinths, and Luna still exist? Yes. And where is the evolutionary logic of it? There is none. Man has reshaped himself to please himself. This is his oval spheroid phase. Later he will choose to be a vile goat. Still later he will be Hanmer. All of us, swept up by the time-flux. 'My son,' Clay says. (Daughter? Niece? Nephew?) Impulsively he tries to slip his hands between the bars to embrace the solemn spheroid. He is dealt a jolt of force that sends him sprawling many yards away, and he lies there, stunned, while some twining plant wraps tendrils about his thighs. Gradually he regains his strength. 'I'm sorry,' he whispers, approaching the cage. 'I didn't mean to intrude on your space. I was offering friendship.' The spheroid is dark amber now. The color of fury? Fear? No: apology. Another vision fills Clay's mind. Spheroids cage to cage, spheroids dancing, spheroids conjugating with ropy extended strands. A hymn of love. Try again, try again, try again. Clay extends one hand. It goes between the bars. He is not jolted. The surface of the spheroid puckers and whirlpools and a thin tentacular projection arises and clasps Clay's wrist. Contact. Trust. Fellow-victims of the time-flux. 'I am called Clay,' Clay says, thinking it vehemently. But all he can get from the spheroid is a series of vivid snapshots of his world. The universal language must not have been invented yet in the spheroid's time. It can communicate with him only in images. 'All right,' Clay says. 'I accept the limitations. We'll learn to get along.'

The tentacle releases him. He withdraws from the cage.

He concentrates on forming images. Handling the abstractions is difficult. Love? He shows himself standing beside a woman of his own kind. Embracing her. Touching her breasts. Now they are in bed, copulating. He depicts the union of the organs, explicitly. He stresses such characteristics as body hair, odors, blemishes. Keeping the coupling couple coupling, he produces an adjoining image of himself atop the female Hanmer, performing the same rite. Then he shows himself reaching into the cage and permitting the tentacle to wind around his wrist. *Capisce?* And now to show trust. Cat and kittens? Child and kittens? Spheroid without cage, embracing spheroid? A sudden response of anguish. Change of hue: ebony. Clay edits the image, returning the spheroids to their cages. Intimations of relief. Good. Now, how to convey loneliness? Self naked in broad field of alien flowers. Flickering dreams of home. Scene in twentieth-century city: bustling, cluttered, yet beloved.

'We're communicating now,' Clay says. 'We're making it.'

The long night ends. By azure dawn Clay sees a whole flora that had not been there at sundown: spiky trees with red ribs, looping coils of sticky pulsing groundcreeping vines, vast blossoms twice the diameter of a rowboat, within which little hammerheaded anthers bob and nod, scattering diamond-faceted pollen. Hanmer has returned. He sits crosslegged at the far end of Clay's slab.

'We have a companion,' Clay says. 'I don't know if the time-flux caught him or if I dragged him here myself. I was making some experiments inside my head. But anyway, he's—'

Dead?

The spheroid is a withered husk glued to one side of his cage. A trickle of iridescent fluid has dyed three of the bars. Clay is unable to rouse the spheroid's now-familiar imagery. He goes to the cage, tentatively pokes two fingers into it, and feels no shock.

'What happened?' he asks.

'Life goes,' Hanmer says. 'Life comes again. We'll take him with us. Come.'

They walk in the direction away from the sunrise. Without touching it, Hanmer pushes the cage along before them. They are passing now through a grove of tall square-topped yellow trees whose red leaves, dangling in thick clusters, writhe like annoyed starfish. 'Have you seen beings like this one before?' Clay asks.

'Several times. The flux brings us everything.'

'I gathered it was also an early form. Close to my own time, in fact.'

'You may be right,' Hanmer says.

'Why did it die?'

'Its life went out of it.'

Clay is growing accustomed to Hanmer's style of answer.

Shortly they halt at a pond of dark blue fluid in which round golden plaques solemnly swim. 'Drink,' Hanmer suggests. Clay kneels at the edge. Scoops up a careful handful. Peppery to the taste. It fills him with a keen expansive sadness, a consciousness of lost opportunities and missed turnings, that threatens in the first instant to overwhelm him; he sees all the possible choices that any moment presents, the infinity of darkened blurred highways marked with unintelligible roadsigns, and he finds himself fleeing down all those roads at once, dizzied, over-extended. The sensation presses. Rather, it refines itself into a more exact nature, and he realizes that he is gifted with a new means of perception, which he has employed metaphorically instead of spatially. He drinks again. The perception deepens and intensifies. He accepts glimmering images: eleven sleeping nightcrawlers in a shallow tunnel just behind him, blood pulsing like sparks within Hanmer's compact body, the misty formlessness of the dead spheroid's rotting flesh, the crisp crustacean interiors of these little golden swimming plaques. He drinks again. Now he sees the inwardness of things still more precisely. His zone of perception has become a sphere five times his own height, with his brain at its center. He assesses the structure of the soil, finding a layer of black loam over a layer of pink sand over a layer of jumbled pebbles over a layer of slippery tilted blocks of granite. He measures the dimensions of the pool and remarks on the mathematically perfect curve of its floor. He calculates the environmental stress caused by the simultaneous passage of a tiro of small batlike things just overhead and the growth of six cells in the roots of a nearby tree. He drinks again. 'So easy to be a god here,' he tells Hanmer, and observes the tones of his voice ricocheting from the surface of the pool. Hanmer laughs. They move on.

4

His new senses fade before midday. A dim residue remains; he still can see a short distance into the ground, and he is aware of events behind his head. But only cloudily. Things are too transient in this world. He hopes they will find another pool, or that the female Hanmer will return, or that the spheroid's time of death will end.

Ahead of them now lies a natural amphitheater: a wide deep bowl contained at one end by a cluster of great black boulders encrusted with blue lichens. Five members of Hanmer's race sit near the boulders. Three females, two males. Hanmer says, 'We will do the Opening of the Earth, I think. The time is right.' The day has become quite warm; if Clay were wearing clothes, he would want to remove them. The lazy sun hangs close to the horizon, and fat beams of energy come rolling bumpily down the amphitheater's slope. Hanmer does not introduce him to the other five, who seem to know of him already. They rise and welcome him with sleepy smiles and shortwinded bursts of song. He has difficulty telling one from another, and even in distinguishing Hanmer from the other two males. A female glides toward him. 'I am Ninameen,' she says. 'Will you be joyous here? Have you come for the Opening of the Earth? Was it painful to awaken? Do I attract you?' She has a singsong voice, high and fluty, and she holds herself in what Clay sees as Japanese postures. She seems daintier and more vulnerable than the female Hanmer. The remnants of his enhanced perceptions show him the ticking sensuality within her: tiny translucent petcocks are spilling golden hormones that stream toward her loins. Her accessibility disturbs him. He feels suddenly ashamed of his nakedness, of the long dangling organ at his thighs; he envies the men of Hanmer's species for their shielded sex. Ninameen turns and sprints toward the boulders, looking back once to see if he is following. He remains where he is. Hanmer, or one whom he takes to be Hanmer, has chosen a female and lies beside her in a pocket of low spongy grass. The third of the females and the other two males have begun a little mincing dance, with much laughter and frequent embracing. Ninameen, capering atop a boulder, pelts him with scraps of lichen. He runs after her.

She is incredibly agile. He glimpses her slim golden-green body always ahead of him as he scrambles over the black rocks; he pants, he sweats, he coughs in fatigue. Satyr-like, he erects. She peeks from unexpected crannies. A tiny breast showing here, a flat buttock there. Pursued this way, she seems almost wholly human to him, although there are reminders of the gulf between them when he pauses to consider the flat-fronted face, the scarlet eyes, the spidery many-fingered hands. He knows, from the glimpses he had had before his perceptions grew dull again, that her inner anatomy is monstrously strange, a series of neat rectangular compartments linked by narrow pearly channels, bearing no more resemblance to his own internal workings than do his to those of a lobster. Yet he desires her. Yet he will have her.

He reaches the summit of the biggest boulder. Where is she? Looking about, he sees no one. The boulder's top is hollowed to form a shallow crater; rainwater has filled it and black threads drift on the surface, quivering and making buzzing sounds. He peers in, thinking she has submerged to hide from him, but sees only his own image, reflected not from the surface of the water but from its obsidian depths. He seems tense and clumsy, a Neanderthal inflamed with lust. 'Nina-meen?' he calls. The sound of his voice makes bubbles rise and his reflection is lost.

She giggles. He finds her hovering ten feet above his head, resting quite comfortably belly-down in the air, arms and legs outspread. He is able to sense the rivers of not-blood flowing in her not-veins, and he feels the breeze of thwarted gravity that her levitation creates.

'Come down,' he calls.

'Not yet. Tell me about your time.'

'What do you want to know?'

'Everything. From the beginning. Do you die? Do you love? Do you put his body inside hers? Do you quarrel? Do you dream? Do you forgive? Do you—'

'Wait,' he says. 'I'll try to show you. Look: this is how it was in my time.'

He opens his soul to her. Feeling like a museum exhibit, he gives her views of automobiles, shirts, shoes, restaurants, un-made beds, hotel lobbies, airplanes, potted palms, telephones, highways, ripe bananas, atomic explosions, power stations, zoos, dental drills, office buildings, traffic jams, municipal swimming pools, shooting galleries, and newspapers. He shows her movies, lawn-mowers, grilled steaks, and snow. He shows her church spires. He shows her parades. He shows her tooth-paste. He shows her rocket launchings.

She tumbles terribly from the air.

Desperately lurching, he breaks her fall and lands beneath her, grunting at the impact. Her cool body clings to him, trembling, and her fright is so intense that panicky images leak through from her mind to his. He sees, through a bleak haze of distortion, some gigantic cyclopean gray wreck of a stone building, and five enormous creatures sitting in front of it, dinosaur-like beasts embedded in mud, lifting their great heads slowly, snorting, shaking the ground with their complaints, and there is Ninameen groveling before them, as if praying, pleading for absolution, and the colossal reptilian things grumble and wheeze, shake their heads, drag their immense chins through the muck, and slowly Ninameen sinks, sobbing, into the ground. The image melts. He cradles the frightened girl as gently as he can. 'Are you hurt?' he murmurs. 'Are you ill?' She shivers and utters a miserable little purring noise. 'I misunderstood,' she whispers finally. 'I couldn't understand your poem and it frightened me. How strange you are!' She draws a multitude of fingertips over his skin. Now he is the one to shiver. She slips down to lie at his side, and he kisses her throat and lightly touches one of her breasts, admiring the quicksilver texture of her skin, but as he starts to enter her he abruptly imagines that she has begun to shift toward the male form of her species, and he loses firmness as though his sensory inputs have been disconnected. She pushes against him, but no use: he does not rise. Helpfully she does switch to the male form, making the change with such swiftness that he cannot follow it, but things are no better this way, and she goes back. In a thin urgent voice she says, 'Please. We'll be late for the Opening.' He feels her burrowing along the track of a thick sluggish nerve in the fleshy part of his back; she bursts through the webs of resistance, tickles his brain, catalyzes him into virility. Then she winds one leg around him and, before the impulse eludes him, he drives himself to her depths. She clasps him as though she would ingest him. Why do these beings have sex at all? Surely they can find more immediate ways of making contact. Surely it can have no biological purpose at this late date in human evolution. Surely this simple animal pleasure must be as obsolete as eating or sleeping. He conceives an agreeable fantasy: they have reinvented copulation for his benefit, and have equipped themselves with these vaginas and penises in a kind of masquerade spirit, the better to understand the nature of their primitive guest. The idea delights him. Hips thrusting, he embellishes it by trying to visualize Hanmer's people in their normal asexual form, blank as machines between the legs, and while he does this Ninameen slyly sends a burst of ecstatic sensation into him using the part of him within her as a direct conduit to his cerebellum; he responds with a quick hot spurt and lies back, dazed and drained.

'Do you want to help us do the Opening of the Earth, now?' she murmurs when his eyes open.

'What is it?'

'One of the Five Rites.'

'A religious ceremony?'

His question hangs like frost in the air. She is already scrambling down the boulder. He follows her, ponderously, wobbly-legged, getting caught in crevices; turning, she tenderly lifts him with a smile and a glance and floats him to the ground. He lands on his feet in the warm damp soil. She tugs him forward, toward the center of the amphitheater, where the other five have already gathered. All of them are now in the female form. He is unable to tell which is Hanmer until the others brandish their names at him in a jingling rush: Bril, Serifice, Angelon, and Ti. Their slender naked bodies ripple and gleam in the bright sunlight. They arrange themselves in a circle, holding hands. He thinks he is between Serifice and Ninameen in the ring. Serifice, if Serifice it is, says in a lovely tinkling voice, 'Do you think we are the evil ones or the good ones?' Ninameen giggles. From across the circle, the one who he believes is Hanmer calls out, 'Don't confuse him!' But he is confused. Temporarily purged of his lusts by Ninameen, he is obsessed with the strangeness of these people again, and wonders how he can feel sexual interest in them when they are so alien. Is it something in the air? Or will any handy hole suit the purpose when the time-flux seizes you?

They are dancing. He dances with them, though he cannot imitate the free swiveling of their unhinged limbs. The hands clasped in his grow cold. He sprouts an icy knot of uncertainty in his belly, knowing that the rite of the Opening of the Earth is now beginning. A fierce rush of activity flutters in his skull. His vision fogs. The six of them rush toward him and press their chilly bodies against him. He feels their rigid nipples like nodes of fire on his skin. They are forcing him to the ground. Is this a sacrifice, and is he the victim? 'I am Angelon,' Angelon croons. 'I am love.' Ti sings, 'I am Ti. I am love.' 'I am love,' sings Hanmer. 'I am Hanmer.' 'I am Serifice. I am love.' 'I am Bril.' 'I am Angelon.' 'Love.' 'Ninameen.' 'I am love.' 'Serifice.' His body is expanding. He is becoming a net of fine copper wires engulfing the entire planet. He has length and breadth but no height. 'I am Ninameen,' sings Ninameen. The planet is splitting open. He penetrates it.

He sees all.

He sees the insects in their nests and the nightcrawlers in their tunnels, and he sees the roots of the trees and shrubs and flowers twining and twisting and extending and he sees the subterranean rocks and the levels of stratification. Precious minerals glisten in the planet's sundered crust. He finds the beds of streams and the floors of lakes. He touches everything and is touched by everything. He is the sleeping god. He is the returning spring. He is the heart of the world.

He descends into the deeper strata, where pools of oil seep sadly through layers of silent shale, and he finds golden nuggets budding and bursting, and he wades in a clear sweet rivulet of sapphires. Then he drifts into the part of the planet that had been a home for man in one of the generations that followed his, and he wanders in awe down empty streets in clean, spacious tunnels, while obliging machines clatter forth and volunteer to serve his every need. 'We are the friends of man,' they tell him, 'and we accept our ancient obligations.' The planet shudders and the time-flux blows, and for one stunning moment he sees this city inhabited again: tall harried-looking mortals crowd its corridors, pale, slab-faced, not very different from the men and women of his own era, except that their bodies tend to be attenuated and flimsy. He is not sorry to drift through their level into the authentic bowels. Here is the blazing magma; here are the inner fires. Not cold yet, old planet? No, not by plenty. Moonless I am and my seas have shifted, yet at the core I glow. His friends are close beside him. 'I am Bril,' Serifice whispers. 'I am Angelon,' says Ti. They all are male and they have extruded their members from their sheaths. Have they come to fertilize the Earth's core? Clouds of billowing blue steam erupt and hide his companions from him, and he wanders onward, swimming up through porphyry and alabaster and sardonyx and diabase and malachite and feldspar, spearing through the tissues of the world like a sentient needle, until the surface grows near. He emerges. Night has come and his friends lie exhausted in the amphitheater, and swarms of droning golden wasps bedeck their limp bodies, three male, three female. In his exaltation Clay discovers that he can walk in the air. He rises to a height of perhaps thirty feet and, grinning, takes great clumsy strides. How easy it is! He merely must maintain a distance between himself and the ground. Yes! Yes! Yes! He walks the length of the amphitheater. He lets himself float down until his toes nearly touch the shrubs, and boosts himself on high again. Step and step and step. It is worth being blown who knows how many millions of years off course, to be able to walk the air like this, not in some intangible incorporeal form as before, but in his own tingling body.

He comes down. He sees the shimmering metal cage of the spheroid, with the lifeless, shriveled spheroid slumped within it. He goes to it and lets his hands rest on the brilliant bars.

'No one should be dead on the night of the Opening of the Earth,' he says. 'Find your strength again! Come! Come!' He puts his hands on the spheroid's prickly corpse. 'Can you hear me? I call you back to life, son, daughter, nephew, niece.' From the depths of the opened Earth he summons new life and pumps it into the spheroid, which gains in fullness, resuming its old plumpness, growing smooth and firm once more, turning purple, turning red, turning pink. It lives again. He detects its wordless emanations of gratitude. 'We humans stick together,' he tells the spheroid. 'I am Clay. My era is a little earlier than yours, before the race changed its shape. You see, though, that later epochs brought a return to the original arrangement. Those sleepers there – our hosts—'

Hanmer, Bril, Serifice, Angelon, Ti, and Ninameen waver and grow dim, oscillate from male to female and female to male, stir, subside. They are still enmeshed in the ceremony of the Opening of the Earth. He wonders if he should have remained

38

with them, but decides that if he had, he might not have had the pleasure of his airwalk, nor would he have resurrected the spheroid. It has been a day of wonders. He has never known such joy before.

Even when the hideous goat-men shuffle into sight, Clay's delirium of happiness is unchecked. He bows to them. 'I am Clay,' he explains. 'Of all those caught by the time-flux, I seem to be the most ancient. The spheroid is of an era subsequent to mine. These, of course, are the current dominant variety of man. And the three of you, I take it, come from some inter-mediate period when—'

Mumbling ominously, the goat-men advance on him.

They speak to one another in a dreary language of mono-tones and move slowly forward crabwise, scuttling on wide angles. They fill the air with the odor of rot. Clay fights off dismay, telling himself to beware of exterior judgments; these too are the sons of man, and in some vanished era must have represented the summit of human striving. I will be naive: I will be charitable: I will be loving. They are quite close to him now, thrusting their faces at him, exhaling foul vapors, spatter-ing him with gluey spittle. He gags and coughs. They keep their short thick arms clutched up against their white hairless chests; the fingers, blunt and stubby, trail driblets of peeling skin, and there are no nails. They rock rhythmically on their enormous thighs. Clay sees their eyes flash with indisputable malevolence. The weeds that sprout at their feet are choking the amphitheater with coarse growth. 'Can we discuss this?' he asks. 'It is the night of the Opening of the Earth. Let us be loving. Let us be receptive. How can I help you?' The crea-tures edge closer to him. Waves of genuine menace emanate from them. Troubled, he attempts ro rise from the ground, but their arms flicker forward to seize him and hold him down. They begin to shove him back and forth, one heaving him toward another, and a thin rattling sound of soiled laughter comes from them. A game! Hare ringed by hounds! 'You mis-understand,' Clay says. 'I'm a human being, an early form but still – deserving – of – respect—' The shoving grows violent. They loom above him; his head reaches only to their chests.

They stomp their feet fiercely, making the ground shake. Teeth now glitter.

Hanmer, Ninameen, Ti, Serifice, Bril, and Angelon sit up to watch. They make no move to interfere.

Only the spheroid shows resentment as the goat-men buffet Clay. It chatters angrily at them. But the goat-men can no more understand the pink spheroid's language than can Clay. They continue to push Clay about. His skin stings where their touch has slimed it. As they shove, they murmur insistently at him. What are they saying? He imagines that they are telling him, *You will become as we are. You will become as we are. You will become as we are.* Is that cracked shriek their laughter? What sinister swing of events produced these things from the human gene-pool? They are the skeletons in tomorrow's closet. They are the joke the future will play on all the utopian dreamers. Clay sinks to the earth under their pummeling. The tangle of quick-rising weeds envelops him and he struggles for breath. They kick and batter him. He vomits. And yet he takes heart from the knowledge that these beasts are only a transient phase in the story. Mankind will pass through them, purged, and go on to become god-like Hanmer. It is comforting, though godlike Hanmer at present offers little comfort. Buoyed, Clay crawls through an opening between the flailing feet and scrambles down the slope of the amphitheater toward Hanmer and his friends. 'You! Hanmer!' he calls. 'Call them off me! Can't you control your own ancestors?'

Hanmer laughs. 'They are in the service of Wrong at the moment, my beloved. And so they are beyond my control.'

The goat-men have observed that Clay has eluded them. They turn on the spheroid instead, but they are hit by defensive shocks the moment they touch the cage, and, grunting, they move away and shuffle toward Clay again.

How can he escape? The bruising he can tolerate, but not the reek, not the sickening ugliness. Stumbling, slipping, he runs off into the deepening darkness, circling the boulders and plunging into a dim forest beyond. He can hear the snorting of the goats behind him: *hhruhf, hhruhf, hhruhf.* A hasty stride sends him into some concealed body of water; he feels the wetness at his shins, tries to back out, trips on an unseen obstacle, falls headlong forward. There is a great splash. Something plucks at his body from below. He goes down.

5

Breathing water is not as difficult as he anticipates. He fills his lungs with the stuff, really drawing it in until every wrinkled puffy crevice is saturated; then he draws energy from it. The panic swiftly passes. He adapts. He is in a black pond five times as deep as it is wide, and the water is cold. He paddles slowly across its middle with little flipping pushes of his feet, while he expels the final blobs of air from his body. The other occupant of the pool waits patiently, letting him become acclimated. *I am Quoi*, it tells him after a while, sending the information to him in a stream of blue and green and red bubbles that cross the bottom of the pool as though on phosphor dots. *I am an enemy of Wrong. You are safe here.*

I am Clay.

I will shelter you, Clay.

He perceives his environment with growing clarity. The waters of the pool are sharply divided into nine zones, each having a distinct temperature, salinity, density, and prevailing molecular form. The meeting place of zone and zone is plainly marked by a quivering interface of unmistakable and unambiguous resonance. Above the iron band of tension at the surface of the pool hover three smears of jiggling red mist streaked with rusty yellow: the foiled goats, glumly peering downward. Clay himself occupies the fourth zone from the top. Three zones beneath him is Quoi, manifesting itself in the form of a tubular emerald glow. Clay refines his perceptions and discovers that Quoi is a massive squidlike being, elongated, tipped at one end by five slender tentacles and at the other by flattened perfunctory flukes. A placid but powerful intelligence is apparent in it; the emanation of its sensibility is a turquoise halo clinging to its black, lustrous skin, and Quoi's thoughts bubble through the depths like flakes of many-colored snow, swirling, blending, clashing. Clay approaches it more closely. *The time-flux brought me here*, he says. *Was it the same with you?*

No. I am native.

More than one intelligent species here, then?

A great many, says Quoi. *We Breathers, to begin with, and then there are the Skimmers, the Eaters, the Awaiters, the Interceders, the Destroyers, the—*

Too fast, too fast! Show me a Skimmer!

Quoi shows him Hanmer, agile, sleek, ambiguous, subtle, shallow.

And an Awaiter?

Misty image, something deep in the soil, like a giant animated carrot, but more interesting.

An Eater?

Huge fanged mouth. Row on row of teeth receding into the shadowy interior. Saucers for eyes. Bleak, bitter soul tick-tocking within. Scales. Claws.

All these, Clay says, *are considered human?*

These. Yes. And the others.

He is baffled. The logic, again, is absent. *Why so many forms evolving simultaneously?*

Not simultaneously. Successively. But without the disappearance of the old forms. We are better at survival in these times.

The Skimmers are the newest form?

Yes, says Quoi.

And dominant? And superior?

Newest.

But with powers that the older forms don't possess, Clay insists. *Not merely a difference of shape. Yes?*

Quoi admits that this is so.

And the rest?

Survivors.

Did your form evolve close to my time?

No.

Clay shows Quoi the goat-men. *These?*
Closer to you than me.
Ah.
He tries to assemble and absorb his new data. Skimmers, Eaters, Awaiters, Breathers, Destroyers, Interceders: at least six species occupying the world at once, representing six successive eras in the growth of mankind. Yes. The Skimmers the current stage; the others mere debris of the past, still hanging around. Yes. And the goat-men, and the spheroid? Extinct forms, swept up by the time-flux and carried here. Yes. And himself, soft ape peeled of his fur? The same. His species gone, his time's deeds obliterated, only the genes enduring, shining seeds squirting across the millennia, ineradicable, inextinguishable. How many forms, he wonders, lie between himself and the oldest of these stubborn survivors? He comprehends a glowing chain of humanity stretching through the epochs. We are an impertinent life-form. We change, but we do not perish. We are forgotten, yet we remain. How can we fear to anger the gods, when we outlast them?

Triumphantly Clay glides from level to level in Quoi's pool. He revels in his awareness of the gradations of his surroundings. Here the water is cooler and more slippery than here; here he tastes coppery salt, here he tastes glistening lime. Here he compresses. Here he expands. Here he must turn edgewise and press to burst through the wall of molecules. He sees himself transformed: he is something slick and glossy, like a seal, with a tapering snout and powerful flippers. Surge! Thrust! Dive! Soar! He races to the surface. The goat-men still hover, brooding, dropping driblets of drool into the water. To the goats: 'Come drown with me!' No. They stay. He stays. Submerged, he drinks wisdom from Quoi.

What do you do? Clay asks.
I examine.
Everything?
Lately I explore the nature of communication. I study the interchanges of love and travel its channels. Was there love in your era?
We believed so.

43

Did you have the flowing, the twining, the exchanging, and the merging?

The terms are not familiar, says Clay. *But I sense the sense.*

We will talk of these things.

Gladly.

But as Clay accedes, Quoi falls silent, and for a time Clay cannot find it in the pool. Then he sees the Breather moving slowly at the very bottom, rooting in the mucky floor. Black bubbles rise. Has Quoi lost interest in him? Quoi sends a flicker of reassurance. *I will show you our way of love.*

Quoi presents a vision.

Here is another pool, black and chilly and deep. Here another Quoi swims slowly in its lower regions. Between Quoi and Quoi there glows a fiery, brilliant streak of harmony. Here is a third Quoi in a third pool. Quoi is linked to Quoi and Quoi. Here is a fourth. Here is a fifth. Here is a sixth. The pools are capsules of cold darkness, driven like spikes into the planet's skin, and in each capsule there is a Quoi. Linked. Through Quoi, Clay becomes aware of seventy-nine Quois girdling the Earth. It is the entire population of this species, although once there were more, when Quois ruled the planet, in another epoch. No Quois now are born. No Quois die. The clumsy monsters, sealed in their watery pits, specialize in a stable sort of survival. And there is love between and among them. Look now! The white-hot spear of connection, leaping from pool to pool! The heavy bodies flow; the tentacles coil and uncoil; the flukes lash the water, roiling the neat stratification. Yet it is not an ecstatic physical thing. Rather it is a somber communion, sexless, metallic. The Quois twine soul about soul. The Quois exchange the stuff of life-experience. The Quois merge to become Quoi. Clay, participating vicariously, feels such keen misery that his flippers droop and he plummets three levels. Did it come down to this, then, humanity evolving into entombed squids trading melancholy boredoms by remote transmission? What could possibly happen to a Quoi in its pool? Such a creature dropped into the water; such a chemical change happened at such an hour; such bubbles came forth from the underlying detritus. Here lie we, seventy-nine strong, telling

44

one another things we have known for millennia. Clay weeps. Yet as he enters more deeply into the union of the Quois he perceives the richness of it, the many dimensions, the supple parallaxes of so multiple a joining. The Quois are old married folk; they derive pleasure from the mere accumulation of one-nesses. Such we were, and such we did, and such came to pass, and this species burst upon the world, and that one, and this other one, and the time-flux blew and now has brought us Clay, and we love, and we love, and we love, and we are Quoi. And Clay is Quoi. Clay loses himself in this watery dream. His borders dissolve. He blends into Quoiness. He has never felt so secure. He lies on the bottom of the pool, enquoied, beneath five atmospheres of pressure. Centuries go by. He breathes cautiously, letting bright streams of water slide into his body, giving forth the cloudy depleted product. He is aware of the sleepy turning of the many Quois in their separate wells. How deep is their love! How flawless! The contact breaks and he is alone, shattered, bobbing ungovernably toward the surface. He hears the raucous laughter of the waiting goats; he sees their red and yellow emanations hovering above. They will seize him. But Quoi takes him first, calmly, benevolently embracing him, and Clay regains control. *Are you well?* Quoi asks.

I am well.
You see our mode of life now?
I see it.
May we then examine yours?
And Clay says, *You may, yes.*

6

He finds himself crawling on hands and knees to the shore of the pool. Morning has come. The goat-men have vanished. His body rids itself of its water; he fills his lungs with air and offers himself to the bright sunlight. The trees here have golden leaves. He takes a few tentative steps. In moments he has remembered walking. Now he inspects his body. The coarse covering of hair that he had shed early in his wanderings has grown itself again. His foreskin is gone. He bears the scar of an appendectomy. His thigh is bruised. He has been returned to his original form. Are they mocking him? He was primitive enough in his edited state; and he had come to take pleasure in the smooth youthful hairlessness of his chest and thighs and groin. Now, seeing the rosy tip of his cock again jutting from those dense black curls, he feels profound embarrassment over his nakedness. He covers himself with outspread hands. But can he hide the hairy buttocks too? The matted chest? He puts his hands here, here, here. He rubs his cheek against his shoulder: sandpapery stubble there. Forgive me, I am an animal. Forgive me, my body betrays me.

His hips sprout tight white briefs. He sighs, relieved, hearing distant applause at this concealment. He adds a crisp shirt. Socks. Trousers. Necktie. Jacket. Handkerchief in breast pocket. Black shoes of synthetic leather. Wallet bulges against left thigh. Attaché case in right hand. Scent of aftershave lotion on sleek cheeks. He finds an automobile and enters it. Places attaché case beside him. Key in the ignition. *Vroom!* Right foot taps accelerator. Right hand grasps wheel. Power steering; the car slides easily out into the street. Horns honk. He honks gaily back. The day is overcast, but the sun will burn through. He touches the stud that closes his windows, and gets the air-conditioner going, for that bus is going to ride in front of him all the way to the thruway interchange, farting noxiousness at him. And so it happens. But he turns off at last, going around the ramp, pausing at the gate to pick up his toll ticket. His rear-view mirrors show him the towers of the city, smog-wrapped, but he will soon be escaping from all that. He is on the approach ramp now, gently building up velocity, and he is doing fifty as he extrudes himself into the traffic flow. Shortly he is at sixty-five, then seventy, and he holds it there. With a jab of his finger he starts the radio. Mozart burbles from the speakers in the rear. The *Haffner*? The *Linz*? He should know them apart by this time. He edges over into the far lane, the fast lane, and coasts along, watching the posts of the median whiz by. A green sign advises him to turn off here for downtown; he laughs at it. In minutes he is beyond the city limits. And yes, the clouds are gone; there is the sun, there is the soft blue sky, sliced every minute or two by the shining wings of a jet rising from the airport on his right. Green fields now flank the thruway. Stands of poplar and maple flutter farther back. He opens his window and lets the sweet summery air enter. He is almost alone on the road, now, out here in the outlying districts. And what is that, up ahead, standing by the side of the road? A hitchhiker? Yes. A girl? Yes. A naked girl? Yes. His old fantasy. Obviously she had had difficulties getting a car to stop for her; she has stripped, and he can see her clothes draped carelessly over the top of the suitcase on the ground beside her: slacks, blouse, panties, bra. He slides his foot onto the brake. Even so, he is unable to stop close to her, overshooting by at least three hundred feet before he finally pulls to a halt on the shoulder. He starts to put the car into reverse, but she is already running toward him, suitcase in hand, garments fluttering behind her, breasts bobbling prettily. She is quite young: no more than twenty, he guesses. Her golden hair is straight and silken, nearly shoulder-length. Her skin has the pink flush of health and youth; her blue eyes sparkle. She has round, taut, full breasts, set high on her ribcage and close together. Her waist is narrow, her hips possibly a trifle too broad. Fine golden fleece covers her loins, with one central swirl rising like an arrow toward her small deep navel. Breathless, she arrives at his car.

'Gee, hi!' she cries. 'I thought *nobody* was going to give me a ride today!'

'It can be rough on the thruway,' he agrees. 'Get in. Here, give me that.' He takes her suitcase and puts it on the rear seat. Her clothes are still bunched in her hand; he takes those from her, too, flinging them atop the valise. She nestles in beside him. He has costly upholstery and she wriggles in pleasure, he supposes, as her bare buttocks come in contact with the seat. Reaching across her breasts, he locks the car. She smiles eagerly at him. 'Where are you heading?' she asks.

'Just out for a drive. I've got all the time in the world.'

'Great,' she says.

The car leaps forward. Soon he is doing seventy again. He gets across into the fast lane. As he drives, he steals glances at his passenger. She has tiny pink nipples and faint blue vein-lines in her breasts. Nineteen at best, he decides.

'I am Clay,' he says.

'I am Quoi,' she tells him.

'Have you ever had a truly meaningful emotional relationship with a man?' he asks.

'I'm not certain. There were one or two—'

'That came close?'

'Yes.'

'But in the end all kinds of defensive walls went up, and you found yourselves embracing at arm's length?'

'Yes, just like that!' she says.

'It's been like that for me too, Quoi. The brittle banter, the quick flip witticism, the clever talk that substitutes for any true intimacy of soul—'

'Yes.'

'But there's always hope—'

'That the next time—'

'That *this* time—'

'Really the one.'

'Yes.'

'Yes.'

'Really the one.'

'If we could truly trust—'

'Open ourselves—'

'Not just physically.'

'But the physical part is important too.'

'As an aspect of the deeper thing, the love thing, the opening of souls.'

'Yes.'

'Yes.'

'We understand each other beautifully.'

'I've been thinking the same thing.'

'It doesn't happen this way often.'

'So fast.'

'So certain.'

'No. It's rare.'

'It's beautiful.'

'That's what I was thinking.'

'Such complete understanding. Such a – a tuned response—'

'A flowing. A twining.'

'An exchanging. A merging.'

'Exactly.'

'Who are we to fight destiny?' he says, and turns off the thruway at the next exit. He runs his right hand over the firm cool roundness of her thighs as the car glides around the exit ramp. She keeps her legs pressed chastely together, but smiles at him. He caresses the gentle curve of her belly and takes a dollar bill from his pocket. The man at the toll booth winks. 'There a motel near here?' Clay asks. The tollkeeper says, 'Take a left on Route 71, quarter of a mile.' He nods his thanks and heads for the motel. It is a squat plastic-looking structure, a green-walled U beside the road. The girl waits in the car; Clay goes to the office. 'Double room?' The clerk reaches for the registration forms. 'Overnight?' he asks, and Clay says, 'No, just a couple of hours,' and the clerk looks past Clay's shoulder into the car, staring as if counting the girl's breasts, and after a while says, 'Credit card?' Clay gives him an American Express card. The clerk writes up the charge; Clay signs the ticket; he gets his room key; he returns to the car and drives it around back to the room. It faces a courtyard in which a small heart-shaped swimming pool has been cut. Children splash in the pool; their mothers doze in the sun. As they get out of the car, the girl looks toward the pool and, sighing, says, 'I like kids a lot, don't you? I want to have dozens of them.' She waves cheerily at the children in the pool. Clay taps her buttocks and says, 'Let's go in.' The room is dark and cool. He turns on the light and turns down the air-conditioner. The girl stretches out on the bed, lying on the olive-toned bedspread. Clay goes into the bathroom and comes out naked. 'Don't turn off the light,' she says. 'I like it to be on. I hate secretiveness.' He shrugs affably and joins her on the bed. 'Tell me all about yourself,' he murmurs. 'Where you grew up. What you want to do with your life. The kind of books you read. Your favorite movies. The places you've traveled. The foods you like. Do you care for Cézanne? Bartok? Foggy days? Football? Skiing? Mushrooms? Christopher Marlowe? Does pot make you happy? White wine? Have you ever wanted to sleep with another girl? How old were you when your breasts grew? Do you have painful periods? Where are your sensitive places? What do you think about politics? Do you have hangups about oral-genital contacts? Do you like animals? What's your favorite color? Can you cook? Sew? Are you an efficient housekeeper? Did you ever do it with two men at once? Does the stock market interest you? Are you religious? Can you speak French? Do you get along well with your parents? When did you have your first serious sexual experience? Do you enjoy flying? When you meet someone for the first time, do you automatically assume he's a decent sort until you have evidence to the contrary? Do you have brothers or sisters? Were you ever pregnant? Are you a good swimmer? Do you spend a lot of your time by yourself? Which do you like better, diamonds or sapphires? Is a lot of foreplay good for you, or would you prefer a man just to go right in? Do you ride horseback? Can you drive? Have you ever been to Mexico City? Can you shoot a gun? He strokes her breasts and catches the stiffening nipples between his lips. He runs his fingertips along her thighs. He inhales the fragrance of her cheeks. 'I love you,' she whispers. 'I feel so *complete* with you.' Her eyelids flutter. 'I have to tell you: I've never done anything like this with anyone before. I mean, so total. So utterly.'

She spreads her legs. He covers her with his body.

'The act of sexual intercourse,' he says, 'is basically rather simple. It consists of placing the male organ, the penis, within the vagina, which is the female organ. By agitating the penis within the vagina, stimulation builds up within the male nervous system until a reaction is triggered whereby the male discharges semen, a fluid that contains the sperm cells. The sperm cells travel up the vagina and enter the complex network that is the female reproductive system. If a sperm cell encounters an ovum, or egg cell, fertilization takes place and a child is conceived. The moment when semen is discharged from the penis is usually accompanied by sensations of pleasure, followed by relaxation, for the male. This moment of ecstasy is known as the orgasm. In the female, orgasm is not accompanied by any release of fluid, but there are certain other bodily responses, such as spasms of the vaginal muscles, dilation of the pupils, and a feeling of physical exhilaration.'

'Yes. Yes. Yes. Yes.'

He goes through the familiar movements and the girl makes the familiar responses. His eyes are closed; his face presses against the side of her neck. He can hear, but only faintly, the quiet comments of those who watch from the depths of pools: the comparisons, the contrasts, the criticisms, the clarifications. Occasionally he can feel the coldness of the water slicing through the sweet warmth of the girl's soft skin. His seed streaks forth. Her muffled moans of gladness climb in pitch, turn ragged at the edges, shred and sever, and slowly subside. The gleaming dark eye of the ceiling winks. A breeze blows through the fading walls. The motel is shimmering and beginning to dissolve. Urgently he battles to keep it together. He clasps the girl, kisses her, whispers words of love. They congratulate each other on the intensity of their shared emotions and on the truth and beauty they have discovered in one another's souls. This is love, he tells his silent watchers. The eye winks again. He is slipping away, he is being drawn back from this. He continues to resist. He staples himself to reality with thick authoritative phrases: Gross National Product, Reciprocal Trade Agreement, Roman Catholic Hierarchy, German Federal Republic, Eastern Daylight Savings Time, United States Postal Regulations, Southeast Asia Treaty Organization, American Federation of Labor. It is no use. The center cannot hold. The girl dwindles and diminishes beneath him, her breasts deflating, her internal organs becoming gaseous and puffing out through her bodily orifices, until nothing more than her two-dimensional image lies on the bed, a mere filmy coating clinging to the rumpled sheets. Then that too is gone. He clutches the mattress, unwilling to let himself be drawn back, yet aware of the inevitability of his defeat. The building around him disappears. He glimpses his car parked nearby, and runs to it, but it vanishes. The paved courtyard has been unpaved. The telephone poles, billboards, newspaper vending machines, and ornamental junipers are gone. He feels fire in his chest. He is drowning. He is sinking deeper and deeper. His body is being transformed. He slips toward the lower reaches of the dark pool, and there is Quoi, massive, thoughtful, grateful. Clay can no longer remember the shape of the girl's face. The taste of her on his lips is increasingly bland. The memories are going. The demonstration is over.

7

At last he leaves Quoi's pool. It has been peaceful and instructive there, and except for a few rebellious impulses coming upon him at unexpected moments he has adapted well both to his metamorphosis and to the static nature of his submerged existence. He has enjoyed his frequent communions with Quoi, and his view, through Quoi, of the other members of Quoi's species around the world. But now he knows it is time to go. He rises to the surface and hovers there a moment, head down and back bent, summoning his strength; and with one quick convulsive thrust he flips himself up out of the water.

He lies gasping on the shore for what seems like a long time, as the water drains from his system. He decides he is ready to admit air to his lungs, but when it rushes in it scorches him terribly, and he expels it. More cautiously, he imagines his head englobed in glass, and allows the molecules to part with great precision, so that one little blip of air slips through, and then another, and then another, and then the helmet is full of holes and the stream of air is continuous and he is breathing it normally. He stands. He offers himself to the sunlight. He wades out a few feet into the pool and peers down, trying to find Quoi and say goodbye, but all he can see is a dark uncertain mass far below. He waves to it.

As he walks away he sees Hanmer sitting in a cup-shaped black flower of giant size.

'Freed from captivity,' Hanmer says. 'Breathes the air again. You were missed.'

'How long was I gone?'

'Long enough. You were *enjoying* it down there.'

'Quoi was courteous. A good host,' says Clay.

'If we hadn't called you, you would never have left it,' Hanmer says, a pout in his voice.

'If you hadn't let the goat-men chase me, I wouldn't have fallen into the pond in the first place.'

Hanmer smiles. 'True. A hit, a very palpable hit!'

'Where did you get that line?'

'From you, of course,' he says blandly.

'You wander in and out of my mind as it pleases you?'

'Of course.' Hanmer leaps lithely from the floral cup. 'In a manner of speaking, Clay, you're a figment of my imagination. Why shouldn't I invade your head?' He trots over to Clay, puts his face close, and says, 'What was that old Quoi doing with you?'

'Teaching me about love. And learning from me.'

'You could teach it?'

'Love as it was in my era, yes. How it was for us.'

Colors flash across Hanmer's face. He closes his eyes a moment. 'Yes,' he says finally. 'You told it everything, didn't you? And now it's all over the world, every Breather knowing everything about you. You shouldn't have done that.'

'Why?'

'You can't go spewing your secrets everywhere. Have some discretion, man. You have obligations to me.'

'I do?'

'As your self-appointed guide,' Hanmer says, 'I have certain claims on any revelations you may care to make. Remember that. Now come with me.'

Hanmer walks off, showing his crossness in the choppiness of his stride. Clay, irritated by his companion's peremptory manner, is tempted not to follow. But too many unanswered questions clog his throat; he rushes after Hanmer, catching up with him in several minutes. They walk silently side by side. Ahead of them stretches a double wall of flat-topped red bluffs, between which lies a narrow plain. The dominant vegetation of the plain is a wavy ribbonlike plant that rises from the soil in a series of individual leafless fronds three or four feet high; the fronds are soft, fluttering in the breeze, and they are so nearly transparent that Clay has difficulty seeing them except at certain angles. They remind him of strands of clear seaweed surging with the tides. When he nears them, the plants fill briefly with color, flooding with a deep wash of reddish-purple that just as swiftly ebbs toward transparency. Only after he is actually walking in the grove, picking his way between one timid plant and its neighbor, does Clay realize that Ninameen, Serifice, Bril, Angelon, and Ti are camped among the fronds.

'Is this all you ever do?' Clay asks Hanmer. 'Loll around in the sun, wander from valley to valley, dance, change sexes, hold rituals, tease strangers? Don't you study things? Put on plays? Tend gardens? Compose formal music? Examine the great ideas?'

Hanmer laughs.

'You're the summit of human evolution,' Clay says forcefully. 'What do you *do*? How do you fill all your thousands and millions of years? Is dancing enough? Quoi called you Skimmers; I think it thought you were shallow. Did Quoi misjudge you? What is there about you that lifts you above plants and animals? Is the texture of your life as simple as you've let me think it is?'

Hanmer turns. He rests his hands on Clay's shoulders. His scarlet eyes seem sad. 'We all love you,' he says. 'Why are you so agitated? Take us as we come.'

Ninameen, Ti, and the other Skimmers spring up about Clay, chattering like happy children. All but Angelon are in the male form. He has no difficulty, this time, in recognizing them. 'Why were you with the Breather so long?' Serifice demands. And Bril asks, 'Were you angry with us?'

Hanmer says, 'He is troubled because we live forever.'

Serifice frowns. His nostrils flicker, his mouth clacks. He touches Clay's elbow and says, 'Explain death.'

'Why should I explain anything? What do you explain to me?'

'Hostility!' Ti cries. 'Belligerence!' He sounds delighted.

'No, really,' says Serifice softly. 'I want to know. Will this make it better?' And he changes to the female form. Serifice rubs her little breasts against his side. 'Tell me about death,' she murmurs, stroking his chest. He thinks of the blonde girl panting and gasping as he nails her to the motel-room bed, and he is not stirred by the grotesque golden-green alien creature wriggling alongside him. Bulbous red eyes. Universal joints. Flat fishy face. Child of man many times removed. 'Death,' Serifice purrs. 'Help me understand death.'

'You've seen death here,' Clay says, avoiding Serifice's caresses. 'The spheroid – suddenly withered in its cage. That's death. An end of life. What can I say?'

'It was only temporary,' Serifice objects.

'But it was death, while it was happening. If you want to know about it, why not ask the spheroid?'

'We did,' Ti says. 'It didn't understand what we meant.'

'It was gone,' Angelon says, 'and then it came back. It couldn't tell us anything more than that.'

'Neither can I. Look: suppose I pull a fish out of a stream and eat it. The fish dies. That's death. You stop being what you are. You aren't aware of anything going on afterwards.'

'A fish isn't aware of much even during,' Serifice objects.

Bril says, 'How often did people like you die?'

'Once. Only once. When you stopped, you didn't start again.'

'Is that the way it was for everyone?'

'For everyone.'

'You, too, then?'

'I was caught by the time-flux before I died. At least, I think so. As far as I can tell you, I was still alive when I was taken from then to now. So I'm no expert on death.'

'You saw others die,' Serifice persisted.

'Occasionally. But it wasn't educational. Their eyes no longer saw. Their hearts no longer beat. They didn't breathe, think, move, talk. I have no idea what it felt like to *them*, either the dying or being dead.'

'Didn't you feel their absence?' Serifice asked.

'Well, yes, if they were people you knew closely, or someone famous, some artist or doctor or statesman who was in a way a part of your own life. You were aware that something was missing. But millions of unknown strangers died every day, too, and there wasn't any impact at all on those who didn't—'

'They *went out of the world*. Those who hadn't gone would naturally feel their absence. Yes?' Bril asked.

'No. Look, are you asking me if we were all connected, like the Breathers are, like I suppose you are, so that one man's death diminished all of us? We weren't. I mean, except in a metaphorical sense. We were each of us an island. When we *heard* about someone's death, and it was someone we had known directly or indirectly, we felt a loss, yes, but we had to be told, we had to have the information given us in words, do you follow me?'

They stare at him solemnly. White tongues slide across their thin lips. They drive the tips of their fingers into the soft soil in a plain gesture of dismay.

'You do follow me,' he says, seeing their sudden somberness. 'Of course you do. If Hanmer can pull a line of Shakespeare out of my head, you can pull the nature of the human condition out, too. You don't need to ask me all these questions. You understand.'

'Tell us,' Angelon says, kneeling with head bowed between thighs, 'what it was like to live knowing that you would have to die.'

He considers that. At length he says, 'Most people came to terms with that fairly well. They accepted it as something beyond their control. The thing to do was to pack as much life as you could into the time you had, to waste none of it, to find someone to love and something to build, to win your immortality the best way you could, by creating something or by creating someone, and keeping yourself healthy so you could extend your life as long as possible. And actually I think the time given was enough for almost everyone. Toward the end,

I suspect, a normal man had had all he wanted of it; his body was slowing down, and probably he was sick a lot of the time, even in pain pretty often – you know what sick is ? You know pain ? – and he was just going through the same old routine, bored with it, the getting up and the eating and the working and the sleeping, and his family was grown and gone from him, and, well, I suspect the end wasn't that much of a hardship. Of course, there were the thinkers and the artists who felt they still had more to give the world, and they didn't want to go, and there were the ones who stayed alert and vigorous into old age, and had so much more to see, and those who had curiosity in them like a fire, wanting to know what would happen next year and the next and the next and on into eternity, and they resented going too. And also there were plenty who were taken too soon, before they had even started living, the ones killed in accidents or carried off by childhood diseases or shot up on the battlefield, you know, and there was real injustice there. But by and large, I think that after sixty or seventy years, the average human being was ready to go, and didn't take it as a terrible affront to his ego to be turned off. Is any of this comprehensible to you ?'

'Sixty or seventy years ?' Serifice says.

'The usual lifespan. Eighty wasn't unusual. Some made it to ninety. More than that, a few.'

'Sixty or seventy years,' Serifice says. 'And then you stop forever. How beautiful. How strange. Like flowers ! Now I see you clearly. Your suffering. Your wonder. Your distance. Clay we love you more. You give us such pleasure !' She claps her hands. 'Look, now ! In your honor, Clay: I will attempt to die.'

'Wait,' he gasps. 'Listen – no—'

She sprints away, through the field of waving transparent stalks. The other Skimmers, smiling serenely, move closer to Clay, who stands watching her in bewilderment. Several of them touch his skin. They make some minor rearrangement within him so that he can see as they see, and he perceives the sixness of them, the sextuple unit T-Bril-Hanmer-Angelon-Ninameen-Serifice, their souls quivering in a single shining suspension.

Spider-fashion, using dozens of busy legs, Serifice scrambles up the sheer face of the red bluff to the left. She loses patience in the last dozen yards of the climb and simply drifts to the top, coming to rest nine feet above the ground, perched on a clear gleaming spike of air. She begins to spin on her vertical axis. The rest of the sixness commence a singing, so that a yellow cloud of music forms around Serifice, punctuated by quick red slashes of discord. Serifice flings her arms wide. Her face is transfigured by joy. Her axial velocity increases. Her angular momentum mounts. In her turning she spins a glass web that tugs him inexorably toward the sextuple unit of Skimmers. He can barely see her now, except at odd moments, when she intercepts the sunlight at the precise intersection and bursts into glittering visibility, a whirling vortex of ecstatic consciousness. She spins. She spins. She spins. She spins. She spins. She spins. Now, as she whirls ever more giddily, the essential reality of her starts to break up. She eddies randomly from the female form to the male. She! He! She! He! Her! Him! Her! Him! Hers! His! Hers! His! She! She! She! He! He! He! We! They!

'No, Serifice,' he screams.

The four syllables, as they leave his anguished lips, turn to cords of fine glass strung with prismatic beads, and, flying outward from him, form lines that leap across the gulf to Serifice. But he cannot snare her. The yellow song of the sixness now is shot through by the snubnosed blue bolts of a song that is Serifice's alone. She! He! She! He!

Pop.

The fabric of the air ruptures and there is a sharp swooshing sound as something sweeps through. Clay sinks to the ground, rubbing his forehead in the pebbly soil and clutching, for support, two of the gently waving transparent fronds. An insistent thought drums at his temples: *Five. Five. Five. Five. Five.* Where is Serifice? Serifice has gone to discover what death is like. Ninameen, Ti, Bril, Angelon, and Hanmer remain. Thunder rumbles. The sky turns orange. Serifice is gone, and a whiplash resonance from her vanishing trips him into wild oscillation, making him tumble end over end until the valley and its tender seaweeds melt away and he dangles above a blistered desert, all red and orange and white in the searing sun, with hissing crackles of static rising from its tortured sands. There he hangs, confronting the fact of Serifice's suicide, until Hanmer, in the female form, finds him and softly brings him back to his proper place. 'What of Serifice?' he asks, and Hanmer whispers, 'Serifice is learning about death.'

8

He is inconsolable. He did not cause it, but he feels that the guilt is his, having stirred in Serifice an irresistible curiosity about the phenomenon of inevitable termination of existence, and he trembles for the damage he has done to the sixness. All through a long day he mopes apart, kicking at the soil, awakening sleeping trees, tossing pebbles across ravines. The others confer. At length Ti comes to him and says, 'Will you let me make you happy again?' She is in the female form.

'Leave me alone,' he mutters, thinking she is offering her body.

Ti understands. Fluttering hastily over to maleness, he says, 'I can show you something interesting.'

'Show me Serifice.'

'Serifice has gone from us. Why do you mourn her this way?'

'Someone has to mourn. I've had more practice than any of you.'

'You make us unhappy with your mourning. Is death so terrible that you must tarnish the sky with sadness?'

'She had all of forever to live. She didn't have to go.'

'Which makes her going all the more beautiful,' says Ti. He presses Clay's hand firmly between his. 'Come with me and let me divert you. We've gone to some effort to find a way of cheering you. It would distress us if you refused what we have.'

Clay shrugs, assailed by this new dimension of guilt. 'What is it?'

'Books.'

'Really?'

'And things. Ancient things made by other races of mankind.'

He is aroused. Serifice is almost thrust into unimportance. He looks sharply at Ti and says, 'Where? How far?'

'Come. *Come!*'

Ti runs. Clay follows. They trot past the other four Skimmers, who are sprawled decoratively on the ground, eyes closed, limbs drooping relaxedly. As he jogs along, Ti takes little leaps on an invisible trampoline, cutting off arcs of the jaunt with sharp vertical bounds. Ti comes down female from one of these leaps. She is fractionally more voluptuous than the others, with wider hips and distinctly human-looking buttocks; but of course the whole texture of her body remains bizarre and alien to him. He imagines that he can see Ti's bones like soft white bristles passing through her flesh, carrying sensations and colors rather than serving any structural purpose. They come to a place of scrubby yellow trees growing on a subtle slope; the land just ahead rises as though tipped up by a firm hand from beneath, and gray streaks of talus come screeing down the side like strands of the giant's hair. The sun is low now and shadows have deep edges. The sky is a trembling red. Midway up the slope, to the accompaniment of unseen trombones, snuffling bassoons, and oily saxophones, Ti begins making flickering gestures with her outspread hands, and an opening appears just ahead of them. He beholds the mouth of a circular passageway, twice his height in diameter, that leads far into the earth. Ti dances forward. He goes after.

The walls of the passageway are crystalline and glow with an inner luminosity that bathes his face and Ti's with cool green brilliance. The tunnel curves and curves again, bringing them finally to a low-roofed banjo-shaped room in which the echoes of their barefoot footsteps thump and swirl like ponderous motes of dust. Clay sees shelves, cabinets, containers, drawers, and closets. Frozen with wonder, he dares not go forward. Ti opens a glass-faced cabinet and withdraws a sparkling ruby cube the size of her head. He takes it carefully from her, surprised at its lightness.

The cube speaks to him in an unintelligible language. The cadence is strange: a liquid rhythm, rich with anapests, made more powerful by unexpected caesuras that split the lines like random hatchets. Undoubtedly he is hearing poetry, but not any poetry of his era. A skein of sound unreels. He struggles to catch even one familiar word, some root with roots in the epoch of man, but no, but no, it is all delicate gibberish, more mysterious than the things a Finn might say as he murmurs in his sleep. 'What is it?' he asks finally, and Ti says, 'A book.' Clay nods impatiently, having guessed that: 'What book? What are they saying?'

'A poem of the old days, before the moon fell.'

'How old?'

'Before the Breathers. Before the Awaiters. It may be an Interceder poem, but it isn't in any language the Interceders ever spoke.'

'Can you understand it?'

'Oh, yes,' Ti said. 'Yes, of course! How beautiful it is!'

'But what do the words mean?'

'I don't know.'

He ponders her paradox, and while he does she takes the cube from him and restores it to its cabinet; it seems to vanish in the inner dusk. Now she gives him an accordion-pleated box made, apparently, of rigid plastic membranes. 'A work of history,' she explains. 'The annals of a former age, describing the course of human development up to its author's time.'

'How do I read it?'

'Like this,' she says, and her fingers slide between the membranes, lightly tapping them. The box sets up a low humming noise that resolves itself into discrete packets of verbalization; he bends his head toward it to catch the quanta of knowledge. He hears: '*Swallowed crouching metal sweat helmet gigantic blue wheels smaller trees ride eyebrows awed destruction light killed wind and between gently secret in spread growing waiting lived connected over shining risk sleep rings trunks warm think wet seventeen dissolved world size burn.*'

'It doesn't make sense,' he complains. Ti, sobbing, takes the box from him and puts it on a shelf. Going to a closet, she brings forth an arrangement of glossy metal plates, fastened by a punch-rivet in one corner.

'This?'

'Very ancient,' she says. 'It isn't easy for me to make out the title. Yes: here: *Mass Transport Planning Techniques in the Ninth Century*.' She gives it to him. Ninth century after what, he wonders. The metal plates are covered from edge to edge with tiny engrossed hieroglyphs, which hurl blurts of spectrum at him as he tips the plates now this way, now that, catching shards of light in the minute crevices. The colors, bouncing into his eyes, leave imprinted images. He sees impossible cities of sky-stabbing towers, webbed by mazy bridges far above the ground; in capsules rocketing at implausible velocities across these bridges sit purple-faced caricatures of humanity, lumpy-bodied, heavy-shouldered, with domed heads and feeble eyes. Words accompany the images, but, tilt the plates as he may, he can never quite get the commentary to come straight at him. Signal after signal ricochets from his cheekbone or his forehead and sputters away into some murky corner of the room. After a while he grows weary of this oblique text and returns it to Ti.

Next she offers him three thumb-sized tubes of what seems like diamond or pure quartz, within which a greasy fluid lolls in caverned chambers. He shakes the tubes and the fluid, roiling, sends slow pseudopods creeping into this miniature passage and that one. Meanwhile Ti has taken from somewhere a looping golden filament mounted on a thin silvery plaque; she puts her lips to the plaque and cold light surges from the filament. 'Hold the tubes against the light,' she instructs him. He does so and the beam, diffracted through the inner labyrinth of the transparent tubes, hammers messages into his brain:

FLOWERS TRIUMPH.
INFINITY CAN ALSO BE DAMP AND MOIST.
BEWARE CHANGE, FOR IT IMMOBILIZES THE SOUL.
THERE IS WINE IN TRUTH.
THE SKULL LAUGHS BENEATH THE SCOWL.

'What is it?' he asks.

'A religious text,' Ti explains. The messages continue to flood his mind with metaphor, and he stands transfixed, trembling, his skin ablaze. In a few moments Ti casually takes the tubes from him and flips them into a closet.

'Show me the rest,' he demands hoarsely. 'Show me everything!'

She gives him a black helmet carved from a single chunk of polished stone. It contains, on its inner surface, a host of feathery cilia. He dons it; the cilia sink into his scalp; he finds himself able to detect the motion of atoms and the vibrations of molecules. The universe becomes a mist of dancing colorless dots, glistening in hazy clouds and occasionally emitting brusque bleeps of energy. He trades the helmet for a film of quivering bubble-stuff which, when placed over his eyes, allows him to perceive the structure of the planet in terms of units of distinct density; here are bars of blue light representing a certain mass, here are auburn globes representing another, here are gray rectangles within which screaming electrons are ground too close. Ti deprives him of this and replaces it with a tiny fragile-walled bowl out of which a river of ivory pins begins to pour, spilling across his feet and covering the floor; he cries out and the pins leap back into the bowl. She presents him with an assemblage of singing wires whose ends overlap in unlikely ways, creating a small peephole of crosshatched nothingness. He squints into it and views the murky orange denizens of some star's heart. Ti's next toy is a slender yellow spindle marked from tip to tip by finely graved parallel lines: this, she says, is the last key ever manufactured on Earth. 'What door does it fit?' he asks, and she smiles apologetically, telling him that the door no longer exists. Then she shows him a coppery disk that holds all the poetry composed in a certain ten-thousand-year period early in the world's history, but later than his, and she lets him briefly grasp the sticky handles of a machine whose function is to turn lakes into mountains and mountains into clouds, and then she touches a knobby wand to his forehead, allowing him to discover that this chamber is not the only repository of ancient artifacts on this hillside, but rather that a whole series of chambers exists, on and on, each packed from floor to ceiling with the treasures of ages past. Here are the musics, poetries, fictions, philosophies, sciences, and histories of civilization upon civilization; here are the machineries of departed human species; here are maps, directories, catalogs, indices, dictionaries, encyclopedias, thesauri, tables of law, annals of dynastic succession, almanacs, almagests, data pools, handbooks, and access codes. Dusty chambers are stuffed with archaeological relics, the gatherings of each civilization that picked the bones of its predecessors. Deeper in, near the heart of the maze, he catches sight of actual paper books, spools of magnetic tape, information films and flakes, all the humble recording devices of his own primitive era, and he shivers with wonder at the survival of such things through unknown eons. His mind floods with a million million questions. He will spend his next three infinities in this hill, mining the past for knowledge, reconstructing all that the inhabitants of this era have coyly declined to tell him. He will put together a coherent semblance of human history from the time of man down to the epoch of these sons of men, and at last it will all be clear and orderly. As Ti takes the wand from his forehead, the vision of multiplicity fades, and he says to her, 'Can we explore those other chambers?'

Her smile is sad. 'Perhaps another time,' she says. 'We must leave now.'

He is reluctant to go. Breaking from his stasis, he kneels to peer into cabinets and to draw things from shelves. He is inflamed by this treasury of lost millennia. What is this? And this? And this? How does this intricate and dazzling machine work? What are these sly and enthralling sounds? What truths lie embedded in this block of sparkling glass? And in this nest of rods? This cluster of orbs? He will load his arms with wonders. He will carry forth from the cave enough mystery and enough magic to occupy him for a dozen cycles of investigation. 'Come,' Ti says, looking annoyed. 'You mustn't demand too much. This hasn't been easy.' He shakes her off. 'Wait. What's the hurry? Let me—'

A slab of marble engraved with almost-recognizable symbols

64

clouds and blurs in his hands. The room loses its symmetry of form as the roof first slants, then melts and drips at one corner. The shelves grow misty. Delicate, intricate objects, as clean and sharp as if they had been fashioned only the day before, lose their precision of form. All is in flux. 'Come,' Ti whispers. 'Come out, now. We've stayed too long.'

The floor heaves. The walls grumble.

He flees with Ti. The thought that some convulsion of the planet will destroy these miracles, just as he has found them, drives ninety metal spikes through his throat. Scrambling, sliding, they emerge in the open. Dusk has come. Rubbery-winged birds swoop and screech. He looks back, terrified. No passageway is in sight. Clutching Ti's arm, he cries, 'What's happening? Will everything be lost?'

'Everything was lost long ago,' Ti says.

He does not understand, but he cannot make her explain. He follows her down the slope, into the plain where the transparent fronds wave; here, in the night, they take on a dazzling glow, filling the air with buzzing brightness. Hanmer, Nina-meen, Angelon, and Bril lie where they had been before, and stir as if rising from a long sleep. They stretch, they blink, they seem to yawn. Serifice is not there, and Clay realizes that he had totally forgotten her death during his interlude among the artifacts. He tumbles down beside the Skimmers. Still blazing with that vision of antiquity recaptured, he says hoarsely, 'Such things I saw! Such marvels!'

'You stayed too long,' Hammer says, a trace of regret in his voice.

'How could I leave? How could I tear myself away?'

'Of course. Of course. We understand perfectly. You're not to blame. Yet it was something of a strain for us, toward the end.'

'What was?'

Hanmer gives him a mild smile instead of an answer. The Skimmers get to their feet. Each of them carefully plucks a glowing frond; the fronds make little clucking sounds as they come, roots and all, from the soil. Clay senses that they are not being killed, only borrowed a while. Hanmer picks an extra

65

one and gives it to Clay. Single file, the Skimmers march off into the night, each carrying its frond aloft like a torch. All but Hanmer have assumed the female form. Clay is third in the procession, with Ti just in front of him and Ninameen behind him. She comes up close and brazenly rubs the tips of her breasts against his bare back by way of greeting: chilly gongs clanging in his spine. 'Do you feel better?' she asks. 'We were so unhappy for you. The way you were when Serifice went.'

'The longer I'm here, the less I comprehend.'

'Did you like the things Ti showed you?'

'Wondrous. Wondrous. If I could only have stayed longer – if I could just have taken a few of them out with me—'

'Oh, no. You couldn't.'

'Why?'

Ninameen hesitates a moment. 'We dreamed them for you,' she says finally. 'Bril, Hanmer, Angelon, me. Our dream. To make you happy again.'

'A dream? Only a dream?'

'And dreams end,' says Ninameen.

9

A furry mist engulfs them; the undulating fronds give a thick pink light now. Briefly it rains. Far away, perhaps high on some unseen but lofty mountain, some female creature begins to sob, and sends the sound of it floating over them, a series of disturbing maroon wails. 'What is that?' he asks Hanmer, who says, 'It is Wrong, weeping in the hills.'

'Wrong?'

'Wrong. One of the powers whom we propitiate.'

'You have Gods?'

'We have those who are larger than ourselves. Such as Wrong.'

'Why does she weep?'

'Perhaps for joy,' Hanmer suggests vaguely.

The sound of Wrong's sobbing dies away as they plod onward. The light rain ends and a muggy warmth descends, but Clay, soaked, shivers nonetheless. He starts to feel fatigue for the first time since his awakening. It is an odd metaphysical kind of weariness whose nature puzzles him. He has not eaten or slept at all in this era, yet he is neither hungry nor drowsy; and, though he has walked a great many miles, his muscles are not sore. But there is now a new heaviness in his bones, as if they are turning to steel in the marrow, and his head is a burden for his spine, and his organs droop and sag against the walls of flesh that contain them. Eventually it strikes him that what he is feeling is a quality of his surroundings rather than of himself: an emanation, a kind of radioactivity, oozing from the rocks and bleeding out of the soil. Turning to Ninameen, he says, 'I'm getting tired. Are you?'

'Naturally. It happens here.'

'Why?'

'This is the oldest part of the world. Age lies piled in clouds all about us. We can't help breathing it as we go through, and it dulls us.'

'Wouldn't it be safer to soar over it?'

'It can't harm us. A passing discomfort.'

'What is this place called?'

'Old,' Ninameen tells him.

Old it is. His body thickens. His skin puckers. He sprouts a coat of coarse white hair on his chest and belly and loins. His genitals shrivel. His ankles complain. His veins bulge. His eyes grow bleary. His breath comes short. His back is stooped. His knees are bent. His heart races and slows. His nostrils wheeze. He tries not to breathe, fearing that he is inhaling age like some poisonous fumes, but dizziness overwhelms him after just a moment, and he is forced to gulp in the murky air. The same thing is happening to his companions; the sleek waxen skin of the Skimmers now is cracked and wrinkled, their fluid stride is a silly shuffle, their eyes are dull. The breasts of those in female form have become ugly dugs, flat and pendulous, with blackened, eroded nipples. Their mouths hang open, revealing gray toothless gums. He is troubled by these changes in them; for, if they are ageless and imperishable, should they be altering even now as they pass through the valleys of Old? Or are they tactfully corrupting their flesh for his benefit, so that he will not feel ashamed of his own deterioration? They have told him so many gentle lies that he has ceased to trust them. Perhaps they are dreaming again on his behalf. Perhaps his entire adventure is nothing more than one of Hanmer's own dreams, an uneasy stirring between one dusk and one dawn.

He struggles forward. Silently he begs them to grant him a reprieve from this place. How easy it would be, he thinks, for them to summon their pale spark-shot clouds and spring up from this dismal slough in lovely flight! But they insist on walking. He moves ever more slowly. The gleaming frond that lights his way has caught the contagion of senescence; it buckles and bends, and its glow is stale. Their path is ascending, making the going all the more difficult. His throat is dry and his tongue, swollen, is a lump of old cloth in his mouth. Gummy rheum drips from the rims of his eyes and trickles across his chest. He is reminded of the goat-men, scaly and hideous, covered with scums.

Animals cackle in the underbrush. The frond's faint light shows him toothy mouths yawning at the base of every tree beside the path. Dark-blooming flowers exhale an odor of digestive fluid. There is a drumming in his temples; there is a coldness in his gut. Twice he falls, and twice he scratches himself to his feet unhelped. Old. Old. Old. The universe itself is dying; the suns have gone out, the molecules lie in quiet heaps in the void, entropy has won its long war. How much longer? How much farther? He can no longer bear the sight of his own wizened body, and, quivering, he tosses his frond away, glad to be rid of illumination. But Bril, recovering it, puts it back in his hand and says, 'You should not condemn it to root itself in such a place.' And Clay's soul fills with pity and shame, and he keeps his grip on the frond, while trying now to look neither at himself nor at the others.

All colors have washed away. He sees everything in shades of black, even the frond's glow. His bones bend with every step. The coils of his intestines are patched and flaky. His lungs are shredding. With a fierce effort he drives himself forward to Hanmer – parched, withered – and mutters, 'We'll die here! Can't we get out faster?'

'The worst is behind us,' Hanmer says in a calm, unaltered voice.

So it is. They still are deep in night, but Old's bleak domain now reluctantly gives up its grip on him. Resurrection is gradual and prolonged. The throbbings and pantings and gaspings slowly cease; the symptoms of physical decay fade moment by moment. Clay's body straightens. His eyesight clears. His skin becomes smooth. His teeth return, budding in his swelling gums. His manhood triumphantly rises. Yet not even its flagpole firmness can ease him of the memory of where he has been and what he has undergone; he still feels the claw of time on his shoulder, and forgets no detail of his descent into ghastly age. He walks with care and husbands his strength. He spends breath cautiously. He is obsessed with the fragility of his inner framework. He hears the scratch of bone on bone, the harsh rustle of dark blood pushing through thickened arteries. He has little confidence in his revival. Is the ordeal truly over, or is this restoration of strength only a dream within a dream? No. He is indeed given his youth again, though tempered by somber intimations of mortality. 'Are there many such places in the world?' he asks, and Ninameen says, 'There is only one Old. But there are other districts of discomfort.'

'Such as?'

'One is called Empty. One is called Slow. One is called Ice. One is called Fire. One is called Dark. One is called Heavy. Did you think all our world was a garden?'

'How did such places come into being?'

'In the old times,' Ninameen says, 'they were established for the instruction of mankind.' She giggles shrilly. 'They were very serious in those days.'

'But surely you have the power to remove these places now,' Clay suggests.

Ninameen giggles again. 'We do, but we will not. We require them. We are very serious in these days, too.'

Ninameen's body is firm and supple again. Her breasts are high; her thighs are taut. Once again she moves in a ready flowing stride. Her golden-green skin has regained its inward glow. So too with the other Skimmers, who have returned to buoyancy and vigor.

A light now appears in the sky.

It is not the rising sun. Unless he has wholly lost his grasp of direction, they have been walking westward this night; but the light lies before them. It is a cone of luminous green, rising from a point at the foot of the slope they now descend, and widening to fill much of the heavens; it is like a geyser of pale radiance spurting aloft. As the wind sweeps through it, it stirs swirls of a grayer color, whirlpools of light within light. Accompanying this outburst of brightness is a rushing, whispering sound, reminding Clay of the song of distant water. He also hears a sort of subterranean laughter, resonant, slippery. A few minutes of further descent and he has a clearer view of what is ahead. Where the hill blends with the valley a glassy coat covers the ground; the whole valley seems to be sealed in this layer of glass, which stretches off toward the horizon. In the center of this, from a circular fumarole, the towering shaft of green light issues. Behind that wavering, flickering luminosity he can dimly discern some massive shape, possibly a low broad mountain. There is no vegetation in sight. The aspect of everything is forbidding and unearthly. He turns to the Skimmers for an explanation, but their faces are so rigid with concentration, they walk now with such trancelike concern, that he dares not puncture their meditation with questions. In silence they proceed downward. Ultimately he feels the slick cool glass beneath his bare feet. As each Skimmer steps out on the glass, he pauses, turning to set down his frond along the border between glass and earth. Clay does the same. The roots scrabble eagerly toward the soil even before they touch. The frond establishes itself, and, in the light of the green upwelling cloud, its transparency takes on subtle newnesses.

Gliding over the polished floor, they move in a wary arc around the fumarole, skirting it to the south. He plainly sees the opening now, strangely small for so huge an effect, a circle no greater than the circumference of his outspread arms, surrounded by a raised rim a foot in height. And through this the green brightness bursts in pulsating blares, as though expelled rhythmically from some factory in the core of the world. Everything here seems artificial to him, the work of one of the species of the sons of man, probably ancient from the viewpoint of the Skimmers yet no doubt fashioned long after the things of his epoch had vanished.

Now they are in the green cloud itself.

The air is electric. His pores tingle. A sour smell drills upward in his nostrils. His naked body sweats and steams. Silent and solemn, the Skimmers remain aloof, and he continues to respect their mood of withdrawal. The group is roughly parallel to the fumarole. As he comes past it, entering into the rear of the cone of greenness, he is able to see the massive shape to the west with greater clarity. It is no mountain. Rather it is some sort of monolith of flesh, a giant living Moloch, squat and enormous, huddled behind the greenness. The being sits in a colossal curving plate, metallic of texture and deep scarlet in color, which holds it above the level of the ground. Reflections from the green cloud slide along the sides of this cup, staining the scarlet with green, mingling with it in places to create a lustrous, overwhelming brown. Brown too is the color of the crouching being. Clay sees its leathery skin, thick and glossy and ridged like a reptile's hide. The shape of the creature is froglike, but it is a frog of dreams alone, without eyes, without limbs: a tapering promontory, long-bodied, blunt-snouted, with a high vaulting back, fat sides, bulging belly, pedestal-like underparts. It sits motionless, like an idol. He cannot detect even a trace of breathing, yet he is convinced the thing is alive. There it rests in the glare of the green upsurge, giving the impression of being millennia old, vastly wise, a watcher, an absorber, a colossus encalmed. The tip of its snout rears at least five hundred feet in the air. Its gigantic hindquarters are lost in shadows. If it were to move, it would shake the planet. Baleful, monstrous, a living hill, it guards the glassy valley with frosty fervor. What is it? Whence came it? He consults his meager knowledge of the human species of these latter days, as garnered from Quoi the Breather: is this an Awaiter? An Interceder? A Destroyer? Some species not described to him? He cannot easily believe that this thing can be counted at all among the sons of men. Though humans in the fullness of time may have chosen to transform themselves into goats and squids and spheroids, he cannot believe that they would have sought to become mountains. This must be some synthetic monstrosity, or some visitant from another galaxy stranded on Earth, or some relict of a Skimmer's troubled dream, accidentally left to linger in the world of reality.

Hanmer leads the way. They walk cautiously along the southern rim of the tremendous dish in which the being rests. Colors reverberate from it, smearing the bodies of the marchers with streaks of red and green and brown. When they have come nearly past it, the thing at last displays a sign of life: from it emerges a terrible rumbling moan, barely at the threshold of audibility, that causes the ground to quiver and fissures to spring up in the glassy floor. It is a smothered roar of such fierce anguish that Clay shatters with compassion. He has heard trapped animals make such outcries in the forest when caught by the leg in steel-jawed snares. Other than this grim sound, though, there is no hint of animation about the creature.

He questions Hanmer when they are safely beyond it.

'A god,' Hanmer tells him. 'Left by a former age. Bereft of worshipers. An unhappy entity.'

'A God?' Clay repeats. 'Do gods have such a shape?'

'This one does.'

'What were its worshipers shaped like, then?'

'The same,' Hanmer says, 'only smaller. They lived eleven eras and sixteen eons ago. Before my time, I mean.'

'After mine.'

'It goes without saying. They created their god in their own image. Left it sitting in this plaza. Beautifully glassed over; handsome lighting effects. Those people knew how to build. Achieved rare longevity for their structures here; the world is so very changed, but this remains. However, they do not.'

'Human?'

'So to speak.'

Clay looks back. He sees the geysers of green light; he sees the mighty rump of the abandoned god. The ground trembles as the deity cries out again. Tears burst in Clay's eyes. A wild impulse seizes him: he makes the sign of the Cross as though he were standing before a holy altar. His gesture astonishes him, for he has never regarded himself as a Christian; but nevertheless the act of submission has been performed, and the outlines of his swift motions of the hand linger, glowing in the air before his eyes. Instants later the frog-mountain bellows again, even more terribly. Landslides begin; rocks fall in thundering avalanches; the glittering glassy crust over the valley is sundered in a hundred places as hidden fault lines yield. Over that monstrous basso boom comes, again, the high-pitched sobbing of Wrong, and laughter tumbles from the skies. Fear engulfs him. He cannot move. He sprays his toes with his own hot urine. He expects a momentary earthquake. Hands grasp his wrists: Ninameen, Ti, Bril. 'Come,' they say, and, 'Come,' and again, 'Come,' and lift him away, as the first beams of morning roll in like the returning tide.

10

It is day. They are in a splendid gorge, camping on a protruding lip of black rock jutting out over the riverbed hundreds of feet below. The air here is mild and sweet. Birds circle in the flat blue sky. The heavy sun lies low on the horizon.

'We will do,' Hanmer announces, 'the rite of the Lifting of the Sea.'

Clay nods. Fatigue and terror have gone from him with the coming of the sun. He feels alert, receptive, open to new experiences. Sexual desire is surging within him once more; he wonders if he can persuade one of the Skimmers to couple with him. The entire group has been chaste, so far as he is aware,

73

since the disappearance of Serifice. An intentional abstention? Or merely a rush of other things to do? Lolling by the edge of the ledge, loins turned toward the sun, he finds himself strongly aroused by the nearby breasts and thighs and buttocks. The Skimmers still seem like strange plastic mannequins to him, but the flow of passion that stiffens him is the authentic article; however they have managed it, these beings have contrived to present themselves to him as human. Would he have responded like that to any of the other species? Drive his rigid shaft into a spheroid's jellied harbor? Clasp himself to a goat-woman's foul udders? Get himself off in a frog-girl's rump?

Hanmer says, 'Will you share this ritual with us, friend?'

'If I can.'

'You can and will. We ask only patience and restraint.'

He promises. Ninameen, Angelon, and Ti, who are in the female form this morning, sprawl face-down on the ledges and with delicate ease bend their bodies into hoops, heads against toes, knees flexed outward in a manner impossible for Clay's species, buttocks upturned in a frank offering of the sexual parts. 'We must join ourselves in this,' Hanmer remarks, and as he steps toward Ninameen his member slides from its place of concealment; he slips it into Ninameen's exposed slit as coolly as if he were plugging in an appliance, and grasps her by the haunches to steady her in her contorted posture. Bril just as calmly enters the body of Angelon. Hanmer flicks his hand toward Clay in genial impatience. 'Yes, I see,' Clay says, and, seizing Ti's plump rear, glides the tip of his wand to its goal. She makes a soft sound. He leans forward, lacking the suppleness of the two Skimmer males but having an advantage of dimension over them, and presses himself into her to the hilt. The six of them form an odd group on this lofty ledge, a tableau of acrobatic eroticism, held motionless, like statues of impassioned sprites. Seeing that Bril and Hanmer are not making the plunging motions of intercourse, but merely stand behind their partners, united and frozen, he does the same. He waits. Where is the signal? When begins the rite?

Imperceptibly it commences. The five Skimmers emit an

oblique humming sound, so faint that less of it is within the universe than without it; their song is scarcely a molecule in breadth when Clay becomes aware of it and hardly spans a photon's depth from edge to edge, but steadily the sound insinuates itself into the world of phenomena, taking on form and color and mass as it invades his continuum, thickening in timbre, rising in pitch, so that ultimately it is a thunderous column of tone suspended above the gorge, a hammer of gray-black sound that rises and falls in devastating impact, and the crescendo continues, the song gains every moment in dimension, growing more rounded, now, more sleek, developing subtle highlights that flash and sizzle in its center, and Clay, fearing that the weight of it will destroy him if he does not defend himself, timidly lends himself to it, finding an unoccupied rung of pitch within the now tremendous mass and claiming it. As he joins the song he looks uncertainly at his companions, afraid that they may feel he is marring their effort, but they smile their encouragement, Hanmer, Bril, even the contorted females twisting their heads backward to nod warmly at him. He takes comfort from this and lets his output swell to match their volume. The cavities of his skull resonate as the mighty droning sound blasts through him. He becomes one with them. He understands their unity, a thing even more intense than that which links the Breathers in their various pools. Now that he has entered the circuit he no longer is afraid of taking a false step. When Ti begins a series of interior spasms, adopting a complex and exquisite rhythm, he realizes intuitively that this is not his cue to move. He remains in stasis, allowing her to gyrate around the axis that he is providing for her. The physical sensations are acute, but he sustains himself with a patience he had not known he had; and when it seems to him that he can no longer refrain from motion, that he must plough her or die, it is simple for him to shunt his excitement's excess to Hanmer and Bril, who dispose of it for him. He waits. Ti moves. A machine has been created on this ledge: he is one of its six parts. Now he is past the point of immediate stimulation; his entire body throbs and glows, but he is glassily calm. The sexual energies have spread

75

through him. His penis has totally absorbed him and there is no longer a Clay, but simply this one rod, this erect member plugged into the circuit. Then even an awareness of sexuality disappears. He is a pattern of black lines and white blobs. He is a jaggedness on a graph. He is force without mass. He is mass without dimension. He is acceleration without velocity. He is power. He is potential. He is response. He is creation.

It is the time of the Lifting of the Sea.

Pink ribbons leap outward from the ledge, vaulting across the land to the great green globe of water. He follows. He becomes a river of pure sensation rushing in lightning zigzags down the continental slope. Here is the sea, a sleepy giant crushing its bed. Clay embraces it. He senses it all: the heaviness, the greenness, the saltiness, the turbulence, the calm, the warmth, the chill. Here are waves lashing a transparent beach. Here are secret valleys and slime-festooned peaks. Here is blackness. Here is brilliance. Here is light, dancing down to the sparkling polyps. Here are the creatures of eternal night, trawling for nightmares. Here are some fugitive children of mankind, altered, hidden, raging in the depths. Here are the cords that bind the planet. Here are the seams of the soul. Here is a winged thing flapping through a realm of shimmering sand. Black spines twitching on a green-encrusted rock. Random claws clasping quivering fleshy tubes. Mouths. Teeth. Surging masses of troubled water. Fragile tawny cells tossed on tides. Silent slippery currents eroding drowned gulfs and bays. The plankton ballet. The symphony of the whales. The weight. The weight. The weight. The sea stirs, questioning the intruders. But it is proper. The rite is necessary. Those who have come from the sea must return to their source. Arms plunge into the ocean's rocky bed. Hands seize the levers of control. Bodies go taut. Ah, yes, yes, yes! The sea rises! Easily, proudly, confidently, they lift it, tugging it in one coherent fishy mass until it erupts from its age-old place. They hold it high overhead. A salty rain begins to fall. Stray weeds and urchins tumble loose, but everything is caught and restored to its rightful position. The liquid sun bathes the bubbling mucky bottom. The roots of the planet's skin lie exposed. The sea's voice has joined their song, overlaying it with thick blurred tones and tender booming crashes. Burbling trumpets sing sweetly. The Skimmers rejoice. The power of the sons of man is made manifest. The circle of the seasons is closed. On the surface of the levitated sea-sphere, prickly protrusions rise and swiftly sink as gravity's shifting spikes perturb its harmony. Now the sphere descends, while those who have lifted it gather ecstatically at the mathematical center of the hemisphere, taking it lightly on their shoulders, tucking in the stray strands of kelp and the occasional unruly eels. Is this the moment for the blaze of completion? No. No. Not yet. The sea subsides. The distant murmur of its echoing flesh grows more faint. It returns to its bed. Easily, easily, easily, all its contents undisturbed, the vast swimming things still nosing in the dark, the drowned cities of antiquity once more concealed, the tracks of lost explorers hidden, the vessels of the millennia blanketed with familiar silt. The demands of the rite have been met. Those who lifted are free now to resume individual identities and pursue individual ecstasies. He slides out of the linkage. He hears the soft rumbling of the relieved ocean as it spreads its rim over the world's coasts. He comes out of his stasis, ready now for the fulfillment that he postponed for the sake of the event.

His body still is joined to Ti's. She moves; he moves; the passionate friction begins. Together they have slipped to the floor of the ledge. His legs part; his back arches; her weight descends on him. He feels her cool lips against his. Ti's hands clasp his breasts and stroke his hardened, fevered nipples. Ti thrusts into him, sliding again and again into the lubricated cleft, probing deep, knocking at the gate of his womb; he has never been invaded like this before, and the penetration is strange and terrifying, although he finds pleasure in it. Gasping, he caresses Ti's strong, muscular back, her taut waist, her flat buttocks. He draws up his knees so that the union can be even more intense. The stone is cold against his back. A curious sense of dislocation troubles him even in the midst of his frenzies. His hips buck; his pelvis heaves. Waves of ecstasy radiate from his loins, shivering into his thighs, his

77

belly, his chest, his skull. He explodes with sensation. But it is not over. Can Ti continue? Yes: goading him toward the next explosion. Ti's body pushes down fiercely against him. He feels Ti's chest against his breasts, he feels the hard shaft of her drilling into him with steady friction. Another explosion. Yes. Yes. Enough! He is lost; he is baffled; he is dazed. He locks his thighs around Ti's hips and cries out for the final frenzy. Ti rams deeper than ever, battering at his kidneys, his ovaries, his intestines, all the hidden machinery of his inner flesh, and then comes the flood of fluid gushing from Ti's member, the cascade spurting from her and striking him with sudden surprising power, and he submits and surrenders and allows the full climactic fury to overwhelm him. It has ended. Ti subsides. After a while, Ti rolls off him. Frowning, he lies as before, belly-up, knees flexed, legs spread, and tries to comprehend the reasons for the feelings of disorientation that have obsessed him since the finish of the Lifting of the Sea. Slowly he comes to realize the nature of the situation. He has assumed the female form.

II

Unmanned by this sea-change, he rises to take inventory. The rite, he sees, has transformed them all: Hanmer and Bril now are female, Angelon, Ninameen, and Ti male. For them no chaos, though; for him, otherwise. He surveys himself. He has lost perhaps six inches in height – no taller than Hanmer is he, now, and the angle from which he views the world is different. Flesh has pooled at his hips. He runs his hands from his armpits to his haunches and is amazed at that outward-sloping contour. He squeezes the meat and is dimly aware of the body structure buried within, the hidden pelvic girdle. He has breasts. They sway when he moves his shoulders. From above they seem pear-shaped, tapering to small dark nipples. They appear farther apart on his chest than he expects breasts to be;

putting his hand between them, he runs up and down the wide track of the sternum, feeling only flat boniness. He searches his memory. Do breasts indeed belong over here in the corners, sprouting almost from his armpits? He exaggerates. They are normally placed. He has never studied breasts with quite this degree of intensity before, he tells himself. Nor from quite this angle. He puts his hands over them. Squeezes. Traps the nipples between fingers. Pushes the mounds of flesh close together to create a deep deceptive valley. Cups them from below, savoring their heft. He has not touched true female breasts since his awakening; he realizes now how different the feel of a female Skimmer is from the feel of genuine *Homo sapiens* flesh. Yet he is not unduly aroused. These breasts are his own.

He releases them. He sweeps his hands downward over the gently curving belly. He ponders the mysterious internal anatomical tangle, the vena femoralis, the vasa ovarica, the uterus, the os pubis, the vasa iliaca externa, the fornix, the cervix, the fallopian tubes, the Graafian follicles, the infundibula, the mesovaria, the infundibulopelvic ligaments. He wonders if he would be fertile if there were someone to impregnate him. Surely not Ti (how do they bear their young in this time? do they have young at all?) but some other captive of the time-flux, coming upon him, topping and entering him, filling him with swimming sperm, the embryo blossoming, the uterus expanding – is it possible? He shivers. He touches his thighs, so satiny, so strangely smooth, and, hesitating just a moment, sweeps four fingers of his right hand inward to his groin. The absence of his accustomed genitals alarms him far less than he would ever have thought likely. The familiar swinging organs are gone, yes, leaving a void, leaving this open empty place, but yet he does have something else here, after all. He pushes the tight, springy pubic floss aside and, wonderstruck, touches the slit, the knob, the moist inner place, telling himself: these are my labia minora, this must be the clitoris, here are the labia majora, this is the vaginal opening, this the mons veneris. I shall squat hereafter to void my urine. I shall be the penetrated and not the penetrator. He sees a view as

79

through a fluoroscope: his body jammed up close against another, and a thick long object stuck deep into him, nudging his organs out of place. How odd. He parses the grammar of his metamorphosis: not *to fuck* but *to be fucked* is how it shall be. I must learn to hold my thighs open for prolonged lengths of time; I must master my inner muscles; I must school my back to new horizontal postures. Shall I menstruate? Is it going to be painful? How can I keep from bruising my breasts as I move carelessly about? Is my walk feminine enough? Should I mince and prance? Will I wrinkle early? Henceforth will I deal with situations in a different way? He closes his eyes. He leans against the side of the cliff, shaking his head, running his bewildered hands over breasts, belly, thighs, loins. The change is getting to him now. He remembers Ti on top of him, thrusting herself inside him. Is that how they all see it, his fellow members of the female sex? An invasion? A battering ram? They must like it more than that. A million million million years and they're still doing it; my reaction can't be typical. A result of my male orientation. Or just an ex-virgin's initial hostility. And even I got pleasure from it. Though feeling insulted and assaulted.

Will I ever change back?

He puts both hands to his crotch. He tries to remember his lost maleness. What a good feeling it was to grow hard! And the anticipatory tickle, and the throb, the hammerblows, the spurt. Gone. Now he will merely soften and flow, and receive.

Hanmer, male again, approaches him.

'How beautiful you look,' he says. 'How strange. How elegant.'

Clay wishes he could hide his body.

Hanmer moves closer. 'May I touch you? May I examine you? We admire your other self, but we value this new one. Is it an accurate rendition of the original?'

Clay makes a thick sound of assent.

'I love you,' Hanmer says calmly.

'Please.'

'We should celebrate once again. We have had a very successful Lifting of the Sea.'

'Perhaps another time.'

'Postponement would be cruel. Here. Here.' Hanmer touches Clay's breasts. The small slender fingers seem like a thousand arthropodal digits as they bristle against his nipples. He indicates his displeasure. Hanmer saddens. 'We must share sensations,' he says. 'Come. Let me enter you as you once entered me.' Clay remembers: a Hanmer turned female, soon after their meeting, a warm and delicious companion, swiftly to disappear. Clay had not objected to Hanmer's transsexualization then. It had not seemed improper to couple with one who had been so lately male. But now he cannot yield when the cases are altered. He will not be had. A tough lay; an iron maiden; he tries to cover his nakedness, one arm flung across his bobbing breasts, one hand spread over the base of his belly. A paragon of pudicity. Hanmer utters the melancholy smile of the disappointed roué, beating a prudent retreat in the face of invincible maidenhood; he will not force him, for the game may not be worth the candle. Eh? Eh? Clay's eyes flutter. Golden bees buzz round his head. He turns. He rushes away, down a steep path toward the river at the foot of the gorge. Brambles snatch at him, snagging one soft breast and leaving a red track. He grows winded quickly. The path twists and shifts angles, so that within moments he can no longer see the ledge on which the Skimmers lie. They have not followed him. Naked, jiggling, too fleshy, he speeds downward.

He falls the last ten feet of the way and is stunned a while. Then he rises. He is alone. Pulling himself together. The walls of the gorge like slabs of black glass above him. The sky a distant crack. No trees here, only small red phallic fungi sprouting on the steamy riverbank. He makes his way between them, trembling to crush one beneath his heel.

The river is not quite as he expects rivers to be.

Its basic color is blue, but it is tinged with bright streaks of red, yellow, and green, as though it carries a swarm of tinted particles that just barely reach the threshold of visibility. The effect is a dazzling one of perpetual change, as the rainbow hues sweep and crest and mingle. Where fangs of rock jut above the flow, a dazzling spray is hurled into the air.

He kneels on the bank, leaning forward to look closely. Yes, tinted particles, discrete and distinct, no doubt of it; this may be water, but it has passengers. A torrent of jellyfish? He cups his hand and scoops up a small quantity of water. Sparkling lights play in it; things flash. Quickly, though, the colors die. The water now dribbling out between his pressed fingers is water-colored, no more. He empties his hand and tries again. Again the same: he scoops something up, but the something does not remain.

Clamping hands against a rocky overhang, he puts his face near the flow. Now he can hear a hazy chattering sound, as of the river talking to itself in a dim monotone. And its colors are brilliant. They do not seem to come from particles *in* the river, though, so much as they appear to be components *of* the river, segments of its actual bulk. There is an overlap of identities between the bits of color and their carrier. He sees the river suddenly as a living thing, on the borderline between the animate and the inanimate; these are its cells, its corpuscles, its homunculi.

Shall he enter it?

He finds a sandy place where the river is accessible and wades out into it. Ankle-deep, he watches the tickling colors coruscating around his feet. He feels an invitation to proceed.

Deeper. Thigh-high, now. He splashes water over his breasts and shoulders. He rubs it on his face. He takes another step; the bottom is smooth and firm. His buttocks now touch. His loins. Come, he tells the river, give me back my balls. The dark pubic triangle is bright with river-colors. Something odd is happening to his feet, but he can no longer see them. He goes deeper. Navel-high. He shivers. He is being lifted and swept away. With a splash he topples face-forward into the current. It is fiery against his breasts. Burn them, yes, sear them off! He kicks his legs; he swims. Then he relaxes. Why work? He is going downstream regardless. He drifts. His mood eases. He feels some mild regret, now, about wanting to give up his new femaleness so swiftly. Why the panic? Why the haste? Should he not learn first what it is like to wear such a body? He has always been receptive to new experiences; he

82

has taken pride in that. Was it not just a short while ago that he was trying to bring about this very transformation in himself, simply to see if it could be done? And now it has. And he is fighting it. Choked with horror because Ti had poked something into him. Refusing Hanmer. Surly, ungracious, ungiving. A bitch. A tease. He is dense with sorrow, suddenly. He has not begun to explore the possibilities of this body. Is being had so much more repugnant than having? Does it shock you to be plugged after a lifetime of plugging? Are you unable to adapt? Are you rigid in your orientation? Why not lie back, spread, let them in? Expand your awareness. Come to understand the Other Side. Yield. Yield. Yield. You can have your pecker back some other time.

He attempts to get out of the river.

But he is unable to reach the shore. He thrashes his legs ferociously, he windmills his arms, he cuts the water with cupped hands, and still he sweeps serenely downstream. The shining rocky bank gets no closer. He seeks bottom with his feet, trying to anchor himself for a landward crawl, and finds no bottom. He bobs along. He fights more fiercely and the result is the same. Exhaustion spears his skull. He gulps oceans. The brilliant corpuscles of the river permeate his intestines.

He is trapped in a swirling tangle of brightness. His thighs are chained. The river will not let him go. But ahead looms a chance for escape: a sleek gray dome of rock rising in mid-channel. He will let himself be swept into it, and he will somehow scramble up onto it and rest until he is strong enough to fight the current. Yes. The boulder approaches. He braces himself for the impact. Hit it shoulder-first, he decides. Protect the sensitive breasts. He sees himself tossed high, a flurry of kicking limbs, white meat, dark hair, rosy nipples, vacuum at the crotch. Cling. Cling. But it does not happen that way. He rockets toward the stony mass and it cleaves his body; without pain he is neatly divided, part of him flowing to the left of the boulder, part to the right; he unites beyond it and continues his effortless journey.

Now he understands.

The river has eaten him. This body, this arrangement of organs and flesh and muscle and bone, this heap of calcium and phosphorus and hydrogen and whatnot, is an illusion. These breasts are an illusion. These plump alluring buttocks are illusions. This hairy triangle is an illusion. He has become one with the sparkling flow. He has contributed his body; he now is composed of the same sparkling particles, hovering on the borderline between life and nonlife, that he admired when first he came to this river. Nor can he distinguish the particles that are he from the particles that are not. All are one in this stream of life.

Is escape possible?

Escape is not possible.

He will go on and on and on, borne by the speeding current, until he reaches the sea that so lately he has helped to lift. And he will pour forth and be scattered on its vast bosom. Will his consciousness then remain intact, when he is tossed like a million million colored dots into those unfathomable fathoms? Already he is losing himself. Already too many tiny blazes of alien fire have mixed themselves with his dissevered substance. He is diluted. He is dissolving. He has given up all sense of himself as female or as male, and barely remembers himself as metabolizing organism; gone are breasts, gone are balls, gone are eyes, gone are toes; only twinkling corpuscular particles remain. To die a pointillist death: how ethereal! To lose oneself in a rush of dazzling lights! The universe shimmers. He endures a Brownian motion of the soul. He is distantly aware of the migrations of his former components through the body of the river: there goes one looping strand shooting ahead, there one sinks, there one is caught in a whirl-pooling bywater. He is aware also of the terrain through which the river passes. The gorge has disappeared, and he travels in flat, alluvial country, rambling over a broad flood-plain, elbowing around unpredictable meanders, bypassing mudwalled islands. Night is coming on. The waters hurry. He is dismembered, disintegrated, dispersed, dissected, disjoined, dissociated, disunited, disrupted, divorced, detached, divided. By darkness the river takes on a fiery brilliance; its light illuminates the entire alluvium. He descends. The sea is near. The river has entered its delta. What deposit shall it make here? What silt is to be dropped? Ahead lie many channels; this stream finds its way deviously to Mother Sea. He will be further subdivided. He will be wholly disbanded. The waters sing. Shiver with brilliant fury and furious brilliance. His fellow corpuscles cry hosannah to him. Destiny, here. Peace ahead. Apart, asunder, alone, adrift. Go, now. *Nunc dimittis.* Journey's end, here, new journey beginning. To the sons of man, farewell. Go. Go. Parting. Brightness falls from the air. Lights everywhere. Lights! Such a beautiful glow. These colors are my selves. This red, this green, this yellow, this blue, this violet. Easily, easily, easily, lighting my way through the night, down, down, unresisting, a last flicker of brightness before I go. What's this? Dropping out, here? The heaviness of me. The mass. The coarseness. I am silt. I am to be the delta. Can it be so? Yes. Yes. Yes. Yes. Adhering here. Stick. Cling. Coagulate. Conglometate. Cohere. Here. Here. Here. I thicken. I accumulate. I consolidate. I amalgamate. I incorporate.

What unexpected coalescence befalls him?

His giddy voyage has halted short of the sea. He has precipitated out of the flow; his momentum is spent at last, and, particle by particle, he tumbles and heaps against the fringed shore of some small isle. He collects himself. He does not join; he does not regain his human form, male or female; he is merely a mound of washed-up fragments, like the tiny larvae of crustaceans cast up by the tide. Mixed with his matter are some alien particles that he has somehow carried with him to this place; he feels them amidst him like blades. He suspects that this entire island is constituted of the river's cast-offs, and the mud of which it is built is not mud but dropped organic matter such as himself. What now? To remain here, rotting in the dark? He still is lapped by the river along one side, but he is not eroded now: he has been ejected. Can he move? He cannot. Can he perceive? Only dimly. Can he remember? He can remember. Will there be a further change in his nature? He does not know. He is at rest. He is debris. He will await new developments.

'I also wait,' declares a mighty voice.

Who spoke? Where? Another pile of refuse brought here by the river? How can he reply?

He has no way of replying.

If I can hear, he insists inwardly, I can speak. And I can hear. He says, therefore, 'Can you help me? Can you tell me what I've become?'

'You are pure potential.'

'And you?'

'I wait.'

'Let me see you,' Clay asks.

A vision comes: he sees a creature of great size planted in the reddish sandy ground of the island. Only the head and shoulders rise above the surface. The head is flat and broad, with great dish-sized eyes and no other features; it sprouts necklessly from the wide enormous shoulders. He sees also the portion of the being that is buried in the ground. It is long and limbless, with a rough porous skin, and a surrounding mantle of fibrous filaments that appear to function as roots, draining nutrients from the sand. Clay recognizes the creature as one of the Awaiters of whom Quoi the Breather had briefly told him. For all its vegetable appearance, then, it is animal, and, more than that, one of the several species of humanity that coexist in this epoch. The vision blurs and goes.

'I am human too,' Clay says. 'Was.'

'Still are.'

'But what am I, now?'

'A constellation of possibilities. You are still in transit, though your passage now has halted. What would you be?'

'Myself again.'

'You are yourself.'

'This is not my true form.'

The Awaiter seems to laugh. 'How can you say what your true form is?'

'The form in which I started my journey.'

The Awaiter shows him a series of shifting forms: an infant Clay, a pubescent Clay, Clay grown, Clay asleep, Clay awake, Clay alert, Clay dull, Clay naked, Clay clothed, Clay altered

86

by the cleansing creek, Clay a Breather in Quoi's pool, Clay female, Clay dissolved by the living river, Clay heaped at the delta. 'Which is you?' the Awaiter asks, and Clay says, 'All,' and the Awaiter says, 'These and others. Why limit yourself? Accept experience as it comes. What would you be?'

'Choose for me,' Clay says, and so he is transformed into an Awaiter.

12

He takes up residence in the moist cool mud. He is unable to move; the concept of having the power of motion is strange to him. He is content to remain embedded, drinking such nourishment as he needs through his fibrous roots, and watching the splendid rippling hues of the river as it flows past his dwelling. His fellow Awaiter lives not far away. Clay is constantly aware of the Awaiter's thoughts: a great strength, a profound calm, a passionate intellect, and, pervading everything, a degree of rock-bottom melancholy, a sadness over the thingness of things.

He does not know how old the Awaiter is, and he swiftly sees that it would be foolish to ask, for time interests the Awaiter only for its negation. 'We will study,' the Awaiter tells him, 'the virtues of timelessness.' Nor does he dare inquire at what point in human history it was thought desirable to take on this form, and for what reason. He accepts all things passively. He has learned to expect infinite variety.

Passive is as passive does. 'What is your goal?' he asks the Awaiter, and the Awaiter says, 'To await.'

'Are there many of your kind?'

'Many.'

'Are you in contact with them?'

'Rarely.'

'Do you feel loneliness out here?'

'I feel freedom.'

Clay has exhausted his questions. He studies the river. His eyes are like antennae draining images from every side; he sees the mountains, the sea, the clouds, the clinging velvet mists. The sun rises and sets and rises and sets, but he does not integrate these changes with the idea that time is passing. They are mere phenomena of lighting. Time does not pass. Not-minute flows into not-minute, and the not-minutes mount into un-hours, which pile into anti-days and contra-weeks and non-months, and these into the antithesis of years and the converse of centuries. These intervals of timelessness are interrupted, occasionally, by some sluggish thought that makes its way by slow sticky drips to the depths of his consciousness. He is not offended by the new pace of things. It seems quite delicate and perfect and lovely to function this way, since he has the opportunity to examine every facet of a notion, turning it this way and that, rubbing it, tapping it, biting it, probing it. Frequently an entire negative span of non-eons elapses between each exchange of thoughts between himself and the Awaiter beside him. It is not necessary to speak a great deal. It is necessary only to think, and consider, and apprehend, and understand. He sheds much of the unneeded luggage of his mind. He casts off the fallacy of forward movement, the absurdity of striving, the inanity of aggressiveness, the idiocy of acquisitiveness, the error of progress, the misconception of speed, the aberration of pride, the hallucination of curiosity, the illusion of accomplishment, the mirage of consecutiveness, and a great deal more that he has carried about much too long. Firmly planted, amply nourished, fully content with his state, he passively masters dazzling universes of thought.

Among his new insights are such things as these:

All moments converge upon now.

Stasis contains and surrounds dynamism.

It is an error to imagine that there is a linear sequence of events.

Events themselves are mere clusters of random energy upon which we impose our erroneous sense of form.

To battle entropy is to pluck at one's own eyes.

Every river returns to its source.

The only doctrine more spurious than that of determinism is the doctrine of free will.

Memory is the mirror of untruth.

To construct physical objects out of given sensory data is a pleasant pastime, but such objects are without verifiable content, and therefore unreal.

We must realize, *a priori*, that all *a priori* notions about the nature of the universe are inherently false.

There are no necessary conditions and no causal relationships; logic therefore is tyranny.

Once he has come to an intimate understanding of these premises, all restlessness leaves him. He is at peace. He has never been so happy as he is in the Awaiter form, for he realizes now that joy and sorrow are merely aspects of the same delusion, no more tangible nor significant than electrons, neutrons, or mesons. He can dispense with all sensation and live in an environment of pure abstraction: away with textures, colors, tones, tastes, and distinctions of form! He does not merely repudiate the messages of the senses; he denies their reality altogether. In this new atmosphere of tranquility he recognizes swiftly that the Awaiters must be considered the highest aspect of human life ever to evolve, since they are most fully in command of their environment. The fact that the human race continued to change after the development of the Awaiters is a trivial paradox, based on a faulty comprehension of the randomness of events, and he wastes little time analyzing it. These Skimmers, these Breathers, these Eaters, all these latter-day forms are pitiably unaware of their irrelevance to the non-structure of the non-universe.

He will never leave this place.

Curious strains develop in his complacency, however. His fellow Awaiter, for example, often radiates dull tolling tones of doubt that are oddly at variance with an Awaiter's grasp of philosophy. The river sometimes rises and spews clouds of sparkling particles over the place where Clay is fixed in the ground; these floods momentarily block his sensory perceptions and leave him unduly troubled by the importance of perceiving. Though he transcends these difficulties, he is perturbed by a fundamental uncertainty of purpose that conflicts not only with his awareness of the nonexistence of purpose but with his awareness of the nonexistence of conflict. He passes this opaque point glibly without attempting to deal with it. Time timelessly elapses, shedding itself in a series of self-devouring concentric gray shells. He no longer knows whether he lives in the world's evening or its morning. He does not return to a linear scheme of events until the day when an arrangement of textures and densities presents itself on the island where he has settled and succeeds in penetrating his isolation.

He perceives softness within hardness. He perceives an oval within a rectangle. He perceives sound within silence.

He hears a bristly voice saying, 'Your friends seek you. Will you return to them?'

Clay allows this abstract cluster of coincidental phenomena to take on the illusion of reality. Now he perceives his resurrected companion, the spheroid. He observes the pink jellylike creature intersecting the shining metal bars of its cage. He says, 'It is not true that I can understand your speech.'

'No barrier is eternal,' the spheroid says. 'I am in tune now with the language of the era.'

'Why are you here?'

'To help you. There is a debt of gratitude upon me, for you are the one who returned me to life.'

'I deny the debt. Life and death are indistinguishable states. You merely were confused, and I illuminated you.'

'However that may be, do you want to stay rooted in the ground for the rest of time?'

'I travel as far as I please without leaving this place.'

'I would not injure you,' the spheroid says. 'But I fear you are not your own master. I think you are in need of rescue. Do you remain in the sand of your own free will?'

'Let me explain about free will,' Clay says.

He speaks at length. While he does, the spheroid rolls closer to him. Clay has just reached an explication of the inner nature of the seeming linearity of circumstances when the spheroid extends a bright ring of golden radiation that slices into the ground on all sides of him. He is encompassed by this cone of energy. Deep in the moist sand it presses against the tips of his roots. The tapering point of him flattens on the bottom vertex of the cone. Halting his discourse, he asks, 'What are you doing?' and the spheroid says patiently, 'Rescuing you.' Clay is unwilling to be rescued. 'Violation of my physical integrity,' he declares. 'Arbitrary antisocial behavior. Contradicts the essentially nonviolent nature of this period of human history. Treason against my soul to act on my behalf against my wishes. I beg of you. You have no right. In the name of the debt you owe me. To be left as is. Amounts to rape. Let me. Why won't you let me. Alone? This sphere of force. Compulsion as a weapon of man against entropy. Go. Away.' None of this moves the spheroid from its task. The cone of energy is rotating rapidly. The air sizzles and shimmers as ionization occurs. Clay becomes dizzy. He calls out in appeal to the Awaiter, who takes no action. Clay is rising. There is a sound as of the popping of a cork and he bursts from the sand. He lies at the edge of the shore, a giant stranded carrot, twitching his roots feebly and rolling his huge eyes around. 'You misunderstand,' he tells the spheroid. 'I had no wish to be removed. I had firmly accepted the passive state. This intrusion. The highest degree of resentment at. Unable to proceed with my former researches. Poor return for important favors received. Insist you restore. A moral issue.' The spheroid, humming eagerly, extends pseudopods of pink flesh to stroke Clay's furrowed, fevered brow. A blue cloud settles about the uprooted transient. Tendrils of gray smoke slide into his pores. 'Unforgivable,' Clay says. 'Involuntary termination of metamorphosis. Sheer biological fascism.' The spheroid weeps. Clay is changing, now. He can feel the throb and surge. What form will I assume? Red gills, purple tentacles? Stale coils of flabby meat? Green knobs sprouting from crested skull? He stirs. He sits up. He is bifurcated again. Legs: and a soft tumble of organs between them. He has been resexed. Hands.

Fingers. Ears. Lips. A garden of epithelium. Grumblings in his bowels; concealed microflora undergoing tidal ebb and flow. The war of the white corpuscles. He's himself again.

Gratitude spills through him in an oily flood. The spheroid has saved him from his own passivity. He springs to his feet. He dances on the muddy flat. Joyfully he embraces the spheroid's cage and receives several mild tingling shocks. 'I would have stayed there till the end of time,' Clay says. 'A vegetable.' The buried Awaiter tolls its disapproval of Clay's shallowness. 'Of course,' Clay adds, 'I did gain some valuable insights into reality and illusion.' He frowns, and, pensively toeing the sand, tries to offer the spheroid an example. No insights come. That saddens him. Is it all gone, then, that wondrous torrent of philosophy, that gush of golden data? Was his awareness of illusion merely a delusion? He is momentarily tempted to crawl back into the sand and plug in, one more time, to that fount of elusive wisdom. But he does not. He knows how narrow his escape was. He feels great warmth and affection, almost a sexual love, for his rescuer. The innate humanity of all human things connects us, he knows. The spheroid is my brother who I must not reject. But the Awaiter tells him, sadly, 'I too am human,' and Clay dissolves in guilt, knowing how cruel he is being. 'I'm sorry,' he murmurs. 'I have to make the choice. Wisdom isn't enough. Experience counts too. Anyway' – a hopeful crumb of consolation – 'I might come back. After I've seen more. It's not a permanent leavetaking.' The Awaiter replies, 'It hardly matters. You are in transit. Do as you please: your will is free.' The paradox sends Clay reeling. He nearly stumbles into the all-dissolving river. Landing on his knees a few feet from the flow, he crawls along the shore a short way and flattens himself, anguished, alarmed. The sky darkens. The sun dwindles. He jams his penis into the damp sand. He thrusts his fingers in. He takes a mouthful and grinds the particles between his teeth. Bits of sour quartz, furry silica, digested calcium, the excreted detritus of ages past lying on this shore, fragments of cities, highways, old space satellites, chunks of the moon, all lovingly tossed and shaped by the sobbing sea and flung up here – he wants to hug it all. The spheroid's faint shadow falls on him. 'Shall we go?' it asks. Clay squints up at it. 'Where does your voice come from?' he demands. 'You don't seem to have a mouth. You don't have any bodily openings at all. How the hell can you be human without bodily openings?' The spheroid replies gently, 'Hanmer hopes for your return. Ti. Serifice. Ninameen. Angelon. Bril.'

'Serifice is dead,' Clay says, getting up, brushing the sand from himself. 'But I'd like to see the others again. I didn't really mean to wander away. Let's go.'

13

They march northward, so far as Clay is able to determine. Since the spheroid is no conversationalist, Clay occupies himself with an attempt at a rational analysis of his experiences since awakening. He makes recapitulatory lists of categories. He tallies the varieties of so-called 'human' forms that he has encountered; he checks off the metamorphoses he has undergone; he records the details of each of his voyages beyond the normal sensory capabilities of a twentieth-century man, and tries to discern whether those voyages were illusions or actualities. He examines such phenomena of this era as the ambiguity of sexuality and the impermanence of mortality. During this cool and clear-eyed assessment, carried out with no small effort of concentration, he pays little attention to his surroundings, and it is a while before he discovers how bleak and dismal a part of the world it is that he is now passing through.

Night has come; the full dreariness is hidden from him by darkness. But a faint depressing purple glow rises from the land, showing him enough. He is in a barren, flat wasteland, where the dry crusty ground crunches underfoot, and tiny angular pebbles stab the soles. Great sundered stony wedges command the horizon. He can see no plants, not even the typical spiky growths of deserts. An unpleasant buzzing sound, like the droning of flies trapped against a closed window, issues from gopher-hole openings underfoot; kneeling by one of these for closer listening, he hears the sinister hum curving and recurving in subterranean burrows. A sense of intolerable dryness prevails. The night sky is fouled with some sort of thin haze, masking the stars. He wonders if this is another of the hells on Earth of which Ninameen once told him, a cousin to Old. Is this the place called Empty? Is it Slow? Is it Heavy? Is it Dark? He picks his way carefully over the gritty basin of this purple plain, fearful of a stumble. This is no place for a naked man to walk by night.

'What is this place called?' he asks the spheroid, after a while. But the spheroid is as much of a stranger to this time and place as he is, and makes no reply.

Clay's throat parches. His skin picks up a coating of fine rock dust. Whenever he blinks he feels his eyelids abrading his pupils. He becomes edgy and hyperwary, sensing imaginary monsters behind every boulder. What sounds are those? The whisper of a scorpion's claws? The dragging of a spiked tail through the forlorn pebbles? The grinding of stones within a reptilian gut? But there is nothing here except night and silence. The spheroid, wheeling merrily onward, is far ahead of him now. Clay forces himself to double his pace, at the risk of cutting himself badly on the rocks in his path. 'Wait!' he yells, hoarse, ragged-throated. 'I don't move on wheels. I can't go that fast.' But the spheroid's command of the language of the era seems to have expired; it takes no notice of his words, and soon is lost from view on the smoky horizon.

Stopping, Clay finds a patch of ground free from sharp stones and squats there. The purple glow – residual radio-activity, perhaps? – is too dim now to guide him, and he will not move on until morning. The risk of sliding into some talused ravine does not attract him. Would a compound fracture of the leg be as troublesome here as it would if he were traversing old Arizona? He does not know. Maybe the jagged white stick of bone would obligingly melt back into place after a time, and the shredded tissues of skin and flesh grow whole in a sweetly dreamlike way. But he does not wish to chance it. A bad dream can end, but not everything is a dream, even here, and he does not care to find himself suffering a genuine fracture in an unreal landscape. He will wait until he can see.

In the unsleeping night phantoms dance around him. Things flutter by dangling on fine metal wires. He hears groans and occasional sobs far away, and something that could be a chorus of large black beetles. The wind is cool and dusty. Transparent fingers tickle the channels of his mind, seeking entry. Slow spirals of pure fear congeal and twist about him. The haze across the sky disappears, possibly devoured by some entity in methodical traverse of the heavens, and the unfamiliar stars blare forth. No comfort from them: our light set out for Earth, they insist, in the time of automobiles and hydrogen bombs, and it has been all this while on its way, buffeted by the dancing molecules between the galaxies, and here it is, and here *you* are. Poor naked fool. When will morning come? Is that a row of insects marching toward my toes? Why is the darkness so close to me?

The first strands of daylight, now. White-hot rods sliding into the sky. A hot wind out of the west. A smear of red on the horizon, sucking all the world's moistness toward it. Dry. Dry. Dry. Ugly rustling sounds. Light. The sky is molten, all copper and brass and zinc, with drooping streaks of antimony, molybdenum, manganese, magnesium, and lead. Pools of tungsten splashing against the rocks. The dawn has a blinding brilliance. He turns away from it, clasping his forearms to his forehead and crouching like an unhappy red crustacean fleeing the pot. The air is a sea of refraction, in which the fundamental atomic structure of matter lies revealed as a series of interlocking circles of green and yellow and brown, turning on their hubs to create dazzling patterns of meshed interference rings. The world swerves on its track. Five primary colors that he has never seen before bombard his eyes. Can he give them names? What will he call this deep cool hue with the velvety walls? And this rigid rectilinear tone, so disciplined, so forbidding? This one is tentative and gentle; this, swollen and brutal;

this, hushed and complex. The colors blend and mingle and occasionally clash. The full blaze of morning begins.

He understands now that he is in a desert where hallucinations rise like heat waves from the rocks. His mind is clear and his perceptions are exact; the imprecisions he experiences are in the environment, not in himself. But the distinction is a fine one. He walks slowly forward, anticipating traps.

The rocks have become bright nodes of pure energy whose rich-textured red surfaces vibrate in patterns that continually change. On one face of every stony mass he sees golden lights circling gracefully. On the opposite face pale bluish spheres are unceasingly born and go bubbling into the air, rising silently to a height of perhaps ten feet and vanishing. Everything shimmers. Everything shines with an inner light. The barren desert floor is now alive with flowers, which grow and shrink as though in tune with some cosmic flow of breath. Incandescence reigns.

His skin is a labyrinth. His hands are hammers. A pulsing blue hose hangs between his legs. His toes are hooked claws. His knees have eyes but no eyebrows. His tongue is satin. His saliva is glass. His blood is bile and his bile is blood.

The breeze is passionately alive, and explodes wherever it touches the ground, kicking up tufts of flamboyant red floss. Time is elastic; a second stretches out to such immeasurable and vanishing termini that it seems ridiculous to compute the sense of it, and then a century collapses with a shy little whoosh into a single crevice of sunlight. Space likewise undergoes extension and compression. The sky bulges and balloons, reaching aggressively into adjoining dimensions, pushing the inhabitants of nearby continua into pinched little pockets of sagging reality. Then it all drops back, bringing down cascades of disrupted nebulae and distressed comets.

Through all of this Clay presses stubbornly forward. Much of what he sees is beautiful and inspiring, though he knows it is meant to terrify him. He cries out amid the trumpets and remains unafraid. But there are truly frightening moments as well: green parabolas belch out of the horizon like annunciators of the Day of Judgment, and blurt forth dismaying crescendos of slippery sound. A forest of hostile umbrellas unfolds. A vault opens in the sky and silvery knives spill from it. The ground billows and sneezes. He perseveres. The desert gives way to black mud and whispering reeds; he is kissed by crocodiles, he is caressed by slimy things. A brooding sense of imminent punishment assails him. Scrawny birds with straggly hair hoot and chatter at him. He strides through a lake of abortions and a dune of monsters. He feels the sun burning his hip and devouring his buttock. He is buried under dark pyramids. He is harassed by cancers that drift up to him in foggy folds and deride his maleness. Creatures made of vertical ribs of gray cartilage make booming sounds at him. He enters a room and finds something green and ropy waiting patiently for him in a dark corner, wheezing and sniffling. He sees a giant scowling face that fills half the sky. These dreams lack beauty, and he suspects they are not dreams. But he goes on.

To the accompaniment of rasping operatic choruses, a tender voice whispers, 'We wish to discourage you. We will amputate, if necessary. We know how to disturb the soul. We have no compunctions. We have no inhibitions. We have no hesitations.' Invisible hands fondle his sexual organs and leave green fingerprints. A catheter slips into him five times within three minutes. Several of his toes shift to his other feet. He defies them with his ductless glands and with his seminal vesicles, and they respond by hollowing him out, turning him into a mere shell, in danger of floating towards that all-consuming sword of a sun at any moment. He adjusts for his buoyancy and even welcomes it, and instantly he is smitten with solidity and becomes a mass of iron; the taste of steel is in his mouth, and he knows that if he is struck he will give forth a metallic ring. He escapes from this by shedding his body. 'Therefore we will delude you with splendors,' they inform him and he hears faint music. In the soft surge and swell of the minor notes there breathes a harmony that ravishes the sense of sound. A resonant organ, with a stop of sapphire and a diapason of opal, diffuses endless octaves from star to star. All the moonbeams form strings to vibrate the perfect pitch, and this entrancing unison is poured into his enchanted ears. Under

such a spell, how can he resist them ? The magic of that melody
bewitches his soul. He begins to rise into the air. Sweeter and
sweeter grows the music; it bears him higher and higher, and
he floats in tune with the infinite – under the turquoise heavens
where globules of mercury are glittering. He turns. He twists.
He twirls. He melts. He fades. He dissolves. He recites snatches
of his favorite poems, declaring:

> Ring out the old, ring in the new,
>   Ring, happy bells, across the snow:
>   The year is going, let him go:
> Ring out the false, ring in the true.

And:

> Make barren our lives.
> And marriage and death and division
> Our loves into corpses or wives;
> Time turns the old days to derision,
> And love is more cruel than lust.
> No thorns go as deep as a rose's,
> Is darkness, the fruit there of dust;
> For the crown of our life as it closes.

And:

> Ships that pass in the night, and speak each other in passing,
> So on the ocean of life we pass and speak one another,
> Only a signal shown and a distant voice in the darkness;
> Only a look and a voice; then darkness again and a silence.

He sees a clear light. He feels the symptoms of earth sinking
into water. He experiences a glimpse of the Pure Truth, subtle,
sparkling, bright, dazzling, glorious, and radiantly awesome,
in appearance like a mirage moving across a landscape in one
continuous stream of vibrations. He sees a divine blue light.
He sees a dull white light. He sees a dazzling white light. He
sees a dull, smoke-colored light from Hell. He sees a dazzling
yellow light. He sees a dull bluish-yellow light from the human

world. He sees a red light. He sees a halo of rainbow light. He sees a dull red light. He sees a dazzling red light.

He enters a world of darkness, a darkness that gradually thickens while he dreams of polar night and everlasting winter.

He passes thence to an unexplored tropical forest. His soul changes to a vegetable essence; he is a giant fern, spreading wide feathery leaves and swaying and nodding in the spice-gales. A strange and unimagined ecstasy possesses him. He is near the end of this passage through confusion, now. He rips himself from the forest's dark floor and goes on, through an utter void of sight and sound. Three intense luminous points stand out on a triple wall of darkness, toward which he silently drifts. Now he can plainly distinguish three colossal arches rising from the bosom of a waveless sea. The middle arch is the highest; the two flanking it are equal to each other. He determines that they form the portals of an enormous cavern, whose dome rises far above him, hidden in wreaths of cloud. On each side of him runs a wall of gnarled and rugged rock, from whose jutting points, as high as the eye can reach, depend stalactites of every imagined form and tinge of beauty. Terrible crashing chords reverberate through the universe as he makes his way toward the cavern's mouth.

He goes within.

The air is cool and tender here, and the thought slowly is borne in on him that he has entered a real cavern, that he has quitted the desert of hallucinations at last. Yet fingers of unreality pursue him even here, flickering in past the entrance to muddle his mind, and he cannot yet tell true from false with any degree of assurance, even here. A door closes behind him. He confronts a vaulted ceiling, slabbed walls, a raised dais of black ivory. Chairs disposed in arcs clutter the entrance. The heavy paneling of the walls is adorned with grotesque frescoes of the birds, beasts, and monsters of this epoch, which are in constant trembling motion, forever changing form like things seen in a kaleidoscope. Now the walls bristle with teeth; now gaudy birds with diamond claws nod from their perches and flutter through emerald cycads; now Breathers and Awaiters sneeze and squirm. Everything flows. Everything twines.

Everything merges. He cuts his way through golden ropes and steps forward. He climbs the dais. Beyond lies a black tunnel. Out of its midst blows a serene breeze coming from some nether chamber. He goes carefully down the far side of the dais and enters the tunnel.

He walks for nearly an hour, he supposes, before there is any break in the darkness. Finally a faint purpling begins. The air grows brighter every few hundred yards. He feels feverish; his head swims. Have bloated balloons of hallucination followed him this far under the planet's skin? The texture of the floor abruptly changes: it had been sleek, like marble or polished slate, and now it has the brusque flatness of concrete. The instant he touches this new flooring the lights flare brilliantly and he finds himself at the vestibule of a vast Gothic hall whose vaults and chambers sweep up and up and up into dimness. On the floor of this mighty room are quaint anachronisms: all sorts of machines and engines, mostly painted a bright green, that make the place look like a generating plant of the twentieth century, except that the wheels, cables, pulleys, levers, turbines, pistons, boilers, compressors, and accompanying apparatus do not constitute any device Clay can remember from his knowledge of the former world. The machinery seems to be working, though. Rumbles and throbs and hums and growls come from the clutter below, and several cables loop and flex as if possessed by the force that flows through them.

To Clay's left is a staircase rising against the wall of the room. He mounts it thoughtfully, watching his step on the narrow treads. When he is perhaps a hundred feet above the level of the machinery he discovers that the staircase comes to a sudden termination; if he takes one more step he will tumble to the distant floor. Looking upward, he sees a second flight of stairs still higher on the wall. And there he is, ascending, a naked man moving slowly, a trifle out of breath. Clay frowns. Instantly he finds himself transported to that second flight, and he is the naked man who now toils upward. Again the stairs halt at the brink of an abyss; again he looks up; again he discovers a flight of stairs still higher, and himself trudging upward; again he joins himself and climbs the third flight. On and on he goes, in reduplication after reduplication, until, after an infinity of stairs, he is lost in the upper gloom of the great hall.

He kneels on a broad slab of pink marble.

He drips drops of hot sweat. He gasps. He coughs. He pants.

He peers over the edge and marvels at the kneading limbs of the clacking machines far below.

He sees several staircases and several Clays climbing them. He waves and calls words of encouragement. A surge of new energy buoys him; he rises, creeps along a catwalk at the very top of the huge chamber, and comes upon a hatch that seems to cry out to be lifted. He lifts it. Beneath is a green haze, cinnamon-flavored, opaque. He slips a hand experimentally into it, fully prepared to have the flesh eaten from the bone; but no, he feels only a sticky warmth. Climb in, the hatch urges. Made for you, made for you! Down you go. A sweet floating trip. He goes in. The haze closes muggily around him like a sweaty fist. Peppermint vapor in his eyes. Wisps of sly greenness twining coyly about his genitals. He floats. Down the chute, down, down, descending at least as far as he had previously climbed, and still farther, into a tunnel that lies beneath the hall of the machines. Gravity is annulled; as he falls he twists and swims, puts his feet above his head, watches his limp organ standing anyway, and in the end drifts to a stop, landing easily upright. He steps from the chute, which pulls away from him with a moist sucking sound. Bright lights here. An underground city, street by street, everything aglow, everything fragrant. Milk-white flames burn in the air, cool, delicious. Galleries stretch outward into the dusky distance. He has been here before. This is the tunnel-world built for the habitation of mankind at a time when the surface of the world was not fit for life. During the rite of the Opening of the Earth, he recalls, he passed through this level, remaining only briefly and then slipping deeper. Now he will inspect it comprehensively. He sets forth.

Immediately he comes upon somberness. Turning a bend in the tunnel, he finds the body of a goat-man on the floor, belly turned skyward. The creature has been partly flayed, and the skin of its middle has been laid back to reveal the interior of the abdominal cavity. Organs have been removed. There is no blood: this could almost be a cunning model of the original. But the goaty smell hovers close, that odor of rot. The death was recent.

Abandon all hope, ye who?

The shining wall opens and a metal man rolls forth. It is shorter and wider than Clay; its body is a simple cone of burnished blue steel, ringed near the apex with a row of sensors – eyes and listeners and heat-scanners and whatever – completely encircling it. Limbs of various sorts sprout from a ring at chest level. There are no legs; it moves on concealed wheels. Clay has seen such robots before also: they are the forlorn servants, abandoned and forgotten, eternally standing in wait. 'Friend of man,' the robot declares in a rusty voice sneaking through a small speaker-grid. 'Accept ancient obligation. To serve. To do bidding.' Clay does not recognize the language but he understands the words.

'Friend of man,' he says mockingly.

'Yes. Miracle of modern craftsmanship.'

'Are friends of men supposed to destroy men?'

'Clarification?'

Clay points to the flayed goat. 'This is a man. Who cut it open?'

'Does not correspond to man-parameters.'

'Look closer. Count the chromosomes. Pluck out the genes. It's a man, whether you think so or not. Genetically adapted, God knows why, to this filthy form. Who killed it?'

'We are programmed to remove all potentially hostile organisms of a lower order.'

'Who killed it?'

'The servants,' says the robot meekly.

'Destroying a man. Not much of a bargain, him, but human. What would you do if a Skimmer came down here? A Breather? An Awaiter?'

'Interrogative.'

Clay grows overbearing. 'Listen,' he says, 'the world is full of human beings who don't correspond to the notions of humanity that were current when this place was built. Some of them may happen to stray in here. I don't want you killing them.'

'A change in program?'

'An expansion. A redefinition of man. Where can I give the order?'

'I will relay it to the central,' the robot promises.

'All right, then: man is hereby redefined as any organism that traces its descent in the true genetic line from *Homo sapiens*, which is defined as the species that construct this tunnel-world. It is understood that the servants of the tunnel-world will make no attempt to molest such organisms if they enter this jurisdiction.'

'Conflict. Conflict. Conflict.'

Red lights flash on the robot's snout.

'So?' Clay asks.

'We are charged with protecting men. But we are also charged with protecting the city. If hostile man-organisms come? Instructions? Definitions?'

Clay sees the problem. 'You will prevent, if at all possible, the injuring of the tunnel-world by intrusive human forms. But you will take the greatest care to isolate and eject the intrusive forms without causing permanent physical harm.'

'Transmitted. Accepted.'

'I am Clay. I am human. You will serve me.'

'Our ancient obligation,' says the robot.

Clay studies the creature, fascinated by his ability to communicate with it. 'Do you realize,' he says after a moment, 'that you may be the oldest artifact of human-kind in existence? I mean, you've got to be practically my contemporary. And everything else from back then is gone. When was this city built?'

'In the eighteenth century.'

'Not *my* eighteenth century, I bet. The eighteenth century after what?'

'The eighteenth century,' repeats the robot complacently. 'Do you want reference access?'

'You mean, an answer machine?'

'Correct.'

'It might help,' Clays says, feeling a wild peak of hope. 'Something to fill me in on parts of the story. Help me reconstruct. Where is it? How do I ask things?'

'Will you follow?'

The robot reverses itself and rolls away down a silver-walled corridor. Clay trots after it, seeing as he runs tantalizing glimpses of strange instruments through windows in the walls. The robot pauses in front of a gray device that flowers cuplike from a pillar. 'Reference access,' it coos, beckoning Clay close with soft flashing lights. 'Hello,' Clays says. 'Look, I've been caught in the time-flux, and I want some information. About the development of civilization, about the course of history. I come from the twentieth century A.D., but I haven't been able to hook that up with any other epoch, not even the one in which the tunnel-world was built, and perhaps you can put things together for me. Even if you haven't been scanning events subsequent to the tunnel-world civilization, you can at least tell me what went on between your time and mine. Yes? Can you hear me? I'm waiting.' Silence. 'Go ahead. I'm waiting to hear.'

Clanks and groans come from the gray cup. Scrapings and hisses. A few tentative words, well articulated but incomprehensible. Trial efforts at communication. Then:

'Toward the close of the first postindustrial era a catastrophic social upheaval resulted in the total demolition of all the constructs and assumptions under which the old urban societies had operated. A restructuring epoch known as the terminal chaos of the collapsed environment. New architectonic concepts. Our present system from this point. However, an inherent manifested itself giving rise to a fundamental oscillation of chronology. May be able to date instability in the revised societal framework eight or ten centuries, intentions that ultimately brought anything experienced in previous erosion. Reached its most severe level world seemed desirable. Fortunately, skills and techniques made possible of the new urban system in a destruction far more potent than human apocalypses. Environmental and abandonment of the surface, the accumulation of mechanical, the swift and efficacious duplication underground cities, and late in the eighteenth century of the present era transfer of the population began, accompanied by a thoughtful genetic inferior heredity, social blemishes, screening to eliminate diseases, and other nondesiderata. We now enhanced human infrastructure. We, the resilience of the species, and conceivable catastrophies that may immediately result of this was the Time of Sweeping, which imposed upon a series. Can take pride in. The renewed have created, which demonstrates: gives us hope for withstanding all yet await us in the epochs to come.'

After a short while Clay says sadly, 'Thank you,' and turns away. The robot is at his elbow. 'No use,' Clay murmurs. 'No damned use. Just as well.'

'To clothe the naked,' the robot says. 'Another urgent obligation. Do you wish clothing?'

'Am I so ugly this way?'

'Humans cover their bodies when in the streets. For those who lack, we supply.'

Clay does not respond, and the robot takes his response for assent. A section of the wall behind Clay irises open and a second robot appears. It lifts a snoutlike hose and sprays Clay with a single honking blast of pigment and fabric. When he recovers from his surprise Clay finds that he now is wearing a tight golden tunic, shoes that resemble transparent envelopes, and a slouchy hat. He has gone naked so long that the clothing instantly begins to chafe and bind him. Not wishing to give offense, he continues to wear it. He walks along the corridor. The first robot pursues him, saying, 'Food? Shelter? Bodily cleansing? Amusements?'

'No.'

'No wishes of any kind?'

'One,' Clay says. 'Privacy. Go away. When I need you, I'll whistle.'

'Interrogative.'

'I'll call. I'll yell out loud with my vocal cords. Better? Now go, please. I ask you kindly. Don't go far, but stay out of my sight until you're summoned.'

Turns. Walks on. Robot rolls away.

Clay peers into rooms and shops. Everything quite neat, a Pompeii for his prowling, no doors locked. In this place a television-like screen offers, at a touch of the level, three-dimensional protuberances that jut and withdraw like bubbles in molten lava. Beyond is an octagonal bathtub whose porcelaneous walls sweat convincing blood at the push of a stud. Green maybe-sausages extrude themselves from a cluster of metal pipes above what is possibly a stove. A bed changes size and shape with frenzied energy, getting bigger, smaller, circular, rectangular. A colossal pink phallus, sinister in its lifelikeness, rises from the center of a black slate floor. A wall dissolves into a shower of mosaic tiles. Nozzles growing like toadstools along a window douse him with perfumes, spices, ointments, and a thin pale fluid that consumes his clothing in a second or two. He enjoys his return to nakedness, although he lingers before the nozzles too long, and one of them squirts a red oil at him that anesthetizes his skin. He puts a finger in his ear: nothing. He cautiously scratches his chest: nothing. He squeezes his penis in his fist: nothing. He cannot feel his bare feet in contact with the shaggy flooring. Is it permanent? He imagines himself casually blundering into sharp things that gouge out his flesh and slice off his toes without his noticing it, until he is reduced to a few shreds of muscle hanging to bare bones. 'Robot?' he calls. 'Hey, robot, come help me!' but before the machine-man can reach him, two nozzles at once spray him, and he feels his nerve cells come alive with such marvelous intensity that he has an orgasm on the spot. Panting a little, he backs away, dismissing the robot with two quick syllables. Going onward, he stumbles between a double wall of mirrors and is caught in an infinite regress, pong and pong and pong from wall to wall as the mirrors turn and shift and buckle, and he drops to the floor and crawls out of range. How have all these things survived, he wonders, when the world has endured so many upheavals of geology, when the continents themselves have been reshaped? He concedes a finite probability that the tunnel-world is illusory. He shifts to a different cluster of streets and galleries; here the architecture is of another style, more brutal, less imaginative than the last, but the ornamentation and surface texture of the structures is of a far higher order. Robots roll out of every corner and offer to serve him, but he keeps his eye cocked for *his* robot, the one following him at a respectful distance, and pays no heed to the others. 'Where did the people go?' he asks his robot. 'Why did they leave? When?' The robot says wistfully, 'One day they were not here any more.' Clay accepts this in good grace. He touches a button and an abstract three-dimensional film cascades from a fluorescent projector. When he releases the button the whole gaudy whirl of colored lights funnels back into the projector in reverse, going whoosh as it vanishes. In another room he finds games of chance: boards that glitter and thump, wheels that spin in erratic orbits, chips, markers, counters, ebony dice, playing cards that melt and sag as he touches them. Beyond is something like a giant aquarium, but there are no fish in it. Then he beholds a child's puzzle, an embalmed tree, an empty cage, and a small sealed box. He passes onward. Jets of live steam warn him away from a tempting womby room with spongelike walls. He avoids a flight of stairs descending into what may be a lower level, for choking clouds of green dust break forth before he has taken three steps down. He comes to a place where robots are disassembling robots. He discovers a mighty screen that shows a view of the surface world: soft hills and valleys, no trace of that grim desert of hallucinations through which he has come. Finally he nudges a nicely pivoted door of thick aluminum-looking metal, and, as it swings solemnly open, the robot scuttles toward him and says, 'Beyond this point there are no safeguards.'

'What am I supposed to understand by that?'

'We cannot protect you if you continue in this direction.'

Clay stares into the newly revealed corridor. It looks much like the one he has just explored, but if anything it is brighter and more attractive. The buildings have subtle, understated facades that gleam with the restrained fire of fine rubies, and he detects a hint of elegant music tinkling in some nearby courtyard. He will go onward. The robot repeats its warning, and Clay says, 'Nevertheless, I accept the risks.' As he takes his first step into the forbidden sector an uncomfortable thought strikes him and, looking back, he asks the robot, 'Will this door close after I've gone in there?'

'Affirmative.'

'No,' Clay says. 'I don't want it to. I order you to leave it open until I come out again.'

'Strict instructions to prevent incursions by inhabitants of—'

'Forget them. This is an *order*. I'm the only man on the planet right now, and this whole place was built to serve men, and you yourself are nothing but a machine designed to make the lives of men happier and more rewarding, and I'm damned if I'll let you defy me. The door stays open. Is that understood?'

Hesitation. Conflict.

'Affirmative,' says the robot ultimately.

Clay goes in. On his sixth step he swings round. The door is still open. His robot waits beside it. 'Good,' Clay says. 'Remember, I'm boss. It stays open.'

As he inspects the classic facades in this wing of the tunnel-world, he comes upon his first sign – other than the goat-man's corpse – that nonmechanical life has impinged on any part of the underground refuge. Eight little green pellets lie outside the entrance to a glossy parlor. Plainly they are the droppings of some rodent of the era. Where the robots do not go, wildlife has taken possession.

Lurking, Clay sees the possible pellet-maker: a ferrety animal close to the ground, moving on stumpy legs and switching a naked purple tail. Its back is lined with eyes. Clay is aware of a cruel and purposeful intelligence within the beast. Not another son of man, this? No. No micron of humanity in it. It is stalking something down the corridor. Clay follows. Beast pounces. Invisible prey, perhaps? The ferret grasps with all feet and tail, plunges jaws into. Munches. Evident enjoyment. Nasty little carnivore, feasting. At length it is through; it drags its unseen victim into an alcove and emerges, dropping more green pellets. Scuttles away. Clay continues.

There is no maintenance here. The air is moist, congested, protoplasmic. Sparkling webs hang from the walls, and clicking predators squat at their centers. Clay confronts one: a hairy blue lobster. It smiles hungrily at him. He slips past its lair and enters a splendid courtyard where a fountain of radiance purrs and gleams. Here are more machines of the kind common on the far side of the door, though he has yet to see two devices alike. Before him is a concave mirror, the depths of which seem temptingly soft and shimmering, like a gateway to fairyland. He puts forth fingertips to touch the silken glass, than thinks better of it and withdraws them. 'What do you do?' he asks the instrument. 'The things here ought to have labels on them, like DRINK ME or PUSH THIS BUTTON FOR GOOD HALLUCINATIONS, or something. Strangers can't be expected to guess at these things. They might get hurt. Or damage something delicate.'

The moment he ceases speaking, he hears a shrill cackling, a gurgling, a bubbling, a babbling, and then there comes from a point within the mirror the sound of his own voice, rearranged and reduplicated and interlocked to form a screaming symphony of devastating intricacy:

'GOOD HALLUCINATIONS things labels have like strangers at at at at at at at can't be expected PUSH THIS BUTTON or or or ought to have DRINK things delicate something damage, damage damage guess might guess guess guess get hurt FOR ME here they can't they they they they they they they hurt or PUSH PUSH PUSH like strangers the here on them on them FOR something to things these something labels BUTTON dam la ex some del age ink cate ic ess an't ings uci ood delicate FOR things utton gers urt et PUSH THIS BUTTON a a a a mage HALLUCINATIONS angers GOOD.'

Followed by silence.

Followed by inverted repetition. Triple fugue. Modulation into the minor. Spiccato. Dazzling dominant seventh. Codetta before third voice enters. Transposition of subject into tonic. Allegro non giocoso. Andante ma non troppo. Largo. Vivace. Solfeggio. The room echoes with the music of his words. 'PUSH!' 'Ood!' 'LUCINA!' 'Ink!' Variations ad libitum. 'Oo oo oo oo oo oo oo.' Sonata quasi una fantasia. Portamento. Sforzando. Sfogato. Fortissimo. He flees. The music pursues him into the corridor. Legato! Doloroso! Dal segno! Agitato! 'Damage! Damage! Damage!' He runs, trips, arises, runs again. The recording machine hurls solid planes of sound after him that split the air into levels, like a pousse-café. He sprints around one corner and a second and a third, continuing to run even after the sounds have died away. Then he skids to a halt. A large beast blocks the corridor. It is tent-shaped, with sagging folds of leathery green skin, and it has about twice Clay's bulk. It waddles on tiny ducklike yellow feet. Absurd little arms dangle from its chest; above them is a slit of a mouth and two large glossy eyes. The eyes startle Clay: they twinkle with a clownish good humor and with undoubtable intelligence, but there is a cold malevolence, too, about their sly flickering movements. The beast and Clay face one another in silence. At length he tells it, 'If you're a human form, I claim kinship. I'm an ancestral species. Carried by the time-flux.' The eyes even more alert, even more amused, but there is no other response. The creature continues to approach. It is big but seems harmless; Clay, nevertheless, naked and unarmed, is cautious, and moves carefully backward. Without turning his head, he gropes for a door, finds one, opens it, steps through, slams it, and leans against it to hold it tight, while following the movements of the corridor-creature by way of a wide window. The large beast makes no attempt to force the door. Evidently it has other prey in mind, for now, Clay sees, it is turning its attention to a nest fixed in a pillar on the far side of the corridor. The mouth-slit has opened, and from it a black trunklike tongue has uncoiled, several yards long, bearing three crooked fingers at the tip. With this it probes the nest, which is fashioned of glistening strands of plastic. As the fingers knock about within the nest, heads bob up: the young, it seems, of one of the ferret-things. Six black snouts weave in obvious fury. They dodge the groping tongue; one of them boldly leaps on it and sinks bright yellow fangs into it, then jumps off, and the tent-shaped thing, stung, pulls its tongue back a few feet, stropping it against the air to cool it. Then the tongue returns and resumes its exploration of the nest. The young ferrets leap and dance about, but this time the tongue strikes quickly, catching one by the underbelly and pulling it down toward the waiting mouth. Small cruel claws scrabble and scratch to no avail. Into the mouth it goes; and in the same moment the mother ferret, returning from a hunting trip, reaches the scene and leaps at the huge predator. Clay hears screeches through the door, but does not know whose. The outraged mother bites and claws and rips. The tongue, flailing like an irritated serpent, goes high and comes down, the fingers seeking the ferret, trying to pluck it away. But the spiky little animal is too quick. Scrambling swiftly, it eludes the blind fingers, biting them whenever they come too near. The ferret finds that its enemy's hide is easily punctured, and it pierces it in several places, finally opening such a rent under one of the larger animal's arms that it is able to burrow through. It enters the flesh of the tent-beast as if it plans to bore a passage to the stomach and liberate its swallowed pup. Now the struggle has been transformed. Snout, shoulders, middle of the ferret vanish into its foe. The tent-beast's eyes have lost their roguish humor; they glisten with agony. The tongue, uncoiling to its full enormous length, whips the wall convulsively. The beast hops and jumps on its duck-legs; it tries in vain to reach the toothy burrower with its useless little hands; it rubs itself against pillars, emits bellows of pain, tips from side to side in clumsy distress. Its doom is certain.

But doom, when it comes, comes from a different distributor. Suddenly there is a third creature in the corridor, reptilian, almost dinosaurian. It strides forward on colossal claw-tipped legs, with thighs like treetrunks. A fleshy tail trails it. Its forearms are short but powerful; its face is extended into a ponderous snout; its teeth are fangs so savage and so numerous that they overstate the newcomer's deadliness, making it a comic exaggeration of all that is most brutal in nature. Above this cluster of sinister blades are two broad bright eyes, icily gleaming. What is this hideous tyrannosaur? What trick of evolution, bending back upon itself, loosed this scaly saurian in these sleek corridors? The monster rears, its head touching the tunnel-world's roof, and it seizes the tent-beast, whipping it aloft as though it has no weight. Two arrogant strikes of the front claws and the unfortunate tent splits, cloven. The ferret bursts free, coated with sticky black blood, and whistles up into its nest. The saurian, stooping, feeds, pushing gobs of meat into its awesome craw. Rending and tearing; snorts of satisfaction. Clay, safe behind his door, looks on, stunned not by the gory killing but by the messages spilling from the monster's mind. It is no reptile. It is another of the sons of man. *Are you of the Eaters?* Clay asks, and the nightmare replies, not pausing in its feast, *So we are known.*

The thoughts of the Eater float like ice-floes on a gray sea. Clay is appalled by the contact. He draws back, shrinking up against the far wall; the Eater is much too big to come into this room, he tells himself. But the door flaps open. The ferocious snout pushes in, though the rest of the Eater remains in the hall. Clay sees himself reflected, distorted, in those glittering eyes.

Man? the Eater asks. *Ancient form?*

I am. The time-flux—

Yes. Brusque dismissal. *Soft pink thing. Useless.*

Clay replies, *Humans were created weak so that their skills and reflexes would develop. If we had had your claws and teeth from the start, would we ever have invented knives and hammers and chisels and axes?*

The Eater scoffs. It nudges its face a little deeper into the room. Clay uneasily contemplates the way the smooth plastic wall around the doorframe is beginning to crack. He would be three mouthfuls for this thing.

I too am human, the Eater boasts.

Having taken on an animal's form?

Having taken on the form of power.

Power lies in transcending your physical weakness through cleverness, says Clay. *Not in giving yourself a beast's raw strength.*

I'll match my teeth against your cleverness, the Eater offers. Pushing harder against the door; obviously insatiable and seeking whatever meat.

Clay says, *Your fellow humans of this era seem to be able to get along without killing. They need no food. Why do you kill? Why must you eat?*

By free choice.

Choice to revert to primitivism?

Must I be like the others?

The others are freer than you, Clay insists. *You are bound by the needs of your flesh. You aren't a forward step in evolution. You're an anachronism, an atavism.* The doorframe strains. *What was the purpose of evolving men out of monstrosities, if men were merely going to turn themselves into monstrosities again?*

Fierce pressure against wall. Creaks within the structure.

The Eater says, *There is no purpose. There is no pattern.* Snaps teeth. Slips one arm into room. *We chose this form at a time when it pleased us to choose it. Should we sit and sing? Should we play with flowers? Should we do the Five Rites? We have our own ways. We are part of the texture of things.* And crashes through the door, ripping half the wall away.

The vast mouth opens. The ferocious teeth sparkle. Clay, who has eyed a small hatch in the corner of the room opposite the door during his colloquy with the monster, rushes to it now, finds that it opens, and, in great relief, hurries through it, escaping. The Eater's roars resound as Clay retreats. He finds himself now in some kind of service core, dark, musty, a series of spiraling passages constituting a baffling maze. His eyes grow accustomed to his new surroundings in time. Animals of a hundred kinds live in these galleries. He does not comprehend the ecology: on what do the herbivores feed? Futile to seek logic here. And through the corridors move Eaters, at least a dozen of them, gathering the harvest. Each has its own territory. There are no trespasses. They hunt constantly, and can never find sufficient meat. Clay learns to detect them, snorting and clattering, long before he comes close, and thus he avoids any danger. Can he find his way back to the door that has been left open for him? Can he return safely to the part of the tunnel-world that the robots maintain?

He wanders eternally in the interlocking corridors. Hair sprouts on his body again. For the first time since he gave his hunger to Hanmer, he feels a faint but definite need of food. He experiences thirst. It bothers him to be naked. He swallows too much dust. Seeking to avoid Eaters, he fails to notice small carnivores, and several times is nipped on the heels and calves. Each passage feeds into another, but he gets no nearer to familiar territory. Despair engulfs him. He will wander in this underworld forever. Of, if he does succeed in regaining the surface, he will find himself merely in that same desert of hallucinations where his guide the spheroid abandoned him. The encounter with the Eater has darkened his spirit. He is oppressed by the notion of such a beast as a descendant.

By way of consolation he attempts to persuade himself that he is maligning the Eaters. He invents a culture for them. He gives himself a vision of the Eaters at prayer, inflamed with zeal and spiritual tenderness. He devises Eater poetry. He shows himself a pack of Eaters gathered at a wall on which paintings hang, and listens to their ideas of esthetics. He conjures up Eater mathematicians, scratching surds in the dust with their terrible claws. His soul floods with compassion for them. You are human, you are human, you are human, you are human, he insists, and he is ready to embrace them in brotherhood. A feeling of love overwhelms him. His consciousness swoons into the Eater world, dim, fantastic, uncertain, traversed by fiery passions, and, glimmering and trembling, trembling and unfolding, he brings his message of love to the monsters, he delivers his Epistle to the Atrocious, and they crowd about him, thanking him for the gift of grace, clicking their fearsome teeth in gentle harmonies, blessing him for seeing the essential humanity within the nightmare flesh. In this rapture he moves serenely through the tangled tunnel-world, and at last he sees bright lights ahead, and steps leading upward, and hears a celestial chord, and a voice tells him, 'Come, this is the way.' He goes up. Choirs of angels sing. He passes through an octagonal doorway and the sweetness of fresh air strikes his nostrils. Nor is this a dream, for he emerges into a meadow of plump golden grass, and his friends are all there, and Hanmer says, 'You are in time to join us for the Tuning of the Darkness.'

14

The Skimmers surround him and welcome him back. All six
wear the female form in his honor; they kiss him and caress
him and wriggle against him. Hanmer, Ti, Bril, Serifice,
Angelon, Ninameen. Serifice? Serifice. They give him no
chance to ask explanations. Giggling, they bear him off to a
shallow pool in the meadow's midst, and cleanse him of the
dust of the tunnel-world. Their hands are everywhere, like
those of giddy harem girls. He cannot see for the splashing.
Serifice? Legs twine about him. He is briefly and playfully
encunted, but the union is broken before he makes a thrust.
Someone explores his armpit. Someone enters his ear.
'Enough!' he splutters, but they continue a while. Finally he
arises, wearing an awkward erection, and clambers to shore,
finding all six of them male and laughing. The spheroid is
perched not far away.

'Serifice?' he blurts. 'Are you Serifice?'

He pulls the slim form close. Serifice nods. There are new
depths in the scarlet eyes.

Hanmer says, 'Serifice, yes. Death bored him.'

'But—'

'The Tuning of the Darkness!' Ninameen cries, and they
all take it up, prancing around Clay and shouting it. Even the
spheroid joins the clamor. 'You went too fast for me,' Clay
says reproachfully. 'You left me behind in that dreadful
desert.' The spheroid, abashed, drops down-spectrum several
phases and pivots uncomfortably on its wheel. But the gaiety
of the others quickly makes such interchanges of accusation
and guilt improper. Their wild dance seems to be a pre-
paration for the coming rite, for he senses them drawing power
from the earth, pulling it in clanging pulsations and wrapping
their bodies with it. A roof of ionization, tingling and hissing,
covers them. A succulent blue glow bleeds from the grass. As

they weave their spell the Skimmers flicker from sex to sex, perhaps unable to hold their grasp while concentrating on these other things. He wanders through the group, ill at ease. The sky darkens; the sun topples as if pushed, and stars begin to burn through the cloud of buzzing electrons overhead as the day ebbs. He comes to Serifice, who is female. She moves back and forth, back and forth, treading an intricate step while never leaving a plot of ground some three feet square. Her arms describe a series of helical bends and twists. Pale sparks drip from her fingertips. 'You were really dead,' he says to her. 'Weren't you?' She does not break her step. With a pretty little gasp she says, 'I'll tell you everything.' He falls into the rhythm of her movements. 'Where did you go?' he demands. 'What was it like? How did you find your way back?' She lifts her arms and showers him with sparks that hum and whistle against his skin. 'Later,' she tells him. 'I'll offer good news of death. But now we must tune the darkness.'

'May I join the rite?'

'You have,' she says. 'You have, you have, you have.'

Now comes a rush of energy from the heart of the world, a bright blue column of it rising like a Maypole in the meadow's midst. Dazzling streamers of force hang from it; Serifice clutches one, Hanmer one, Ninameen, Ti, Bril, Angelon. The spheroid, seeming apprehensive, allows one gleaming strand to penetrate its cage. Clay hesitates a moment. Then he catches a streamer. He perceives a sensation he recognizes: that feeling of dissolving flesh that he experienced when Hanmer took him, long ago, soaring from planet to planet. But the texture of the sensation is closer and tighter now; it is altogether more intense. He is rising, he, Hanmer, Serifice, Angelon, all of them, becoming a single flame, spurting upward and funneling into the heavens, and almost instantly they are beyond Earth's atmosphere. He sees the planet sleepily turning within him, wrapped in folds of blue fleece. A zone of daylight sweeps across it; tiny particles shimmer in that beam. The other worlds cling to the celestial spokes and swing creakingly through their duties. He longs to visit Jupiter again and surrender himself to its weighty blanket. He dreams of swimming through misty Neptune. But there are no local stops on this journey, he soon discovers. The planets zoom away and are lost in the distance, mere points in the night, then not even that. He weeps at this loss of worlds. His tears slide free and go gonging through the firmament, turning ever more rapidly, gaining in momentum, picking up kinetic grandeur, sucking energy from the roots of the galaxy as they roll across the night, and one by one they strike fire and burn with sudden brilliance. They assume the clear luminous self-sustaining blaze of suns. He has created a necklace of stars. 'Yes,' Hanmer says, murmuring somewhere close. 'We are here.'

They hang, the group of them, before the frozen face of the universe.

He wishes now that he had mastered astronomy. These stars bear no labels. How will he know what he visits? What is that terrible red orb, embedded in a huge expanding shell of tenuous gas? What is that fierce blue beacon, ripping space apart with its outflow of power? That clump of smouldering ash? That massy white dwarf? That throbbing orange eye? This triple sun? That cloud of speckled brilliance? 'Their names,' he says. 'Can you tell me?' And someone – Hanmer? – replies, 'Egg, Leaf, Lip, Toad, Blood, Sea, and Stripe.' Clay says, 'No. No. Their old names. Sirius, Canopus, Vega, Capella, Arcturus, Rigel, Procyon, Altair, Betelgeuse. Spica? Deneb? Aldebaran? Antares?' They give him other names, pointing excitedly with flares of energy: 'Cauldron. Thin. First. Flat. Stone. Blind.' Again Clay refuses these names. He seethes with frustration. Where is he? Who are these stars? Beta Lyrae! Tau Ceti! Epsilon Aurigae! Gamma Leonis! He hangs suspended in space with the stars dangling from a dark wall before him. He can touch them; he can caress them; but he cannot name them. Here is one yellow as his own sun, but monstrous, engulfing greedy light-hours of space. Here is a planetless blue scorcher sending savage waves of siren energy into the blackness. Here is some red giant gently gathering a hundred charred worlds to its bosom. And here. And here. And here. Dead stars. Dwarf stars. Double stars. Exploding stars. Brazen stars. Timid stars. Dusty stars.

Comets. Meteors. Nebulae. Motes. Moons. Here are stars that flocculate. Here are stars that do the fevered doppler-dance. Here are collapsing stars. Here are colliding stars. Where does the universe end? What is the color of the land that lies outside its walls? What language do they speak there? What wines do they drink?

The cosmos is full of discordant tones and he drifts, dazed, blown whole parsecs at a gust by the rude clangor of these jostling nameless stars. Each one sings to him in its own cluster of jangling keys. Each one creates a private set of scales. There is no harmony. There is no order. There is no reason. He is lost; he is helpless; he is stunned; he is dwarfed.

Hanmer, ever calm, says. 'It is the Tuning of the Darkness now.'

Which begins. A supreme effort, difficult but necessary. Clay feels the others close about him, embracing him, mingling substances with him: this is not something that can be done by individual exertion. He lends his strength to theirs. They start to organize the stars. The clang and bang and hiss and swoosh and bong and smash of random energies broadcasting at will must be tamed. They work patiently to comb the tangled frequencies. They sort and arrange the clashing colors. They straighten the crooked vibrations and classify the clutter of sizzling radiations. The work is slow and arduous, but there is an ecstasy in it. Entropy is the enemy; we carry the war to his territory, and we prevail. There! Now the glistening rows take form! Now order comes out of chaos! It is not yet finished: fine adjustments are needed, a manipulation here, a transposition there. A few growling dissonances still creep forth. And there are backsliders; not all will hold their places, and some trickle into randomness almost as soon as they have been given their new assignments. But listen! Listen! The melodies are emerging, now! The tuning is supple and cunning; the scales are elusive but convincing, with many a plangent twang, many a slippery interval. The cosmic keyboard sings out. We are the mallets, they are the xylophone, and listen to the song! The tingling, the jingling, the trembling, the glistening: the universe moving serenely on its bearings, the cosmos in harmony.

Now he hangs enraptured before the ringing stars.

Their fire is cool. Their skins are soft. Their music is pure and clean.

And we are the sons of man, the tuners of the darkness.

He looks upon the stars and greets them. He hails Fomalhaut, Betelgeuse, Acherner, Capella, and Alphecca; Mirzan and Muliphen, Wezen and Adhara; Thuban, Pollux, Denebola, Bellatrix; Sheliak, Sulaphat, Aladfar, Markab; Muscida, Porrima, Polaris, Zaniah; Merak, Dubhe, Mizar, Alcaid. He greets El-rischa, Alnilam, Ascella, and Nunki; he strikes joy from Al-gjebha, Al-geiba, Mebsuta, Mekbuda; he sets pealing Mira, Mimosa, Mesarthim, Menkar. All the suns sing in splendid unison: Sadalmalik, Sadalsud, Sadachbia, Saq sakib alma; Regulus, Algol, Naos, Ankaa. He joins the song himself. Look, he tells them, I hover suspended here in space, I who am man born of woman, who came forth and crawled and learned to stand, I who wore gills in the womb, I who was allotted three score years and ten, I who suffered and knew pain and was alone. I stand before the stars. I coax melodies from them. I the wanderer from the sealed past, I the exile, I the victim; here I am. With my companions. With the sons of man. So am I that small? Am I that feeble? Sing! Fill the universe with thunders! Now, woodwinds, brasses, strings, percussion! Now and now and now and now!

He extends across the cosmos from wall to wall. He laughs. He roars. He fondles suns. He whistles. He sobs. He shouts his name. He exults.

And the tuned stars chime.

And Hanmer says quietly, when the moment comes, 'It is done. Now we go back.'

15

'Death,' he reminds Serifice. 'To tell me. You promised. All about it.'

'It was peace,' she says. 'It was being empty. It was like a double sleep.'

They loll in a lake of dark honey, the seven of them. The spheroid alone is missing, having failed to return from the journey to the stars. The honey drips from great wrinkled trees whose crowns dip downward under the weight of their own elixir. It enters the Skimmers through their skins, enhancing their luminous gleam. Clay occasionally tastes a few drops; the honey makes his ears hum. All the skimmers now are female except for Hanmer, who swims in virile circles round the borders of the lake.

Clay says, 'Did you see anything there? Were you aware of anything around you?'

'Empty.'

'But you knew you existed somewhere.'

'I knew I did not exist.'

'What did you *feel*?'

'I felt non-feeling.'

'Can't you be more concrete?' Clay asks, mildly exasperated. 'I want to know what it was like.'

'Die and see,' Serifice suggests.

'Die and see,' Ninameen murmurs. 'Die and see,' says Ti. 'Die and see,' from Angelon, but from Bril, 'See and die.' They all laugh. Hanmer says, 'We all will die. We all will see.'

'And after a while you'll all come back?'

'I think not,' Hanmer says lazily. 'That would spoil it.'

'It is a shining kingdom,' says Serifice. 'All things are there, united, as all colors unite to make white. It was a place outside all places. It was – itself. With bright walls. With whiteness. With sky that comes down past the horizon. And we were all nothing. And soon we forgot ourselves. And I was not Serfice, and they were not whoever they had been, and we glistened. And we glistened. And then I came back.'

'No,' Clay says, splashing the honey in his confusion. 'I don't believe it. Death is death, and afterward there's nothing. The meaning of the word. The end of beingness. It isn't a place. You weren't anywhere.'

'Was.'

'You couldn't have died, then,' he insists.

'Serifice died,' Hanmer tells him, floating with legs crossed.

'I died,' says Serifice. 'And went. And was. And returned. And tell you of it. A place, a place, a place!'

'An illusion,' says Clay stubbornly. 'Like your trips to the stars. Like your sliding into the core of the world. Like lifting the sea. You invented a death-place, and you went to it, and it pleased you. But it wasn't death.'

'It was death,' says Serifice.

Ti and Ninameen swim closer. 'You sour the honey with your quarrels,' Ti says. Ninameen says, 'The solution is simple. When we go to die where Serifice died, come with us, and see it for yourself, and you'll know the truth.'

'I'm no Skimmer,' he grumbles. 'When I die, I'll be dead, and no coming back.'

'You know this certainly?' Bril asks, with surprise.

'I believe it, is all.'

'How can you believe, when you have never been?' asks Angelon. 'Serifice has been,' says Ti.

'We believe Serifice,' says Ninameen solemnly.

He is outnumbered. They debate like children. He can make no impact on their minds. This chatter of death and coming back from death leaves him tense and constricted.

'It was only a little death,' Serifice announces. 'We must try the larger one eventually. He is right and I am also right: it was death, but not *all* of death, that I tasted. And perhaps it was not enough. To find out what death is, we must truly die. When the time comes.'

'Enough,' he says.

'Do we bore you?' Angelon asks.

'Death bored me,' says Serifice. 'The little death that I had. It was beautiful, but it became boring.'

'We are beautiful,' Ninameen observes, 'and perhaps we are becoming boring.'

'You don't bore me,' he tells them. 'You depress me. With talk of death. Of dying.'

'You asked,' Serifice reproaches.

'I wish I hadn't.'

'Shall we unhave the conversation?' asks Hanmer.

Clay stares at him, bewildered. He shakes his head. He

locates the source of his irritation: it is presumptuous, he decides, for these immortals to play games with death. When his own people lived always under the cruel sentence. For us it was no game. He does not like to think that the Skimmers would consider dying. Dying is incompatible with their nature; for them to die would be a breach of esthetics, a failure of natural law. Yet they toy with the idea. They dabble in mortality. They mock his transience with their offer to renounce their jeweled lives. And I love them, he realizes.

'Are you lonely among us?' Ninameen asks.

A lavender cloud slides over them. A sudden passionate rain falls, striking the surface of the honey like a deluge of bullets. Geysers of dark fluid rise and subside. During the storm no one speaks. Green lightning explodes. There is immediate thunder; and riding over its mighty sound comes what seems at first to be a crackle, but which he recognizes shortly as the weeping of Wrong. Will I meet this troublesome deity at last? The sobbing can no longer be heard. The raindrops fall less vehemently. Puddles of shining water lie on the viscous surface of the honey-lake. The Skimmers have gathered close about him, almost protectively.

'Will you dream with us?' asks Angelon.

'What will you dream?'

'We will dream your world,' she says, smiling serenely. 'Because you are lonely.'

16

He closes his eyes, and they take his hands, and they drift on the bosom of the lake, and they dream without sleeping, and he dreams with them, and they dream his world, for he is lonely.

They dream Egypt for him. They dream white-jacketed pyramids and snarling sphinxes, they dream scorpions on the hot red sand, they dream the pillars of Luxor and Karnak. They dream pharaohs. They dream Anubis and Set, Osiris, Horus,

Re the falcon. They dream Lascaux and Altamira for him, the sputtering, stinking lamps of mammoth-fat, the left-handed artist rubbing his ochres on the cave wall, the herds of woolly rhinos, the sorcerer in his skins and paints. They dream him the gilded domes of Byzantium. They dream him Columbus tossing on the sea. They dream him Liberty with the sword held high in her hand. They dream him the moon, with footsteps on it, and motionless metal spiders. A grove of redwood trees; the Eiffel Tower; the Grand Canyon of the Colorado; the coral-crusted beach at St Croix; the Bay Bridge at sunrise; the Riviera; the Bowery. They dream passenger pigeons and auks and dodos and quaggas, the aurochs and the heath hen, the moa and the mastodon. They dream lions and tigers, cats and dogs, gazelles, chipmunks, spiders, bats. They dream highways. They dream tunnels. They dream sewers. They dream subways. Benedictine and Chartreuse, cognac, bourbon, rye, and eggnog. Lincoln. Washington. Napoleon. Pontoppidan. He seizes the fragments as they float by, embraces them, releases them, reaches for the next. The flow is fertile. They dream his friends and his family, his house, his shoes. They dream Clay himself, and send him floating past himself. Stirring, tossing, purring, they hook vagrant images out of the pot and set loose many bygone things. They give him the Crusades, the movies, The *New York Times*, the testing grounds at Eniwetok, the Model A, the Ponte Vecchio, the Ninth Symphony, the Church of the Holy Sepulchre, the taste of tobacco, and the Albert Memorial. The pace intensifies. They smother him in memories. They crowd the sticky lake with pieces of the past. They are fascinated and delighted and appalled by each discovery, murmuring, what is this? and who was that? and how is this called? as they dredge. 'Are you glad to see these things again?' someone whispers. 'Did you think they were beyond recovery?' He moans. The dream has gone on too long.

It ends. Their dream-gifts vanish. At random, he seizes Ninameen, and clasps her close until the spasm of terrifying displacement has run its course. 'Are you frightened?' she asks. 'Are you troubled? Are you sad?'

17

A day and a night and a day and a night and a day, and they enter a land of woods and streams, rugged and broken, patrolled by beasts. Certain patterns seem dear to evolution. He sees something that is almost a moose, though it is crowned with a green-flowered shrub instead of antlers; he sees an almost-bear, paunchy and jowly, made strange only by its spike-crested spine; he sees flat tails strike the water, and thinks of beavers, though their owners have long serpentine necks; he hails a mound of shining quills as a porcupine, a flash of tooth and tail as a bobcat, a tremor of long ears and creamy fur as a rabbit. There are also many for whom he can find no counterparts in the zoologies of times past: a perambulating heap of hairy flesh with five equidistant trunks along its perimeter, a blue vertical thing that bounds along on a single rubbery leg, a flightless bird with chicken claws and crocodile snout, a limbless scaly crawler with three snaky bodies linked in parallel, and more. As they proceed, the weather worsens, which puzzles him, for it is distinctly autumnal here and he has grown accustomed to a world without seasons or climatic zones. A frosty wind blows toward them. Withered leaves whip in the crackling air. The sunlight is thin and strangled; all sounds are sharper; heavy gray clouds load the horizon. 'We near another of the uncomfortable places,' Hanmer explains.

'Which?'

'It is called Ice.'

The place called Ice comes upon them with great suddenness. A thick curtain of close-packed trees bearing bulging blue needles, like those of cancerous spruce, marks the boundary between the woodlands and the awful zone beyond. The marchers push through these trees and emerge into eternal winter. Like a leprous spot on a tender cheek is this incongrous segment of the old Antarctic, somehow mortared into a kinder globe. Whiteness reigns. It stuns; it dazzles. The furious glare stabs his eyes, and he turns away, saying to Serifice, 'Are you sure that this is not the place you went to, mistaking it for Death?' and she replies, 'Death was much whiter than this. And not nearly so cold.'

Cold. Yes. Naked to the polar furies. He will freeze. He will become a pillar of ice, eyes still open, lips clamped, his genitals turned to icicles. 'Must we go forward?' There are limits. What will protect him? The ice is taut and sleek, a blanket over the land, alive with a terrible sheen. Black rocks, fissured and fanged, leap up from it. There are subterranean rumblings and crackings, as of hidden cannons. He hears the birth pangs of crevasses. Yet Hanmer goes out onto the ice and all the others follow. He too. Aching. Frosted. The sunlight plays with ice, leaping over it and straining it at every touch: deep blue here, yellow-green there, and on these ridges the tint is red, the marriage of blood and light. In the frozen silence between underground sounds, masses of fog overwhelm the travelers, and, while he welcomes the soft fleecy wrapping, he fears that he will be separated from the others while they are engulfed, and will perish in this wasteland. For he knows that he is drawing warmth from them. They nourish him as the crossing proceeds.

Figures appear in the mist and cross his path: upright two-legged creatures, slender and elongated, with short malproportioned legs and barrel-like bodies. A thick gray pelt covers them; their bodies are powerfully muscled, with massive necks forming tall pedestals for their high-domed heads. The mouths are well toothed. The noses are strong and hooked. The eyes, bright yellow, gleam with cunning. They look a little like giant otters adapted for a life of walking; but they also look like men transformed for meeting the special conditions of Ice. He fears them. He glances about, searching for his companions; momentarily he cannot find them, and panic heats his soul. 'Hanmer? Ninameen? Ti?'

The gray creatures move in idle sauntering paths, but it becomes clear that they are closing in. There are about a dozen of them, now, and more are visible every time an opening appears in the dense white fog. Clay picks up their scent: sour, grating, a smell of wool left too long in the rain. He feels absurdly naked. He knows that these are no beasts of the wilds, but rather the sons of man in yet one more guise.

'Bril? Angelon? Serifice?'

Something warm touches his elbow: the breast of Serifice. He turns to her, trembling. 'Do you see them?' he whispers.

'Of course.'

'What are they?'

'They are Destroyers.' Simply; matter-of-factly; with full acceptance.

'Human?'

'In their way, yes.'

'They frighten me.'

Serifice laughs. 'You, who debate with Eaters, are frightened by *these*?'

'An Eater is nothing but teeth and claws and swagger,' Clay says. 'And these—'

He hears the familiar sobbing sound sweeping through the fog.

'Yes,' Serifice says. 'Servants of Wrong.'

A fierce gust blows. He huddles, covering his face and his loins. The fog wraps him more tightly. Wrong cackles. Sunlight, sliding over the frozen ground, slips under the fleecy mist to bathe him in blue, glossy green, and velvet black; he feels a flash of golden fire, and then the light is gone. 'Serifice?' he calls. He gropes for her. My lips must be turning blue. My ears. My fingers. He imagines that he could crack his frozen penis off with one snap. His crystalline balls. He shuffles his feet; the ice is a mirror beneath him, cold slick glass. 'Hanmer? Bril?' To dissolve, now. To soar, to leap into space, to hover between the stars – anywhere, anywhere, only not here. What is the area of Ice? This patch of blight. This chilly blemish. The sobbing grows louder. It wrenches the heart; can Wrong really grieve so deeply? For what? For whom? 'Ti? Ti, where are you? Any of you. Ninameen?' To reach them with his mind, to wrap a tendril of supplication about one of them and draw them near. He is too vulnerable. This cold is real. His friends are shallow, mercurial, forgetful; they lost the spheroid coming back from the stars, and said nothing of it; they may not even be his friends. Where are they? Why did they bring him to this place? The smell of rotting wool, a louder smell now, rank, dismaying. He remembers ponds, valleys, meadows, streams, the fragrance of strange flowers, the sweet taste of mysterious waters. He remembers entering Ninameen's warm moist cleft. He remembers old ecstasies and former comforts. Blundering forward, he trips on his own foot and falls headlong: his body blazes from chest to thighs where it touches the ice. Ears caked with sobs. He scratches frost from his skin. The world is darkening now. The light retreats, sucked away westward, draining all color from icefield and fog and sky. And in the blackness new colors come. The aurora erupts; pale electric streams cascade from a pocket of the sky, and draw fiery strands around him in a web of rosy goldness. Playful tremors rack the new night. But there is warmth in the beauty of this storm. He rises, he reaches forth his hands, he tries to seize the aurora and clothe himself in it. Folds and ripples in the night; pearly gray, turquoise, emerald, lemon, cerise; hammers ring on a million anvils; voices cry out; Wrong weeps joyously. He goes forward. He knows now that the Skimmers have abandoned him to fortune, and it hardly matters. Fear has not left him, but he has encapsulated it and bears it like a cyst in his breast. He loves the ice. He loves the cold. He loves the night. He loves the fire in the heavens. He loves those who destroy. He loves his fear.

A ring of Destroyers now surrounds him.

He sees them plainly by the aurora's blaze. Slightly taller than he is, but much heavier, for their muscles are huge and thick slabs of fat lie under their skins. Their gray fur is close-woven and silky. Their paws seem to have retractile claws. These are efficient engines of death, compact and streamlined: not grotesque overblown monsters like the Eaters, so terrifying that they are comic, but rather the essence of animal power, understated, menacing. They remind him now less of otters than of wolverines. But their stance is human, and so is that cold light of knowledge in their eyes. They stand facing him, patient, immobile, their long rapacious arms hanging down below their knees. What do they want? Merely to devour him? They are so very carnivorous; he pictures himself spread out on this primeval plain of ice, intestines bared and steaming, liver and lights aglow, while the Destroyers quarrel over his pancreas, his kidneys, his aorta, his spleen. But that seems too trivial a fate. He tests them, feinting to his left, then pivoting as if to break through a gap in their circle. Their reflexes are, as he expects, superior to his: with barely an indication of response they move to close the gap, and remain as before.

'Can you talk?' he asks. 'Do you understand me? Do you know what I am?'

Thin black lips curl in unmistakable smiles.

'A man,' he says. 'Ancestral species; early form. The time-flux brought me. The Skimmers escorted me. I'm un-adapted and unspecialized, nothing going for me except a brain, and that's no good when you're naked on a field of ice. Do you understand me? Can you talk?'

The Destroyers say nothing.

He rushes forward, not feinting now, simply trying to get past them and run; perhaps he can yet find Hanmer, possibly he can go from this place. For a moment it appears that they will let him pass, but as he breaches the circumference of the group one of them casually snares him by the arm and pulls him back into orbit. They toss him around the circle. He is embraced by one, another, another – a quick bear-hug, nothing affectionate about it, more a gesture of mockery than of love. Now he becomes truly aware of their physical power: he is a heap of straw in their hands. The smell of them inflates his skull. He dizzies. He falls. He no longer notices the cold. It seems quite natural to lie naked on the ice. The aurora fades. The night is triumphant. The Destroyers laugh, and do a clumsy dance, and bay the absent moon. Morning may never come.

18

By morning they have reached the far perimeter of Ice. Marching with Destroyers all about him, he is shielded from the cold by a wall of dense fur; spring comes into his step, and he holds himself buoyantly erect. The bland lightnings of the aurora have come and gone all through the night. He is in the repose that lies beyond exhaustion.

They have met many other Destroyers – moving usually in packs – in their crossing of the whiteness. Bound on taut errands, lashed to unexpressed duties, these Destroyers move about with a purposed look that he has not seen on other beings of this world. The members of one pack greet those of another with appropriately feral growls, which Clay senses are far from hostile in content; but nothing is exchanged that he can recognize as a word. Nor is he able to enter the minds of these grim folk with his thoughts, though he is certain of their strong, cold intellects. They treat him with a kind of amused lipsmacking interest; clearly they are attracted to him, but is it the pleasure of his company they desire, or, ultimately, the taste of his meat? He knows they must have contempt for him: pale hairless beast, almost in a man's shape, so weak, so simple. They hustle him along, bumping him with hips and haunches when he pauses. Day breaks.

By first light he discovers the Destroyers at their great task. Scores of them are at work along the border between Ice and the district beyond. Some are diligently felling trees and uprooting shrubs; they perform this labor with arms and shoulders and chests, and their bodies seem severely strained by its demands. Others gather the debris left by the clearers and pile it in heaps. Still others periodically incinerate these heaps, apparently by sudden intense flares of concentration. A different team, crouching and hopping about, rips up the turf with awesome bared claws, slashing the network of roots and runners and grasses and ropy weeds that binds the sod into something sturdy and able to resist. Lastly comes a quartet of Destroyers, arms linked, eyes closed, walking slowly out of Ice. They move with the greatest effort, as if pushing against a breast-high metal band that bars their advance; but with each struggling step they take, the area of Ice undergoes a minute expansion. A line of frost sprouts on the interface between the icefield and the newly upturned soil. The frost, at first, is only a glittering white film on the clumps of earth; but quickly it takes on substance, deepening, conquering. The dour Destroyers, pressing forward into fertile territory, pull the rim of the glacier behind them. Already the ice is six inches thick at the inner end of the point at which they began their morning's toil, sloping from there to the frost line immediately to their heels.

'Do you mean to freeze the entire planet this way?' he asks.

There is goodnatured laughter. No one replies. The fringe of ice progresses another quarter of an inch. Farther out, a tree falls, screaming. Are there Destroyers everywhere on the glacier's rim, working to expand its dominion? How long will it be before the world is wholly covered?

'Of course,' a Destroyer tells him, 'we lose ground also. The sun beats us back. Our enemies thaw the perimeter. Some days we do nothing but repair the damage of the day before, and often we may pass a week with no net gain in territory.'

'But why *do* it?' he asks.

Laughter again. No reply. Did the Destroyers actually speak? He saw no lips parting. He saw no jaws in motion.

He tours the edge of the ice, accompanied always by several Destroyers who never let him stray. He feels as if he is being shown some throbbing, productive factory. The Destroyers display a pride in their work. Look at us, see how dedicated we are! Keep your idle Skimmers, keep your sluggish Breathers, keep your rooted Awaiters, keep your raging Eaters: we are no sluggards, we are no dreamers! See our zeal as we consume the forest. See the passion with which we extend the ice! We are the committed ones; we are the doers of deeds. And the ice grows. And the soft summer shrinks.

'There were six Skimmers,' he says. 'I was with them and lost them in the fog. Do you know where they might be?' He says, 'Can you tell me why you're keeping me here? I'd be much happier where it's warm.' And he says, 'Won't you ever speak to me? Since you can understand me, why won't you bother to answer?'

At night they take him back into the heart of Ice.

Again the aurora. Again the green and red and yellow splashes, the hissing, the crackling. The groaning deep in the ground. He watches a feast of the Destroyers as he sits clutching himself against the cold. They have captured one of the five-trunked animals and have brought it shambling into their camp; it is elephantine in bulk and somewhat spherical in shape, with long black hair, glossy and coarse, and an uncertain number of thick short legs. The Destroyers surround it. Each lifts its left arm; claws slide from sheaths; the aurora blazes more fiercely and fire descends, playing over the shining yellow blades with somber brilliance. Abruptly that concentrated flow of energy finds its focus, rushing toward the captive beast. The creature's hair rises, revealing large sad eyes, a pimpled purple skin, a baggy-lipped mouth. The five trunks grow rigid and deliver trumpeting cries of pain. The animal falls and does not move. The Destroyers pounce. They have the nostalgia of old carnivores for a world of universal rapacity, and they tug and rip and claw their meat with superfluous fury. One of them, showing a bloody humor, brings Clay what he suspects is a prized delicacy: some internal organ, the size of a fist, with the iridescent green glint of a beetle's wings. Clay looks at it doubtfully. He has taken no solid food since his awakening, and even if he still had need for food, he would hesitate at raw meat. Though this appears not to be raw; it is warm in his hands, not only with animal warmth but with a tingling glow that the aurora's flare must have caused. The Destroyer who offered it to him pantomimes the act of eating, and laughs, and slaps his foreshortened thigh in pleasure. Clay frowns. Instinct tells him to beware the generosity of the servants of Wrong. Will the meat turn him into a Destroyer? Shrink him? Expand him? Poison him?

Hallucinate him? He shakes his head. He begins to hand the morsel back to the Destroyer, and receives such a terrible glare of threat that he kills the gesture at once, and puts the meat to his lips. He nibbles. He admits a single shred of flesh to his mouth. The flavor is extraordinary: rich, pungent, a tinge of cloves and an oystery aftertaste. He smiles. The Destroyer smiles, looking almost benevolent. Clay takes another bite.

Now he feels effects. A metallic taste in his mouth; a band of hot steel pressing against his forehead; a sheet of fire bursting from his pores. He gobbles the meat. Where are the Destroyers? Sprawling in the snow, sated, belching. He no longer fears them. Clumsy beasts. Killer-apes, evolution's prank. Getting a creative thrill out of spreading the ice. 'Build!' he shouts at them. 'Heal! Repair! *Improve!*' They glance up, eyes dulled and contemptuous. He wishes he could strip them of their fur. 'Push back the ice!' he cries. 'Plant greenery! Bring warmth!'

'Idiot,' one Destroyer mutters.

'Weakling.'

'Agitator.'

'Troublemaker.'

'Fool.'

He is buoyant. He is unaware of the cold. He plants his feet on the ice, rears back, drinks the aurora. Red and yellow and green and blue go cycling through his brain. He laughs. He capers. He leaps over one prostrate Destroyer after another. Gluttony has made them torpid. They are coils uncoiled, springs unsprung. He scrambles up a black boulder and looses a bolt of aurora-fire at the perimeter of the ice; it hisses, it sizzles, it melts, it vanishes. He cuts the strip off the border, revealing moist dark soil. While the stagnant beasts lie useless he will obliterate all the ice, and then he will make his escape. Colors and textures shimmer in his inflamed mind. His head swims; he purples with joy and excitement and hurls another fiery bolt at the distant rim of ice. Boiling molecules drift toward the heavens. How much can he remove before the Destroyers cast off their stagnation? Already he has undone nearly all of their day's work. 'See? The feeble prehistoric has his powers, too,' he tells them. 'What dulls your minds catalyzes mine.' He has always wished for the opportunity to do valuable, constructive service. Now he will restore fertility to this frost-blighted area. Let the Destroyers beware; they have let loose a mighty force! Yet already he is past his high. Yellow spiderwebs are congealing over the surface of his brain. The beam of energy that he hurls at the ice has lost its vigor; it droops and barely kindles a glow.

Is there more meat?

He pokes in the mound of bones and shards. Bits of skin, lumps of fat, the dismal deflated trunks, a strand of ligament – the Destroyers seem to have picked the carcass almost clean. No. Here. A wedge of bright red flesh, overlooked. Clay seizes it. Hot against his fingertips. Eats.

Potent again. Sends forth blaze.

He eradicates another dozen square yards of ice before he feels inertia ensnaring him. Reluctantly he realizes he must abandon his task. Escape now, while his captors snore. He runs, sliding and stumbling and occasionally falling, under a canopy of exploding stars. Which way is the exit? The Destroyers are out of sight. The aurora dims and moonless darkness takes root. He fears that in his blindness he will wander somehow back to the Destroyer camp. Wait until morning? Perhaps too late, then. He will be in the grip of demons again unless. But how can he find his way out? There are no landmarks. There is only ice.

He walks on. The cold has invaded his testicles; they clatter together, clicking like marbles in their pouch. The last kinetic shreds of the magical meat dissolve sadly in his gut. By brief auroral flickers he guides himself uncertainly, full of fear, wishing he could stop somewhere to rest and get warm. A quick cigarette. A cup of cocoa. The roof of his mouth turns to hot buttered toast and it maddens him. It is summer, now, in Clayton, Missouri. The hickories and elms are burdened with green. Gently the brook gurgles; trout wiggle on the hook. In the evenings one goes into town: steak and bourbon on Fifth Street, some jazz, then the place just off Lindell, where girls in diaphanous nighties smile, breasts bobbling, pink diaphanous nighties, yes, soft lights, diaphanous, girls with diaphanous crotch and you look for the exit and find yourself.

In the mud.

Primeval ooze. This is the place where, from afar, he was melting ice. The thaw has touched the earth below. All is in quagmire. He swims in slime. The warm gelatinous suspension of spuming soil slides up over his skin. He wriggles forward. It is not unpleasant. The hot silty mire defrosts his genitals. The dark lubricant caresses his refrigerated thighs. He crawls through the vagina of the world. He wallows. He writhes. Here the mud is three of four feet deep, some of it almost liquid, some merely clayey, and the touch of it is voluptuous and delicious. He is leaving the ice behind; he is eluding the sluggish Destroyers. Mud smears his belly, his chest, his face; it engulfs him entirely, and he fears for a moment that he will slip below the surface and be lost, but he finds solid footing underneath and pushes onward. When the going exhausts him, he lies still, pumping his hips gently to drive his throbbing organ into the yielding stickiness on which he sprawls. Then he scrambles onward. I need not be ashamed of returning to the mud, he tells himself. I know who I am. I know what I am. Why struggle to keep up appearances? Only one who has recently emerged from the ooze will feel tight about getting back into it for a while. I am secure in the knowledge of my humanity. If I choose I am free to love the mud.

As the first gray slivers of morning arrive, he frees himself from the morass. *Thuck!* goes the mud as he severs the suction. A coating of slime covers him. Naked no longer. Where is the exit? Ahead, he sees dimly, lies some kind of boulevard bordered by two rows of tall, stately trees. Dawn climbs his back as he sets out on the road. He walks with an easy, relaxed stride. The mud dries and he brushes most of it off, leaving only the dusty residue. There is a sudden swelling of light as the day leaps over him. It is warm here. He is back in the garden-world. He hopes now to find a clear, cool stream where he can wash himself. And then to seek the Skimmers; he does not care to wander guideless.

'You are not guideless,' a growling voice declares.

He discovers that two Destroyers accompany him, padding along gently to his rear, one on his left, one on his right. They are fully alert, as menacing and as intensely physical as ever: their gluttony has refreshed them and they have caught up easily with him. Will they punish him for thawing their ice? He walks a little faster, though he knows how futile that is. The road continues, perfectly straight, an arrow aimed at the horizon; the bordering rows of trees form flawless walls. The day is mild. The sky is cloudless. The Destroyers are silent.

He feels the weight of their terrible pride.

He hears Wrong's lilting sob.

He sees a smear of red in front of him, like sunrise perversely rebounding out of the west.

Shortly comes the smell of ashes and the taste of heat. Bits of cinder float on the air. Waves of distortion assail the straightness of the road. The trees, which have been uniformly upright and tall, now become gnarled stunted things, with charred and twisted branches void of leaves.'Where are we?' he asks one of his Destroyers, and the sleek beast-man perhaps replies or perhaps does not, but Clay becomes aware that he has reached the place that is known as Fire.

19

It is another of the districts of discomfort. Once, maybe, it was a forest, with splendid trees connected by a tight, bouncy network of glistening green vines. But there has been devastation, not just once but continuously. The ground is a deep carpet of ash. He feels the cold clinkers at the bottom and the warmer embers near the surface. The air is soot-stained. Spirals of greasy blue smoke rise from conical heaps of ash at irregular intervals. The trunks of the trees are blackened, glossy with the scars of combustion. The vines hang in angular, disheveled loops, split open where the flames have licked them.

The heat is no longer intense; whatever conflagration has

blazed here has nearly exhausted itself, settling into an amiable low-grade smoulder. Nothing is too hot to touch, though warmth is everywhere. But the place gives the impression of having undergone repeated scorchings. This is a used-up place. It is wholly oxidized; it is completely depleted. A dull ruddy glow gleams beneath some of the ashheaps, telling him that he is wrong about that: if it burns, it still lives. A little. Yet there must not be far to go. Waiting for the end, boys; it won't be long.

He moves through the rubble. Clouds of ash leap up with every step. Haze veils the sun. An acrid carbonized taste invades his nostrils.

'What happened here?' he asks.

The Destroyers laugh. 'This place is Fire,' one of them possibly tells him. 'It's folly to distinguish event from content. There is no isolated incident. This is an inherent characteristic.'

'It just burns, all the time?'

'We encourage it.'

Indeed they do. Clay now sees teams of Destroyers at work on the far side of a hummock of ash. The burned area terminates there, but they are increasing it with much the same sort of diligence they showed in extending the ice. Again it is a task performed in several phases. The advance parties go forward into the lush, steaming jungle and interrupt the life-processes of the vegetation with short bursts of hostile attitudes. Secondary marauders follow close behind, sucking all sap and other moisture from the dead trees and shrubs by energetic reversals of the *elan vital*. This creates a hovering mist of disembodied floral juices which lingers a few moments, finally being drawn off by a humidity-gradient deeper in the forest; the temptation to rush from wet to dry is irresistible. Once this fog has gone, the actual pyrogenesis begins. Expert ignifactors walk among the readied tinder. They are in the pyrophoric state: sparks flicker in their crackling gray fur, and electric halos surround them with glowing gaseous envelopes. The sparks fly across the parched gap; the trees take fire; the red blossom reigns. The hot wind blows outward, driving the small animals of the ruined jungle before it. Clay is awed by the efficiency of the process.

'What is your ultimate goal?' he asks.

'To enlarge Fire to planetary size.'

'But surely this conflicts with your program for adding to the territory of Ice.'

'It does,' the Destroyers readily admit.

'How do you reconcile this conflict?'

'Fire grows toward Ice, Ice toward Fire. When the two meet, we will consider a revision of our policies.'

'And in the meanwhile you'll bring as much of the world as possible into one zone or the other.'

'Your grasp of the situation is excellent,' they tell him.

They prod him forward, past the region of cooled ash, into a part of the jungle where the flame has touched within the last few days. His calloused soles nevertheless are aware of the warmth underfoot. The vestiges of mud that still coat his skin acquire an overlayer of soot. His fingers, lubricated by helpful particles of carbon, slide freely against one another. He feels the fierce blast from the newly incinerated sector. Luscious tongues of flame spurt from the kindled ground. Huge blazing limbs occasionally break free and, shrouded in red, topple from the jungle roof, landing with gaudy splashes of squandered energy. The faces of his escorts glaze with pleasure. Clay watches them warily, looking for an opportunity to escape. But they lead him ever deeper into Fire. Now he is unable to perceive anything that has not been burned. He hears the song of flowing air as it glides in to fill new vacuums. He sees mounds of charredness on every side. There is a great pit here, hundreds of yards across, its slopes hairy with black slag and its bottom a fathomless crater: plainly this must be the mouth of hell. Will they hurl him in? He stands with them on the lip of the pit. Figures move far below, trekking resolutely along the crater's wall; they are blackened, irremediably sooty, and it is impossible for him to tell what species they belong to, other than the species of the damned; there must be at least a thousand of them, each by himself, following a narrow track through the sulfurous abyss. Clay pauses, bracing himself, hoping to be able to dart away before the two Destroyers can seize him and thrust him in. But they appear to have forgotten about him. Carefully, like tired mountaineers descending, they pick their way over the side of the pit, and walking sideways, placing one foot below the other, they begin to go down. Standing on the rim under a glaring red sky, he watches their descent. Soon they are no bigger than dogs, and bits of charcoal cling to their sleek fur. They move serenely, never losing their footing, their powerful, agile bodies always poised and perfectly balanced. Now they are lost to view as a gust of gray smoke bursts from the crater wall; when he detects them again, they are very much deeper in the pit, almost to the level of those who shuffle on the lower tracks, and their bodies are thick with cinder. The odor of singed fur reaches him. There is a rumbling in the earth. A wan flame gleams overhead. Where are the Destroyers? Those two dirty monkeys, slogging through the ash down there? Those carbonized squirrels? He no longer knows which they are; they have taken up their orbits among the others and are lost in the crowd. Puffs of heavy smoke conceal them. The crater roils and exhales noxiousness.

He is alone.

He staggers away from the pit and stumbles through a charred field of stiff weeds and thistles and tufted nettle-bunches. The day is ending, and soon the only light is the faint, foul one of the smoking embers. Trees crash in the distance. Enormous boughs land with the soft sighing impact of wood that has burned from the inside out: dream-branches, dream-light. His feet crunch the cinders, which set up a mournful metallic twanging. The universe is cocooned in black haze. He has been transported to the shell of a dead star; he slogs through a cremated wilderness. Where is music, now? Where is beauty? Where is grace? Where is brightness? This forlorn fire-world corrodes his soul and burdens his body with black particles of ash. A scratchy glow, somber and coppery, pokes at his eyes. He tries not to breathe. The breeze changes and blows heat at him. Here the ash is a thick, soft black powder that leaps up in choking puffs. A savage gloom prevails. All the wondrous multicolored splendor of his days with the Skimmers seems only a fable, now, an arcadian echo quickly disappearing in this place of scorchedness. The flames surge!

The trees crackle! He runs this way and that, driven by some fearful drum that thumps against the fabric of the sooty sky. Out! Out! Out! Out!

It is cooler and cleaner here.

The fire must not have been here lately. He feels a certain peace as he passes into this purer zone. Looking back, he sees Gehenna over his shoulder; all the sky is reddened now, and a funnel of flame pours starward. Against this ghastly light the skeleton of the forest maintains its blackness, but trees lean, vines dangle, panicky figures dart to and fro under the raging flames. Clay turns away from the scene. He goes forward until he hears the sound of running water. What disturbing powers does this brook have? He scarcely cares. He must rid himself of filth. Trustingly he commits himself to the water, wading out until he can crouch and be covered to the neck. The water is cool; it comes from some pleasanter place. He scrubs his skin, uprooting muck and ash. He ducks his head and scrapes his gritty eyelids clean. He tugs at his hair to loosen all that clings to it. At last he emerges, refreshed. The water does not seem to have changed him, except that his skin now gleams, lighting his path for him. He walks on. He prays that he has escaped from the Destroyers at last.

20

This place, he suspects, is called Heavy. It must be one more of the districts of discomfort. He has been in it since shortly after dawn. He finds it among the worst of his trials.

There was no warning where it began, no sudden transition, no sense of crossing a boundary. The effect is something that gathered slowly, mounting with each step, oppressing him only a little at first, then more, then much more. Now he finds himself under the full stress of the place. It is a region of thick-stemmed gray shrubs, broad-leaved and low. A cold mist hovers. The general mood is a colorless one here: hue has bled

139

away. And there is the awful pull coming from the ground, that clamp of gravity hanging with inexorable force to every part of him. How much of this can he endure? His balls are drawn so powerfully downward that he thinks of walking with bent knees. His eyelids are leaden. His cheeks sag. His gut droops. His throat is a loosely hanging sac. His bones bend against the strain. What does he weigh here? Eight hundred pounds? Eight thousand? Eight million? Heavy. Heavy. Heavy.

His weight nails his feet flat to the ground. Each time he pulls one up to step forward, he hears the boingg of reverberation as the recoiling planet plops away. He is aware of the arterial blood lying dark and sleepy along the enfeebled catenaries of his chest. He feels a monstrous iron hump riding his shoulders. Yet he walks on. There must be an end to this place.

There is no end.

Halting, he kneels, simply to get his breath, and tears of relief burst forth as some of the stress is lifted from his body's framework. Like drops of quicksilver the slow tears roll on his cheeks and thump into the ground. He will go back, he decides. He will retrace his steps and seek another route.

He attempts to rise.

On the fifth try he does it, rocking himself and levering up on his knuckles, rump in air, intestines yanked groundward, spine popping, neck creaking, up, up, another push: he stands. He gasps. He walks. Finding the path he had used is no difficult task, for there are his footprints, nearly an inch deep on the soft sandy soil. He puts toes to previous heels and walks. But the gravitational drag does not lessen as he retreats from Heavy's center. Quite the contrary: it continues to increase. He estimates that he is halfway back to the beginning of this place, now; even so, he does not experience a gradual stepdown of the force as he hauls himself through the region of the gradual stepup. Mere reversal of direction gains him nothing. Breathing becomes a battle. His ribcage will not lift except under duress; his lungs are stretched like rubber bands. His cheeks hang towards his clavicles. There is a boulder in his throat. A dry, peripheral voice intones, *The intensity of the pull is a function of the duration of your exposure to it, and not of your proximity to the center of the attractive body*. 'Attractive body?' he asks dimly. 'What body? Whose body? But he plays the words back in his mind and understands. The laws of physics make no provision for such phenomena. But he knows that if he remains here much longer, he will be squeezed flat. He will become a film of molecules coating the ground like November frost. He must get away.

It is much worse.

He can no longer remain upright. He has become top-heavy, and the mass of his skull bows his back; his verte-brae slide about, grinding and creaking. He must crawl. He resists the temptation to lie flat and surrender to the awful force.

The sky is being pulled down on top of him. A gray shield lies on his back. His knees are taking root. He crawls. He crawls. He crawls. He crawls.

'Hanmer, help me!' he cries.

His words are leaden. They spill from his mouth and plummet into the ground.

'Ninameen! Ti! Serifice! Someone!'

He crawls.

There is a ghastly pain in his side. He fears that the tip of his intestine will break through his skin. His fingernails too respond to the pull. His bones are separating at the elbows and knees. He crawls. He crawls.

He crawls.

His gullet is stone. His earlobes are stone. His lips are stone. He crawls. His hands sink into the ground. He wrenches them free. He crawls. He is at the end of his resources. He will perish. He will die a slow and hideous death. The gray mantle of the sky is crushing him. He is caught between earth and air. Heavy. Heavy. Heavy. He crawls. He sees only the rough bare soil eight inches from his nose.

He sees water.

He has come to a pond. Smooth gray liquid awaits him. Come to me, it calls. Shed your burden. On my bosom there is no heaviness. But can he haul himself forward the last five feet? His lips touch the water. His chest scrapes the ground.

He puts his cheek to the surface of the pond: it cradles him, a tough and pliable film. He wriggles, gasping, gravity's worm, fighting for survival. Inch. Inch. Inch. Inch. Coldness against his breast. Heave. Pull. Lurch. In. *In.*

He floats.

Is this water? It seems so dense, so tangible. Heavy water? He drifts in it, free of that crushing force, his legs down deep, his arms outspread. His heart thunders. Here I am, but where am I? And how to get from here to there? The longer he bobs here, he suspects, the worse he makes things for himself, since his exposure to the power of Heavy continues all this while, the gravitational impact accumulating, and when he comes forth from the pond he may be smitten into two-dimensionality in one swift swat. But must he come forth? Perhaps there is another way. He sucks breath.

He dives.

He descends easily. The water accepts him. He goes down through layers of sun-dappled grayness until he finds, near the floor of the pond, a rock-lined chasm three times the width of a man. Though his lungs are bursting, he forces himself to enter it. With choppy nervous strokes he propels himself forward. He is traveling horizontally now beneath the surface of the earth. Will the tunnel prove a blind alley? Will he die of drowning in this black pocket, and is that to be preferred to dying of hypergravitation above? He swims. He swims. He swims. He sees a zone of brightness ahead. He goes up.

He emerges.

21

He has come forth at the edge of paradise. The sun is green-haloed for joy; the air is sweet and tender; birds sing; plants have a happy shimmer. After Ice, after Fire, after Heavy, he can barely believe his good fortune. He sees himself sprawled on that friendly carpet of softly humming grass; he sees himself bathed by cheerful warmth; he welcomes the restoration of his driven body. He rushes forward. There is the sound of a jeering sob. He feels a jarring impact and is hurled back. Is there some invisible wall around this Eden? No. No. He is able to enter. But slowly. Very. Slowly. This too is a district of discomfort. This. Too. He has come to Slow.

The air is transparent molasses. He is its prisoner. There will be no running here, only a solemn gliding stride. Knees pumping high, shoulders pivoting, hair floating free – it seems at first a delight. But the pleasure subtly fades. He discovers the discomfort. The busy brain buzzes, sending impatient commands, and the body cannot respond. Thwarted decrees cycle and sour in his synapses. He wishes to stoop to pick up a jeweled blossom, and he halts as abruptly as if his forehead has banged on glass. He hears a sound, and tries to turn, and must fight against the secret grip. Each motion is a challenge; each is a frustration. There is no pain in this place, but there is no freedom either.

Cross it and be quit of it, then? Yes, certainly. But how long will the crossing take? He tries to adapt. He quells all irritable impatiences. He glides. He glides. He glides. He goes up, he comes down, gently, gently, endeavoring to offer no counterresistance to his resistive medium. Despite himself, he chafes. He frets. He wants to hammer against the liquid golden air. He forgets himself and attempts to accelerate, and gets nowhere. He boils. He sweats. All about him is grace and beauty; the trees sway softly, the sky is honey, the light is sublime. But he is held.

And, he realizes, this place also has cumulative power.

He is moving ever more slowly. The tensile air takes a firmer grasp. The viscosity waxes. To move in slow motion loses its last shred of ecstasy: he is frightened. Lifting his leg is now an effort. Moving an elbow is a battle. Taking a step is a war. This is no agonizing squeeze, such as he experienced in Heavy, but it is creeping immobility all the same; painlessly and gently this place is bringing him to a stop. Panic bursts. He tries to accelerate his crossing. This merely multiples his woes. The more he struggles, the more closely he is webbed.

How much farther? Will he stop altogether, a living statue in this elysian field? Step. Step. Step. He strains to pull his feet free. The invisible wall is all about him. It flattens his nose. It smears his lips. He tries to make himself a wedge and cut through the glue. Perhaps walking sideways, shoulder first? It takes him minutes to turn ninety degrees. At last he is in position. He leans against the luminiferous ether. He pushes. He presses. He slows.

He is barely moving at all now.

Exhaustion is near. He is ragged from struggling. His lungs blaze. Muscles plink and blither in his taut cheek . He orders himself to relax: drift forward, float, insinu te yourself through it. Yes. Easy to say. At least it is less strenuous this way, but he is not making much progress. Another approach: simply let yourself fall. Total release of muscular tension. Then pick yourself up and fall again, looping forward and forward and forward until you are out of this place. He tries it, going limp, leaning outward, letting himself tumble dreamily to the ground. It takes him several minutes to complete the drop. Now: gather your legs under your trunk and rise! But it is not so easy. He might just as well be back in Heavy, for there is an invisible shield pressing down on him. He uncoils, slowly and slowly and slowly, not forcing it, just moving with stern determination, and ultimately he is on his feet again. The maneuver has gained him perhaps a yard and has cost him perhaps four minutes. He stands in place a while, gathering strength; at least standing is no strain, not with the environment bracing him on all sides. Try it again, now? Fall and rise? His descent is even less swift. He is a feather falling through asphalt. Down. Down. Down. Lands. Draws feet up. That takes half of forever. Now rise. As before, but less swiftly. What does he look like to an unfettered observer? A drunken inch-worm? He is on his feet. Possibly he has slowed to one one-hundredth of his normal rate of activity. One one-thousandth. He may pass all of eternity crossing this field. He falls again. He rises. He falls. Twilight begins; a coppery tone tinges the grass. He attempts to rise, but this time it is too much of a battle. It occurs to him that the resistance of the atmosphere may not be so great close to the ground. He will try to crawl, as in Heavy. He crawls. The resistance is no less here. He must insert himself into the vacant space just ahead. Every movement is slowed: his eyelids descend in monumental blinks, his lungs expand in marble inhalations. He crawls. He crawls. He crawls. It is night. Will the blaze of the stars melt his stasis? It will not. Silver beams dance in the air. Should the starlight not be refracted by this intractable medium? Is he not capable of detecting that refraction? Will there be an end to this passage? Oh, so slowly, so infinitely slowly, with such snaily slowness. And soon he will not be able to move at all. 'Bril?' he calls hopefully. 'Angelon?' His voice too is slowed; the vibrations break up into lumpy particles that fall away and lose all resonance. 'Ti? Hanmer? Han Mer? Ser I Fice? Ser? I? Fice?' He is forgotten. He is engulfed by Slow.

There is no possibility now of getting to his feet. It would take a million years. He concentrates on crawling. Right hand forward, right knee, left hand, left knee. Feet drag along behind knees. Head is propelled by shoulders. He completes one crawling step. The crooked light of dawn trickles into his eyes. Right hand forward. It is midday; fire overhead. Right knee. The sun sinks. Left hand by dusky dimness. Night and left knee. Under the stars: rest, store up strength. Right hand forward. Dawn. Noon's blaze. Right knee. How much longer? He will have no passport for forever's customshouse. Shadows lengthen. Left hand. Dawn. Left knee. Night. Dawn. Right hand. Twilight. Right knee. Darkness. Dawn. Left hand. Noon. Night. Dawn. Noon. Left knee. Night. Night. Night. Night. He gives up. His pace now verges on the infinitely slow. In this region of velocity the boundary between motion and not-motion is easily breached from one side, but not from the other. Day. Night. Day. Night. Try again to move, perhaps? Slow triumphs. It is a month from systole to diastole. He studies his fingers and, experimentally, lifts them. He has seen mountains do a livelier dance than that. But somehow he is able to advance a fraction of an inch, ever more slowly creeping forward. And then, miraculously, he finds himself at the farther border of Slow.

He has reached the edge of a low bluff. The upper part of his head projects over that edge, permitting him to see a plateau beneath him. It will be a risky drop to that plateau, but what does the chance of a broken bone or two matter against the chance of coming to a complete halt of the life-processes up here? He has no choice. He must fall. Perhaps the influence of Slow will extend slightly over the margin, so that his fall will be gentled. He succeeds in wriggling another few inches forward. Now he can hook his chin over the edge. With that leverage he pulls himself on. His head dangles into the abyss. At what point will his center of balance be past the tipping point, so that his own mass will free him from Slow? He makes little progress for a while. Possibly the cumulative effect has come too close to the critical point: stasis will arrive and he will hang here everlastingly. But he gains another inch. His breast now is past the edge. He slides his right arm forward during several days and nights. And now. And now.

He falls.

22

Indeed Slow tries to retain him. He slithers over the edge in no great rush, and he drops in a leisurely way, not yet restored to the time-scheme of the outer world. Thus it is that he is able to rearrange himself as he descends, jacknifing out of that disturbing head-first dive and turning so that he will land on his haunches, which he judges are better padded to take the impact than his feet. So he lands, with a smart thump on the rump. He bounces a bit and settles back.

He determines quickly that he is unhurt.

He gets rapidly to his feet, glorying in the sensation of swift motion.

He waves his arms. He kicks out his legs. He jumps in the air. He shakes his head.

There is no extreme gravity here, nor is there a mysterious retarding force, nor is the cold unbearable, nor is there furious heat, nor does he feel overtaken by unexpected senility. He is relieved to find these negative qualities absent from his present place. On the other hand, he can discover few positive qualities here. He stands on a broad, featureless plain which seems to consist entirely of a single slab of glossy gray stone, reaching to the horizon. The sky also is gray, and meets the land in such a manner that he cannot determine where one ends and the other begins. There is no vegetation. There is no sign of animal life. There are no hills. There are no valleys. There are no streams. He perceives an unbroken gray expanse, utterly without content.

He understands that he is not yet free of the districts of discomfort. He surmises that he has come to the place known as Empty.

'Hello?' he calls. 'Hey! Anyone? Here! Where?'

No echo responds.

He kneels and puts his hand to the gray stone. It is neither warm nor cool. He tries to scratch it and cannot. He puts his face close, looking for imperfections, and finds none. It might as well be a seamless sheet of plastic. Rising, he looks back, trying to see the plateau on which Slow is, but it is lost in the general grayness. The sun is not apparent. There is nothing at all here. He is surprised to find even molecules of air about him in this matter-free place: why not total void? But he seems to be breathing. He has at least the illusion of it.

He resigns himself to a traverse of Empty.

Never has he known such isolation. He could well be the only object in the universe. Perhaps he has been caught up by the time-flux again, and swept billions of years farther along, to the era of entropy's triumph, when grayness conquers all. Where will he go? How will he pass the time?

It could be worse. He is not crushed here. He is not immobilized. He is in danger of neither freezing nor burning nor aging. Can he not cope with the loneliness? Is the quality of isolation here anything so different from that which he felt while keeping company with Hanmer and friends?

He sets off, walking. Jauntily at first. Let Empty do what it can to him. Somewhere it has to end. He will stumble forth, as he did from Old and Ice and Fire and Heavy and Slow, and perhaps he will undergo some further trial, or perhaps he will rejoin his former companions, but in any event he will not suffer while he goes. After a time, though, he is not so sure. All directions seem the same here, for there are no landmarks to guide him: he could well be moving in muzzy circles, and he cannot hope for sunrise or starlight as clues. He does not even know if he is advancing or if the grayness beneath him is constantly sliding backward while he moves in place. Centuries might pass without a change here. It is a stasis worse than anything that had gripped him in Heavy or Slow, and as the time slips along in unknowable intervals a foggy despair nibbles at his soul. His mood darkens from moment to moment. Now he knows which is the worst. In this sea of nothing he is crushed beyond even a husk. His life swims before his eyes and he sees nothing at all: no incidents, no crises, no relationships, no events, merely a stream of days and weeks and months and years, gray, featureless, empty. This is an infinite kingdom. This is a continuing city. How can he break free? He walks. He walks. He walks. He does not bother to call for help. This is Empty. This is the slough of despond.

Nothing changes.

He attempts to disengage his mind. He will become a mere walking machine, taking stride after stride without thinking, and perhaps he will come to the boundary eventually, and in that way he will cheat this place of its soul-sucking victory. But it is not that easy not to think. Awareness of his isolation hammers at his mind, kindling lusts and regrets and fears and hopes. He walks. Nothing changes. Does the ground slip backward? Does the sky unite with the land? This is Empty. This is Empty. This is the final death of the heart, the negation even of negation.

He seeks ways of defeating the emptiness. He counts his steps, taking fifty paces beginning with his right foot, then bringing his feet together and starting again, fifty with his left foot. He varies the patterns of paces: eighty and sixty, seventy and fifty, ninety and forty, one hundred and thirty, thirty and one hundred. He hops on his right leg a while. He hops on his left leg. He slinks. He drops into a rigid automatic strut. He pauses and rests, squatting on the gray nothingness. He masturbates. He summons memories of his former life as he walks, imagining the faces of schoolmates, teachers, business associates, lovers. He pictures buildings and streets and parks. He lies down and tries to sleep, hoping that when he awakens he will find himself somewhere else, but he has no sleep left. He walks facing backward. He sings. He recites his catechism. He spits. He broadjumps.

It is all no good. The empty grayness continues unbroken, and waves of miasmatic boredom swirl like smog about him. This is the night land, this is the place that is no place, this is the armpit of the universe, this is the home of the sounds of silence. Every device fails him. His mind loosens at the moorings. He is a mechanical man, taking step after step after step after step, getting no nearer to anything.

'I!' he shouts.

'You!'

'We!'

Not even an echo. Not even an echo.

'Christ Jesus our Savior.'

'When in the course of human events!'

'Fuck! Fuck! Fuck!'

Silence. Silence. Silence.

He will not be beaten. He will go on, no matter what befalls him, though the emptiness stretch from here to the universe's nether rim. He has escaped Old and Ice and Fire and Heavy and Slow, and he will escape Empty also, if he must walk a million years through the clinging murk.

'Clay!' he calls.

'Father! Son! Holy Ghost!'

'Hanmer! Ninameen! Ti!'

His words are swallowed by the air. His bravest roars slide through the fabric of nothingness and trickle away. Yet he continues to shout. And stamp his feet. And clap his hands. And shake his fists. And walk. And walk. And walk. His mood wavers. There are moments when he is so burdened with despair that he sinks to his knees, limply despondent, and closes his eyes, and waits for the time of last things to overtake him. But in other moments he knows that the end of his sufferings lies just ahead, if he will only keep his courage high and march pluckily onward: he is the representative of man in these latter days, and must not fail the high trust placed in him. He walks on, searching for signs. Is that a star on the horizon? No. No. Is that a deepening of the texture of the grayness in some places? Perhaps. Is that a darkness settling in? It seems to be. If this place has the capacity to change at all, it has the capacity to end. He will persevere. Already the quality of the grayness seems definitely to have altered. He must have passed some boundary unawares. The reward of faith: delivered from Empty. His joy in his escape is tempered, though, by a difficulty in perceiving his present surroundings. It is terribly dark here. He walks on and on, neither stumbling into trees or boulders nor sensing any change in the smoothness underfoot, and the darkness deepens until it becomes absolute; he begins to wonder if he has truly left Empty behind, or if this merely is Empty's night, coming down after an infinite day. As he continues he starts to understand what has happened. In truth he has made his way out of Empty, but this exercise of his courage and determination has brought him only to the neighboring territory, which is Dark, no better and probably much worse. Here he has the absence of all those things that were absent from Empty, and he had also the absence of light, so that he mourns even the loss of the grayness. Now he tastes true hopelessness. Empty was a garden of delights next to Dark.

He cannot continue the struggle.

He has passed every test; he has survived every hazard. But he has gained nothing and lost a great deal. Now he surrenders. He will not match himself against Dark.

He sits. He locks his arms around his knees. He stares forward and sees nothing.

Why hast thou forsaken me?

If he could have but one sign, he would try to go on: a single drop of rain, the sound of a distant sob, the passage of a bird close by, a flicker of lightning, a moment of stargleam. But the blackness is complete. He is overwhelmed. He stretches out flat, arms outspread, face to the absent sky, eyes open but seeing nothing. He will do nothing more. He will wait.

He remembers a world of content and form and color. The blazing constellations; the wrinkled gray boughs of trees; a frog's golden eye; the insistent verticals of a furious snowstorm; rich red desert sand at sunrise; the deep rose of a nipple against the pinkness of a breast; a goldfish's lightning-bright frightened flicker in a green pool; high-tension towers dark against a summer sky; a gaudy iguana frozen in a thicket of jacaranda; the aurora's dazzling folds; the sharp sparkle of a welder's arc; New Jersey's dying red sunlight splashed on Manhattan's towers; white scum on a blue stream; the Zen garden's smiling pebbles; the ocean; the mountains; the prairies; the foam. To see none of these things again. To stare with keen eyes into a world gone blind. Where are the trees? Where are the frogs? Where are the stars? *Where is the light!*

A million years of empty blackness roll over him.

'Enough,' he murmurs. 'Enough!'

And lightning splits the sky. And Wrong sobs. And a bird whickers past his nose in a flurry of feathers. And rain lashes his belly. And the stars erupt in the night. And all about him spring up the objects of nature, trees and shrubs and flowering plants, rocks and pebbles, chattering insects, veils of moss, yellow lizards, blue lichens, red toadstools. In the lower sky a pinpoint of light appears and widens, becoming a quicksilver glare, a fiery eye, a radiant sun. Celestial choirs sing. The blue sky, cloud-flecked, blankets him. Color oozes from everything. 'I am Hanmer,' a gentle voice says. 'I am love.' Clay sits up. The Skimmers surround him. They are in the female form. Ninameen strokes his arms, saying, 'I am love. I am Ninameen.' Ti plays with his toes, Bril with his hair, Angelon twines a dozen of her fingers around four of his, Serifice brushes her lips against his cheek. 'I am love,' Serifice whispers. 'I am Angelon,' says Angelon. They draw him to his feet. He blinks. The brightness is too strong for him now. 'Where have I been?' he asks them. 'Fire,' says Bril. 'Heavy,' says Hanmer. 'Slow,' says Ninameen. 'Empty,' says Angelon. 'Dark,' says Ti. 'Where am I now?' he asks. 'With us,' they tell him.

'Where have you been?' he asks. And they say, 'We have been swimming in the Well of First Things. We have discussed death with the Interceders. We have visited Mars and Neptune. We have laughed at Wrong. We have taught beauty to the goat-men. We have loved the Destroyers and sung to the Eaters.'

'And now? And now?'

'Now,' says Hanmer, 'we will do the Filling of the Valleys.'

23

They run off with him. He is hard-pressed to keep pace, and fears they will lose him again so soon after finding him, but they never quite get out of his sight, and after a while they halt in a glade of tall triangular trees with ropy, dangling limbs. The sun is high and hot. They loll with him on tightly woven bluish grass under the strange trees. He has been alone so long that he scarcely knows how to talk to them. Finally he says, 'Why didn't you come for me earlier?'

'We thought you were having a good time,' Hanmer replies.

'Are you serious? Yes, you are. But—' Clay shakes his head. 'I was *suffering*.'

'You were learning. You were growing.'

'I was in pain. Both physical and moral.'

Hanmer strokes Clay's thighs. She says, 'Are you sure it was pain?' and becomes male. 'It is time for the Filling of the Valleys now,' he says.

'One of the Five Rites?' Clay asks.

'The fourth of them. The cycle is almost complete. Will you take part?'

Clay shrugs. These Skimmers, their rituals, their obliquenesses, their unpredictabilities, have begun to bother him. He feels a warmth toward them, yet he wonders if it would not be better to go back to Quoi's pond, to the Awaiter's mudbank, even to the tunnel-world, before some Skimmer prank turns out more grim than the last. He brushes the thought away. They are his guides and his friends. He loves them. They love him. He nods. 'What must I do?' he asks.

'Lie back,' Hanmer says. 'Close your eyes. Make yourself receptive.'

He senses that he is about to lose them again. 'Wait,' he says. 'Don't go. Hanmer, can't we get to know each other better? Can't you let me get behind that jumpy facade? What do you really *feel*? What do you think is the purpose of life? Why are we in this place? Are you ever afraid? Are you ever unsure? Hanmer?' He looks up. Hanmer seems insubstantial, well on the way toward invisibility. Nothing left but the grin. 'Hanmer? Don't go, Hanmer. Don't start the rite yet. Talk to me. If you love me, Hanmer, talk to me!'

'Lie back,' Hanmer says. 'Close your eyes. Make yourself receptive.'

Even the grin is gone. Alone again. He does as he is told.

In a moment he feels hands caressing his body. Soft fleshy fingers trace paths of sensuality across his chest, into the hollow between his neck and his shoulder, up his cheeks, down his earlobes. The tender touch traverses his belly and comes to his flaccid penis, which rapidly rises as the fingers grip the stiffening shaft. Other hands toy with his toes. A sly fingertip delicately prods the root of his scrotum. His breathing grows ragged with excitement. He stirs; he gasps; he arches his back. How cunning the hands are! How light their touch! He feels the delicious caress at his thighs, his loins, his face, his hands, his feet, his calves, his forearms, his throat. Hundreds of hands touching him all at once.

Hundreds?

Hanmer, Ninameen, Angelon, Ti, Bril, and Serifice have but a dozen hands among them. He knows that more than a dozen touch him now, many more. Without opening his eyes, he attempts to isolate each zone of contact and count the hands. Impossible. They crawl all over him. Hundreds.

Frightened, he looks. He sees darkness and a cat's-cradle of crisscrossing fibres. He sees no Skimmers above him at all.

Who touches him? He understands. The hands belong to the triangular trees, which have bent low so that their swaying ropy limbs almost reach the ground. Each limb ends in a hand; each hand now roams his skin. Is it obscene to be handled this way by a tree? He dares not try to creep away. He fears that if he makes a move to withdraw, the hands will seize his throat and tighten. Or tug at his limbs. He would not match his tensile strength against the power of these trees. He submits, fearful. He closes his eyes again. He gives himself to the trees.

The unseen hands stroke him, sliding more and more often to his waist, flicking his balls, rubbing his cock. Idiot, he tells himself. Pervert. To let yourself be jerked off by trees. Get up! Brush their filthy hands away! Where do you go from here? Banging ducks? Sucking horny salmon? He churns with resistance. He is tense, tight, angry. They have their nerve. You ought to have your head examined. Where's your sense? Where's your shame? This is dirt. Show some backbone. Hands off! What kind of queer do you think I am? Away! Away! The apogee of the polymorphous. But he does not move. He shuttles sullen thoughts in the circuits of his skull.

'Love. Love. We are love.'

'Who said that?'

'All things are one. Love is all. Give yourself. Give.'

'No.'

His *no* rockets toward the sun. The world shivers. The clouds blush.

'Yes,' the trees say. 'Yes, yes, yes.'

'Yes.'

'Love.'

'Love.'

'Yielding.'

'Yielding.'

'All.'

'All.'

'Warmth.'

'Warmth.'

He is conquered. He will not fight them. He is into the rhythm of the thing now, feet flat against the ground, shoulders grinding the grass, head flung back, back flexed, buttocks in the air, hips moving. He thrusts his inflamed member again and again into the sweet slippery hand that grasps it. He has no shame. He is pleasure's slave. He hears the choirs singing; he hears the sobbing on high, like the tolling of bells, and the sound descends in luminous golden teardrops. He thinks he is coming: muscles tremble and twitch everywhere in his body, even in his lips. But the ecstatic sensation is diffused over his entire skin, and he cannot concentrate it at his middle, and the impulse sweeps by, leaving him fulfilled but uncome. And the excitement mounts again, for the hand (or is it some other hand?) will not let go of him, and he thrusts and thrusts and thrusts again, and again he finds a cosmic transducer at work, spreading the sheerly erotic currents out into something too general to be sexual, and with a sigh he subsides in a haze of miscellaneous delights. And it happens again, but this time he slides past that point of undifferentiated ecstasy and reaches a place of pure sexual fervor, in which his rod has expanded to fill the heavens and burns with a clear brilliant fire. He feels his lips pulling back as passion mounts: with bared teeth and flared nostrils and rolled-up eyeballs he enters his orgasm and sends fiery jets of jissom trumpeting across the cosmos. He subsides. The tree-hands release him. A great gong sounds. As he sinks back, dizzied, sweat-bathed, he realizes that the Filling of the Valleys has begun.

The Skimmers are banishing inequality from the terrestrial sphere. They are making the rough places plain. Every mountain and hill is made low. As the planet turns, they hover above it, pushing ascensions into declensions, loading gulleys with former mesas, demolishing outcroppings, plugging crevices. All imperfections are slain. The world will become a flawless globe, a gleaming white marble dancing in its orbit.

The transformation proceeds rapidly. Already, whole continents have been leveled. Mighty mountain ranges have crumbled and now are distributed elegantly in potholes and basins. Clay is aware of this without leaving his place beneath the trees, and he knows that in some fashion he has helped to provide the energy with which this titanic undertaking is being carried out. But he does nothing himself. He cannot see the Skimmers, but they must be up there, six swirls of force in space, rearranging and editing the Earth. Nothing will withstand their efforts. They who have already tuned the darkness and lifted the sea and opened the Earth will now fill the valleys, and the world will come a phase closer to perfection.

And now they reach the place where he lies.

And out of the east comes a wave of substance that sweeps over him in a fluid flow and cancels the topographic flaws of his present location. He is sealed into the ground. He is entombed again, but it is different from the entombing he knew when he was with the Awaiter, for then he merely rested in the soil, sending out roots, but now he is actually one with it, fused, part of the planet as it turns. He is without form. He is without independent existence. He is a grain of sand. He is a nub of quartz. He is loam. He is basalt. He is bubbling magma.

He is at peace. He thinks it almost might be possible for him to sleep again.

'Hello?' It is Hanmer, calling from far away. 'Clay? Clay? Hello?'

'I am love,' Ninameen says, from a different direction.

Serifice says, 'Death was a little like this. We will all try it together.'

'Hello,' Ti says.

'Hello,' says Bril.

'Hello? Hello? Hello?' It is Angelon.

They show him sunlight sliding over the Earth's pearly perfect surface. They seem to want him to applaud their work. He does not reply. He is trying to sleep.

'Hello,' says Hanmer.

'I am love,' says Ninameen.

'When shall we die?' Serifice asks.

He remains silent. And Wrong sobs, and cracks appear in the flawless skin of the world. And mountains rise. And valleys sink. And ravines yawn. But it does not matter. 'We have carried out the rite,' Hanmer says. 'What happens afterward is not our concern.'

24

Only one of the Five Rites remains to be performed: the Shaping of the Sky. They will not tell him when they plan to do it or what it will be like. Clay imagines that it will be something brassy and apocalyptic, as the climax of such a cycle of transformations should properly be. Perhaps the world will be truly changed. Perhaps a new species of man will come forth. Perhaps the Trump of Trumps will sound. But they laugh his questions away, and tell him to be patient. 'Anticipation is sin,' Hanmer says gravely.

'Sin? What do you know of sin?'

'Oh, we have our sins too,' says Hanmer.

25

There is a bad geological accident and Chaos breaks through into the world. One of Hanmer's birds brings the news; the Skimmers at once must see it. 'Come,' they say. 'It may be very beautiful, who knows?'

They waste no time walking. The distance is too great. Instead they dissolve and soar, taking Clay up with them. In the form of whizzing gray-green streamers they flock across the sky at an altitude of several miles, casting inverted electromagnetic shadows that sparkle and fizz in the ionosphere. Looking down, Clay imagines that he sees the route of his recent wanderings, but he is not sure. From this height everything is mixed together, and even after Ninameen shows him how to adjust his vision he has his doubts. He thinks a certain gray blotch below may be Empty, but Angelon tells him it is a dead meadow, marshy and cluttered. He sees a pinpoint of blackness and asks if it is Dark, and learns that he is just then flying over the Well of First Things. 'What is that?' he asks, and Hanmer laughs, saying, 'It is the brother of what we will see today.'

They cross an ocean. 'I see Floaters!' Brill cries, and Hanmer decides to let Clay have a look. So they flash down some thousands of feet. Just beneath the surface of the water lie a dozen immense whalish beasts, green flecked with gold: each is at least half a mile long, with a single placid eye the size of a stadium at one end, atop the flat skull, and a pair of shaggy mustache-shaped flukes dangling at the other. Clay is allowed to make contact with their minds. It is like wandering through the coral gardens of a tropical sea: shallow but complex. The thoughts of the Floaters are spiky and gnarled, sprawling in baroque configurations over immense territories of the soul, and covered with a rich many-colored crust of anemones and tubeworms, sponges, barnacles, clams, bristleworms, and chitons. In the interstices of this structure crawl beady-eyed many-clawed crabs of the spirit, limuli with long barbed spines, peaceful seahares and periwinkles, urchins, neritas, starfish. A sparkling bed of pure white sand underlies everything. Yet, as he pushes cautiously through the submerged foliage of the Floaters' minds, Clay realizes that it all is alien to him: he can comprehend nothing of what he touches.

'Are these also human?' he asks.

'No,' Hanmer says. 'Merely beasts.'

'How can they sustain themselves at such a great size? How can they find enough food? How can they keep gravity from pulling them apart?'

'Oh, they are often pulled apart,' Hanmer replies. 'It is not important to them. They rejoin afterward.' They swoop still lower, until they hover almost within touching distance of the enormous browsing islands of meat. Several Floaters swivel the golden platters of their eyes at him. 'Don't land on one,' Hanmer cautions. 'You'll sink in.' Clay explores a Floater's tangled mind at closer range, following paths that branch and rebranch, until he is lost in a forest of gently waving sea-fans. Are there sharks? Are there barracuda? Out of the fumbledness comes a single coherent thought, powerful, intense: a vision of a Floater lying dead on a beach, rotting, blackened, covering vast crescents of the shore, attracting scavengers from several continents. The image splinters and Clay is out of his element again, trapped in the incomprehensible corridors of the coral garden. 'We must go,' Hanmer murmurs. 'Are they not strange? Are they not beautiful? We often visit them. We find them refreshing and original.'

'We love animals,' Ninameen observes.

Up they go. They speed across the glassy sea. Shortly the shore appears, an auburn strand fringed by clumsy close-set trees. It is early morning here. This continent has a rough look of buckled terrain and ribbed mountains; the colors Clay sees from above are gray, blue, black, and dark green. They journey inland for some time and make an abrupt descent into a dissected plain. Ahead of them rises a single great mountain, treeless and smooth. A little more than halfway up its eastern face is a tremendous wound, a place where tons of rock have dropped out, creating a passage to the mountain's dim interior. It is by way of this passage that Chaos has staged its breakout.

'I don't understand,' Clay says softly.

'Just look. Just look.'

He looks. What appears to be a river is gushing from the hole in the side of the mountain. But the fluid that pours out is misty and intricate, carrying in itself a multitude of indistinct shapes. Steam accompanies the dark flow. Patterns form and degenerate within this white halo: Clay sees monsters, pyramids, ancient beasts, machines, vegetables, crystals, but nothing lasts. The Skimmers lead him nearer to the event. They sigh and exclaim their pleasure at the sight. What color is the flow? It seems to be a rich blue streaked with filaments of red, but as he reaches that conclusion he discovers a distinct green tinge, and islands of brownness, and a sort of maroon, and then a freshet of colors he is entirely unable to name. Nor can he identify the shapes he sees. Nothing endures. All is in flux. The stream emerges horizontally, spewing over the mountain's flank to cover the rubble marking the place of the wound, and after several hundred yards suddenly tumbles over the side, racing downward in a series of five or eight cataracts until it strikes the ground. At the foot of the mountain a pool has formed where the flow of Chaos lands. Out of that pool, Clay notices, strangenesses are constantly being born: animals that scramble to shore and run wildly away, clumsy tractors and derricks, self-propelled monoliths. No two objects are alike. Unending inventiveness is the rule here. He sees a shining spear of a beast go careening end over end, and a thick snaky worm with luminous antennae, and a walking black barrel, and a dancing fish, and a tunnel with legs. He sees a trio of giant eyes without bodies. He sees two green arms that clutch each other in a desperate and murderous grip. He sees a squadron of marching red eggs. He sees wheels with hands. He sees undulating carpets of singing slime. He sees fertile nails. He sees one-legged spiders. He sees black snowflakes. He sees men without heads. He sees heads without men.

Each of these miracles rushes across the plain as though if it can only get away from the place of its creation swiftly enough it will be permitted to survive. But each meets the same fate as it variously creeps, crawls, hops, rolls, runs, jumps, slides, slithers, tumbles, dances, or leaps out of the steaming pool. It succeeds in covering perhaps half a mile; then it perishes, turning transparent and speedily losing substance, vanishing within moments. The primordial Chaos calls its creatures back. Again and again some particularly dynamic monstrosity strives to escape its doom by streaking madly across the plain. No use. No use. Reality bleeds out of each; the vigorous become as insubstantial as the sluggish. Clay is swept with pity at the sight, for, while some of the things that Chaos spawns are hideous, many are charming, elegant, graceful, delicate, and lovely, and he has hardly begun to appreciate their subtle beauties when they are gone.

The Skimmers stand arm in arm, watching Chaos' prodigality. Clay is in the group, with Ninameen (female) and Hanmer (male) flanking him. No one speaks. High above them, the wound in the mountain bubbles with boiling fertility. He remembers once having seen photographs taken by oceanographers of a newly scooped netful of plankton: a billion tiny jeweled nightmares spilling forth, glistening little beasts with many eyes and many claws and angry bristling tails, aglow with every stripe of the spectrum during their brief fitful moment of life on deck, then fading, sagging, turning to twitching slime. So here, on a larger scale. The outrageous fecundity of Chaos delights and appals him. To what purpose, all these vanishing wonders? From what source, this parade of shortwinded splendors? And what lies within the mountain yet unseen, if these are the ones that emerge?

'How long will this continue?' he asks finally.

'Forever,' says Hanmer. 'Unless someone closes the mountain.'

'And who would do that?' Ninameen asks, laughing.

'Where does everything come from?'

'There are rivers under the world,' says Hanmer. 'This one has broken out. It is the fifth time such a thing has happened in our lifetimes.'

'Few of the other openings remain productive,' Ti points out. 'The channels change.'

'The channels change,' Hanmer agrees.

'But if the channels change,' says Clay helplessly, 'why do you tell me that this flow will continue forever?'

The Skimmers giggle. An elephantine form waddles out of the pool and disappears. Six skulls appear. Two bloody things, dog-shaped and immense, cavort and howl and leap high, and lose dimensionality before they touch ground again. A platoon of glittering insects emerges, moving toward oblivion in flawless formation. A grinning face is visible in a towering burst of gray steam. There is no end to it. Night comes and the whole plain glows. And Chaos still gushes.

26

He senses a spiritual slippage of his position here. Imperceptibly the Skimmers are losing interest in him. Perhaps he bores them, perhaps their attention-span has reached its limit; whyever, they have withdrawn some of their love. Several times he finds himself suspecting that they actually fear him. Or dislike. But he can point to no special incident.

It is harder than ever to engage them in sustained conversation. Topics melt and blend; themes disappear in midthought; laughter and handsprings too often foreclose formal sequences of information-exchange. He still makes attempts to learn things from them, but less often.

'Will I ever return to my own time?'

'What became of the spheroid?'

'How are new Skimmers created?'

'Where is the home of Wrong? Who or what is she?'

'Why have I been brought here?'

'When do you do the Shaping of the Sky?'

'How old is the world?'

'Where is the moon?'

'Why was I allowed to suffer in the districts of discomfort?'

'Will I ever sleep again?'

'Am I dreaming you?'

'Are you dreaming me?'

27

One afternoon they do the Shaping of the Sky, and they do not tell him until later. It has come to that, now. They do not need his participation. They no longer bother to share their important things with him.

He suspects, while it is taking place, that something unusual must be happening. They are camped along the coast of a southern sea: the beach here consists of fine gray pebbles, coated with the pale green bodies of innumerable jellyfish cast up by the tides. He has always loved the sea. Seeing the Skimmers drawing together for some mysterious unspoken conversation, he goes wading, delicately picking his way over the dead coelenterates and wandering out hipdeep into the warm water. Weedy strands sprout from the powdery bottom; shining fish dart past him. He relishes the feel of the gentle waves against his nakedness. He swims. He dives, and is surprised at how long he can remain submerged. He floats, kicking, letting the sun stroke his cheeks.

There should be a mermaid.

He thinks he can see her approaching. Woman to the waist, fish below. Long golden hair, trailing to pale shoulders. White breasts, firm, full, red-tipped. Fiery green scales. Supple tapering tail, strong, sleek, terminating in agile active fins. She comes to him in a lashing of flukes and bobs beside him. 'Yes,' he says. 'An inevitable result of the fractioning of the human form. Nature follows art. What a lovely thing you are!'

She smiles. She pouts. She kisses him. She puts his hands to her breasts. Mammal above, fish below.

'Love me,' she says, voice like the sound of seashells.

'But how? Where's the harbor?' He explores her scales. She laughs. Even a fish has sexual organs. She gives him no aid; his search is in vain. If he were to clasp her, he decides, he would abrade himself. It is some consolation. He releases her. She remains beside him.

'Are there many like you?' he asks. 'A nation in the sea? Are you an ancient form? Evolved naturally, or by means of genetic manipulation?'

'I am not like the others you know,' she tells him.

'In what way?'

'I am unreal,' she says.

He will not accept that. He reaches for her breasts. But she is gone before he touches her. He dives, eyes staring through the sparkling green water, and cannot find her.

When he returns to the surface he becomes aware that some disturbance has begun. The disappearance of the mermaid, the loss of that grace, that innocence, still clouds his soul with ebbing wonder; but once he admits the end of the vision, he sees more clearly what is happening all about. Far out to sea a cluster of turquoise waterspouts stands on the horizon, penetrating the clear air. They whirl; they grow; they shrink;

they move apart and drift back together; they hurl a spray of fishes and weeds toward the land. Turning, facing shore, he sees the canopy of the sky undergoing quick shallow undulations, its belly bouncing earthward and instantly rebounding. Harsh music chimes and groans: the scraping of huge crickets, the pounding of heavy drums. The sun has undergone a spectral shift and yields a distinctly greenish light, and some of the brighter stars are visible. From the south comes a series of swift unresonant explosions: *pop pop pop pop*, as of sudden compressions and decompressions. The earth trembles. Then the music is gone, the waterspouts fall back into the sea, the sun grows yellow, the stars disappear, the sky becomes rigid, the explosion ends. The event is over, having lasted hardly three minutes, and, so far as he can see, nothing has been altered by that brief magical interval of instability.

He hurries to shore.

The six Skimmers sprawl on a grass-tufted dune a hundred yards inland. They look exhausted, limp, like wax mannequins that have come too close to the flame. They all seem to be in some intermediate sexual form – some with breasts and the scrotal bulge, some with wiry male bodies and the pseudo-vaginal slit, but none clearly in this camp or in that. Nor can he readily tell one from another. Their faces are identical. He realizes that he has been distinguishing Hanmer from Ninameen, Angelon from Ti, Bril from Serifice, more by the quality of the spirit they radiate than by any individuality of feature, and now they radiate nothing he can detect. It is possible that these are not his Skimmers at all, but some other group entirely. He is hesitant as he nears them. When his shadow falls on two of them, he draws back, abashed, as though intruding. For a long while he stands beside them. Their eyes are open; but do they see him?

At length he says, fearfully, 'Hanmer? Serifice? Nina—'

'—meen,' she finishes, stirring lazily. 'Did you have a good swim?'

'Strange. Did you see – things that happened?'

'Such as?' The voice is Hanmer's.

'The waterspouts. The drums. The sun. The stars.'

'Oh, that. Nothing much.'

'What was it, though?'

'Side effects.' A yawn. Rolling over; slim back turned to the sun. Clay stands frozen, arms dangling foolishly. Side effects? 'Ninameen?' he says. 'Ti?'

'Are you unhappy?' one of them asks.

'Puzzled.'

'Yes?'

'The waterspouts. The drums. The sun. The stars.'

'These things happen. We completed the cycle.'

'The cycle?'

'The fifth rite. The Shaping of the Sky.'

'Done?'

'Done, and very nicely. And now we rest.' The voice is Hanmer's. 'Come lie beside us. Rest. Rest. Rest. The cycle is complete.'

28

They give him no satisfying answers. They sink back into their stupor. He feels deserted and betrayed. They had let him share in the other four rites; why not this? They have clipped an experience from his life. And they are bored with him. He steps back, angry and ashamed. He has missed something of climactic importance, he believes. He has, perhaps, lost his chance of seizing the key that opens the box that holds the answers to his riddles. And they do not care. And they do not care.

Irritated, he skips up the side of the dune and begins walking swiftly inland.

The sand twists under his feet, slowing him. He notices, also, little highways on the ground, the tracks of flat gray crawling creatures that look something like scorpions. They pay no attention to him, and several times, crossing the path of one, he comes close to treading on it. He is concerned by this: he does not want to step on anything angry. But soon the sand gives way to coarse reddish loam, tufted by fleshy-looking blue plants, and he sees the crawling things no longer.

He wonders where he will go.

He is not sure yet whether his leaving the Skimmers represents a passing pique or a permanent break. His annoyance with them may ebb; after all, they have given him some extraordinary moments. Possibly he soon will want to return to them. On the other hand, he does not wish to force himself on people who find him dull. He may try to assert his independence. He does not seem to need food or shelter in this world, and he imagines that he can find other companions whenever solitary wandering loses its charm. He believes that he has no hope of returning ever to his own era.

Through most of the morning, as he walks on through a hot dry region of flat wastes and inquisitive purple landsnails, he toys with this notion of surviving on his own. The more he considers it, the more attractive it seems to him. Yes. He will explore every continent. He will search for underground cities dating from epochs not long after his. He will try to gather artifacts and other curios of the sons of man. He will test such new powers as he may have acquired under this bloated sun. He will, maybe, try to manufacture a sort of paper, and set down a memoir of his adventure, both for his own enlightenment and to inform others of his kind who may be blown this way. He will converse with such Breathers, Eaters, Destroyers, Awaiters, and Skimmers as he meets, and the Interceders if he happens to find them, and also any being of prior eras cast up here by the whims of the time-flux: goatmen, spheroids, tunnel-dwellers, and such. A kind of ecstasy comes over him as he savors the freedoms of this intended way of life. Yes! Yes! Why not? The joy of it swells like a balloon in his soul, and, balloon-like, it explodes abruptly, sending him reeling to the ground in shock and loneliness.

He regrets leaving the Skimmers.

He must get back to them and ask them to accept him once more.

Strangely confused, he remains where he is, crouching,

knees and elbows in the dirt, rump up, eyes tracking a great globular snail that is crossing in front of him. Inertia knees his back. Up: turn around, find your friends. Slowly he rises. The soft hot breeze lifts the topsoil, coating his sweaty skin. He runs, heedless of the snails all about. Where is the sea? Where are the Skimmers? He follows the sun. Soil gives way to sand, snails to scorpions. He hears the surf. He mounts the dunes. This is the place. He sees his tracks. He remembers Nina-meen's coltish gaiety, Hanmer's solemn helpfulness, Serifice's mystic depths, Ti's beauty, Angelon's alertness, Bril's tenderness. How could he have left them? They are his friends. And more than that: they are part of him, and he, he hopes, part of them. Well on the way to sevenness. We have shared so much. My momentary anger. Childish. My brothers, my sisters: a little careless sometimes, but it is only to be expected; there's such a gulf of time between us. Could I understand a Cro-Magnon's feelings? Could he interpret a tenth of the things I say? But no reason to split because of that. We must be loving. We must be close.

He comes over the last dune, and sees the shore, and finds the marks where the Skimmers had been lying, but he does not see them.

'Hanmer? Serifice? Ti?'

They are nowhere about.

He shouts. He waves. He runs along the beach. He searches for footprints. No use, no use, no use. They have not left a trail. Soaring up, blazing through the stratosphere, off to Saturn in a single rush, perhaps. Forgetting him. Serves him right. He calls their names without hope. He rolls desperately in the sand. He sprints into the water, hoping to find his mermaid, at least. No one. Nothing. Abandoned. Alone.

Your own fault. But now?

He will trek. The Skimmers have rescued him from loneliness before; they may again. Meanwhile he will go his way, and regret his impulsive bolting, and hope. And hope. Once more he walks inland, this time at an angle to his earlier path, for that wasteland of snails was not pleasing to him. If he ever finds his Skimmers again, he resolves, he will never willingly leave their side. The land here is much like the other place, though not quite so hot; a row of low hills intercepts the brunt of the dry wind. There are snails here too, but of a different species, green with crimson whorls. They leave glistening fiery tracks on the bare ground. More than once, accidentally, he steps on one. These snails crack with a sinister hissing sound that leaves him desolate with shame. He studies his footing, placing each step with care, and becomes so obsessed with avoiding the snails that he fails to notice changes in the character of his surroundings. Some trees have appeared: conical snub-topped ones, short, that seem like hybrids of date palms and toadstools. There are a few feeble streams. And, he discovers, he is approaching someone's house.

House?

Since his awakening he has not seen such a thing. But plainly this is a fraud or an illusion, for what he beholds is a two-story brick structure in the 1940 style, with a roof of gray slate shingles and a green holiday wreath hanging on the knocker of the front door. The path that leads to it is nearly paved, and there is a dark asphalted driveway on the left side of the house, although Clay sees neither a garage nor an automobile. The windows are shielded by frilly white draperies. A windowbox in which geraniums are growing sits on one of the second-floor sills.

He laughs. He doubts very much that of all the structures of the former eras of mankind, this house alone would be the one to come intact through myriads of millennia. It is a prank, then. But whose? 'Ninameen?' he asks, in hope. 'Ti?'

The front door opens and a woman emerges.

Of his species. Young but past her true youth. Naked. Short dark hair, adequate breasts, a little wide in the hips unusually good legs. An easy smile; even teeth. Alert, sympathetic eyes. A minor skin blemish here and there. Not a fantasy creature, but a real woman, imperfect, attractive, promising reasonable delights. She looks just a trifle ill at ease in her nudity, but gives the impression that it will not matter much to her once she knows him somewhat better. He pauses a dozen yards from her door.

'Hello,' she says. 'Glad to see you.'

He moistens his lips. He feels odd about being naked, too. 'I didn't expect to find a house out here.'

'I'll bet you didn't.'

'Where'd it come from?'

She shrugs. 'It was here,' she says. 'I came along walking, just as you did, and I found it. Nice and cozy. I suppose they made it for me so I'd feel at home. I mean, I don't really believe that this is an actual house left over from our time, that just happened to be sitting here umpteen million years. Do you?'

He grins. He likes her open manner. She is leaning against the frame of the door, no longer seeming troubled about her bareness in any way; one hand is jauntily perched on her hip. He sees her eyes pass over him in appraisal. He says, 'No. I didn't believe for a minute that the house was genuine. The question now is whether *you* are.'

'Don't I look genuine?'

'So does the house,' he says. 'Where'd you come from?'

'The time-flux took me and put me here,' she tells him. 'And you the same way. Right?'

Her words make him shiver as though he has just inhaled flames. A woman of his own era? Really? In the same instant he feels joy at finding a true companion, and a curious sense of melancholy at the thought that he is no longer unique in this world, that he must share his role in it with her.

'How long have you been here?' he asks.

'Who can tell?'

He accepts the answer. He would have had to give the same.

'What have you done since your awakening?'

'Wandered,' she says. 'Talked with the people. Gone swimming. Wondered.'

'What year was it when you left our world?'

'You ask too may questions,' she says, no sting in her tone. 'And not even the right ones. Like what my name is. Like how I feel about what happened to me. Don't you care what kind of person I am?'

'Sorry.'

'Do you want to come inside?' A flicker of coyness in the invitation, a flicker of wantonness. He asks himself how many millions of years have gone by since he last went to bed with a human woman, a real one. He finds himself thinking of the smell of her skin and the taste of her lips and the sounds she will make when he goes into her. 'Of course,' he says. 'We don't need to get acquainted out here on your doorstep.'

She leads him into the house. As he enters, he hears a quick catching sound, an unmistakable sob. The house is a shell, a three-sided facade; within it is nothing at all. The woman stands a dozen feet in front of him, her back to him, her arms on her hips; her buttocks are full, with a deep dimple above each cheek. 'How do you like it?' she asks. 'Be it ever so humble.' There is a hollow, mechanical tone to her voice. She laughs. 'How do you like it? Be it ever so humble. How do you like it? Be it ever so humble. How do you like it? Be it ever so—' He rushes forward, berserk. 'You said you were real!' he yells. 'You didn't tell me the house was like this?' He has been cheated. He slams his open palms furiously into the small of her back, knocking her to the barren ground. She lies there, sobbing. He attains a robust erection. He will fling himself upon her and mount her as though she were a dog. He drops on top of her; her buttocks are firm cushions for his thighs. She makes a gasping sound and flexes her back slightly, and as he begins to ram his swollen organ home she disappears, sobbing, and he tumbles with a startling splash into a black pond. There is a Breather in its depths, squidlike, huge, patient. *I am Quoi,* it tells him.

What – how—?

You are welcome here.

His body is changing. He sinks toward the depths, sprouting flippers and gills, ridding his chest of air. It is a remarkably convincing illusion, but he does not believe that it is anything more than illusion.

He says, *You are the same entity who was the woman before.*

I am Quoi, insists the Breather. *Come rest beside me. Let us talk of the nature of love. Do you remember? The flowing, the twining, the exchanging—*

—and the merging, Clay says. *You have the jargon down well. Why are you so hostile?*

170

Because I hate being deceived, he replies.

The Breather seems hurt. A long silence comes; Clay wonders if he should apologize. But he waits. The Breather sobs. Clay says finally, *Show me your true form.*

The dark waters roil. Nothing else happens. He begins to believe he has been unjust to the Breather. In that instant the pond disappears and Clay finds himself on land again, facing a hideous colossal Eater. Fangs clash. Eyes blaze.

'No,' Clay says. 'Please. Don't run through the whole repertoire. Will you be a Destroyer next? An Awaiter? I'm not interested in these games.'

The Eater departs. Clay stands alone, nervously digging his toes into the rough soil. A bush in front of him catches fire, and burns with a harsh green flame, but is not consumed. And he hears the sound of sobbing out of the burning bush. A grim joke, he thinks, and a shallow one. He realizes that he is at last in the presence of Wrong.

29

Out of the bush: 'To help you?'

'What good is it?'

'To be kind to a poor wanderer.'

'Your kindness has a price,' he says.

'No. No. You are confused. You don't know me.'

'Then let me know you.'

'There are ways of helping you. I will.'

'What are you?'

'Wrong,' says Wrong.

'A god?'

'A force.'

'Standing in what relation to, say, the Skimmers?'

'I do not know.'

'You do not know.' Clay laughs. He tastes a wall of oily porcelain around his head. 'Thank you. Thank you very much. What do you want?'

'To help you.' Sweetly. Daintily.

'Help me, then. Send me home.'

'You are home.'

He looks about him. He sees only hot scrubby terrain, unfamiliar, bleak, pocked with alien plants. He tries again, feeling nausea climbing. 'Where are my friends?' he asks. 'I speak of the Skimmers Hanmer, Ninameen, Ti, Bril—'

Wrong flashes him a numbingly brilliant vision: the six Skimmers sitting in a solemn circle, faces drawn and skullish, eyes cloudy, a nimbus of doom crackling above them.

'They are preparing to die,' says Wrong. 'The six of them. It will happen soon.'

'No. No. Why?'

'To die?'

'To die, yes. Why?'

'To discover,' Wrong tells him calmly. 'You know, Serifice has been there already. The journey to the first house of Death. But it was not enough for them. It was not satisfying, do you see; it had the wrong texture. Now they look for the real death, the permanent death.'

'For what reason?' he demands. His voice skids awkwardly from pitch to pitch. He feels terribly young.

'To escape.'

'Escaping what? Boredom? Life in eternal summer?'

'That is part of it.'

'And the other part?'

'To escape you,' says sobbing Wrong.

30

He is stunned. His feet grow gnarled roots; his genitals shrivel; tears cut blazing furrows in his cheeks. This dream has turned sour. The fire in the bush is out, leaving bitter white fumes. Eventually he asks, 'What can I do to make them change their minds?'

'Very little, perhaps.' The voice comes from the area of sky just above his head. So Wrong is still with him, somewhere.

Clay turns, twists, sweats, grimaces. 'Why do they want to escape me? Am I so hideous? Am I such a monster?'

A long pause.

At length a reply: 'You do have a taint.'

'A taint?'

'You know that you carry a great cold wad of cruelty and ugliness inside yourself. You know that you are capable of being crude, vindictive, unfaithful, irascible, jealous, greedy, irrationally hostile, and coarse.'

Clay scowls at the sky. He spits at the indictment. Then, more humble, bowing his head, he responds, 'I am only a primitive. I am a mere prehistoric. I didn't ask to come here. I do my best; but I'm made of sleazy stuff, full of grease and impurities. Should I beg pardon for that? It's not my fault I'm imperfect. Anyway, what does that have to do with the Skimmers and their dying?'

'It is difficult to be with you for long,' Wrong explains. 'You carry much pain within you. Despite yourself, you share this burden with your friends. You have shared it with the Skimmers. You have hurt them. You have been more than they could handle, do you see?'

'I've never been aware of that.' Defiantly, not apologetically.

'Exactly,' says Wrong.

Clay kicks at the baked ground. He plucks up a weed and hears it pop and ping. He tosses it sullenly aside. 'They could have told me all this themselves,' he says, wounded. 'They could have helped me rise above myself. They're like gods, aren't they? They could cope with a mere smelly beast out of the past. And you say they'd rather die. How does running away from me—'

'It is not as easy as you think for them to—'

'—into death help them in any way that could possibly—'

'—change you,' Wrong says. 'They too have their limits. So they will go.'

'*Why?*'

Wrong materializes briefly in the form of a cluster of vertical rods encircling an eye and a sob. 'Out of despair,' she says. 'Out of kinship-shock. They recognize you in themselves. You are the ancestor. They did not know your nature until you came, and now that they know it, they fear you, for you are in them. As you are in all of us. So they go to die. They talk of it as a happy adventure. For them it is: but also, as you realize, it is flight.'

Clay's head spins. There is a fiery throbbing in the back of his throat. He is drowning in metaphysics.

He says, summoning all the intensity at his command, 'How can I persuade them not to do this?'

'You keep asking that.'

'I have to know.'

'I have no answer.'

'Who does?' he asks shrilly, with a vulture gnawing at his liver.

'Who does? Who does? Who does?' Wrong's sob becomes a caw. Clay looks around. He cannot find her. A hot, hard rain begins. He is crumbling. He starts to run, but his feet are gone, his shins are shedding, he must clump around on the bones of his knees. He inhales knives. He sweats acid. He sees a mirage: the Skimmers squatting before him, melting, dying, singing, smiling. *How can I prevent it?* he asks. The words scoot around inside his head, whirlpooling, funneling, disappearing with a whoosh into his neck. Left behind is the powdery residue of an answer: *You might try the Interceders.* Vertebrae clacking, Clay nods. The Interceders. The Interceders. 'Where can I find them?' he demands. But of course he is again alone.

31

He comes to a land where there is no color. Pigment has been drained from everything; he stands at the zero wavelength, fearful of sliding down a crack in the spectrum. Even the sun is without hue, and the light that descends is a fiery paradox.

He walks carefully, wondersmitten. He has seen Antarctica's all-devouring whiteness, and he has seen Dark's fanged blackness, but this place is not like those, for, though black may be an absence of color, nothing here is black, and, though white may be a joining of color, nothing here is white. How, then, can he see anything? 'You aren't fooling me,' he says bravely. 'I know a little about the laws of optics. Color is nothing more than the effect on the eye produced by electromagnetic radiation of a certain wavelength. No wavelength, no color; no color, no vision. So how can I see these things?' He studies his colorless hand. He thrusts forth his colorless tongue. He touches the blank petals of a blank-tinged shrub. *If there can be color without physical extension, can there perhaps also be physical extension without color? Surely you would grant that there is such a concept as an absolute color. You can visualize red, can you not, without visualizing a red object? Yes? Yes? Very well. Color in the abstract, unassociated with mass. Now visualize mass without color. Mere form, minus the distraction of resonances in the visual spectrum. Not so easy? Well, yes, but try, my lad, try, try!* Clay screams at the droning, pedantic voice to get out of his head. It goes, with the sound of ripping wires. A colorless lizard spurts across the colorless ground: he sees the event as a clash of textures. There is something quite Japanese, he decides, about this mode of perception. One must depend on pure form for the identification of objects; the world has the subtlety of a symphony in one key, of a garden of black pebbles, of a single shimmering calligraphic stroke. He relishes this narrowing of the palette. He moves with great gentleness, afraid that a misstep will jar the spectrum alive again. How peaceful this is, how deliciously empty. Even sound is colorless. 'Hello,' he calls. 'Hello. Hello. Hello,' and the words are like glass rods, chaste, epicene. 'Can you tell me where I'll find the Interceders?' He sees rocks, trees, birds, flowers, grass, insects. This is the ghost of the world. This is the shadow of a shadow. He could stay here forever, bearing no responsibilities, purifying his mind, cleansing it of the dregs of old colors, all that gritty dried accumulation of fading greens and yellows and ultramarines and scarlets and myrtles and bistres and vermilions and sepias and bronzes and emeralds and carmines and blues and grays and oranges and indigos and purples and lilacs and cerises and golds and slates. To see a blank sunset spread peacefully across the blank sky, to look into the quiet heart of a blank forest, to think blank thoughts while the wind stirs the trembling blank leaves – but he remembers the Skimmers. He goes onward, passing through a sandy strip and a place where millions of bits of glistening glass, smooth-edged by time, sparkle silently all about, and he enters a district of dense brambles where wicked hooked thorns sprout from thick vines that rise and move about. Sighing and hissing, the vines circle him like moody snakes, making tentative passes at his eyes, his genitals, his calves. 'Go on,' he says. 'Cut me, if you have to, and get out of my way!' Still the vines hesitate. He laughs at them. Then one of them whisks across his hip in a quick kiss, drawing beads of blood, and the sprouting droplets too are colorless, at first, but suddenly they tumble into insistent redness; by that startling bright blaze on his skin he learns that he has crossed the boundary. Color leaps out of everything here, obscenely profuse. He is dazzled. His retinas fold and stretch under the barrage. *Red! Orange! Yellow! Green! Blue! Indigo! Violet!* All texture is lost in the spectrum's furious shriek. Parting with colorlessness is sad; he looks back into that place in the hope of catching one last glimpse of its unique bleachedness, but his battered eyes cannot detect that quality of absence now, and, shrugging, he faces the intense bombardment. Those channels of his mind that had been drained of color residue now fill up again like replenished wells, making thirsty sucking noises as the shattering light pours in. How can there be such brilliance? Everything pulsates. Everything radiates. From the core of a single leaf come a thousand gradations of tone. The sky is a prism, and he dances under its awful beam. His own skin is ashiver with undecipherable, cavernous mazes of light and shadow. His eyeballs are adrift, sliding in his skull. He is learning the limits of his senses: if he does not somehow lessen his receptivity, he will overload and burn out. Close your eyes! Close your eyes! *Close your eyes!* 'To close the eyes is to die a little,' he answers fiercely, and stares at the sun. Go! Do your worst! He flings his arms wide. He hammers his heels into the warm moist yielding soil. His manhood rises. He drinks the many-colored radiation and, gasping, finds room for it within, and pumps his hips and clenches his fists, and defies the giant prism to destroy him. And triumphs. And absorbs. And gluts himself on reds and greens. And enters ecstasy, sending his seed spurting in a soaring splendid arc; it flashes purple and blue and gold as it travels, and where it lands it creates fiery homunculi clad in winding folds of flame. He laughs. A cloud passes in front of the sun. He kneels and stares into a universe he finds within a single oily drop of water and a thick round blue leaf. All the tiny creatures, suffering, loving, rising, falling, striving, losing: he sends them his blessing. 'Where are the Interceders?' he whispers. 'My friends are in danger. Where? Where? Where?' The colors fade. The world returns to its expected hues. Clay is assailed by doubts, phantoms, hags, harpies, phobias, fogs, infirmities, decays, taboos, rigidities, bogies, infections, impotences, pharisees, extremes of temperature, and spiritual distress. He wades through these miasmas as though through an ocean of sewage, emerging coated with slime that withers and falls away at the first touch of the sun. Ahead of him lies a sweeping rocky headland, a single spectacular scarp that sprouts from a commonplace plain and shoots rocketlike to a height of hundreds of feet, forming a long flat-topped pedestal dominating a somber landscape. Nestling at the base of this promontory, far across the plain, are the ruins of some immense building, some great stone structure that even in its disheveled state retains extraordinary power and presence: it is a columned edifice in the classical mode, gray and stolid and self-assured, fitted by style and grandeur to have been the supreme museum of Earth, the repository of all that has ever been achieved on this planet. Many of its columns are smashed, the mighty portal hangs from its marble hinges, its pediments are in disarray, its lofty windows gape. Yet Clay realizes that he has come upon no minor work, but rather a place of enduring significance, and he feels a strange confidence that here he will encounter those whom he has sought. He creeps towards the colossal structure as though he were an ant.

32

He comes upon the building from the west. The side that faces him is a massive unbroken sheet of gray granite, unpunctured by windows, almost untouched by time; only the disruption of the row of ornamental reliefs near the roofline indicates the injuries the years have done. A scaly green lichen clings to the roughnesses of the wall, creating patterns of choked color, continents sprouting on the ancient stone. Weeds have begun to straggle across the portico. The door is gone, but, staring through it, he sees only darkness inside the building. Cautiously he begins to walk around it. As he proceeds, legions of chittering insects fall warily silent, dropping out of the rustling chorus in groups with each step he takes. There are scratchy brown thistles nearly half his height; they jab their ugly brushes at his naked body. Now he stands before the building. He has not realized, from afar, just how tall it is; it rises and rises and rises, claiming so much of the sky that he wonders why it does not topple from sheer giddiness. Yet it is no skyscraper, phallic in verticality. It has the blocky bulk of a proper museum. Nine huge marble steps lead to its main entrance, each step running the width of the building. Clay mounts the first step and the second, and then, losing his courage, decides to complete his inspection of the exterior first.

He follows a pockmarked step eastward and turns the corner. This end is dismal. The columns are shattered stumps, jagged as broken teeth. Green strangling vines lash them together. The pediments have fallen altogether, and fragments of masterpieces, half-buried, jut from the ground. He tries to discover what scenes had been carved there, and, going close to one cohesive sculptured mass, beholds the images of beasts

178

more strange than any he has yet seen, things with bulging eyes and grillwork mouths and rasping skins, monstrosities out of a nightmare's nightmares; with cool fascination he examines this gallery of horrors until, taking it with the impact of an icicle in his ear, he comes upon what surely is his own portrait, delicately carved in gleaming stone. He flees. Turning the corner, he attempts to tour the building's rear; but it has been set close against the sheltering promontory, and there is no fourth side. He retraces his steps, avoiding a sight of that dreadful pediment, and returns to the front face. Shall he go inside now? He backs off, considering. The terraced roof is, he sees, overgrown with vegetation that has taken root in the fissures and niches of the entablature's intricate cornice. A whole forest lives up there: frizzy under-brush, clumps of gay flowering shrubs, streamers of glossy ivy, great-boled trees that must have seen many centuries. Even the largest of the trees, though, is dwarfed by the grand sweep of the roof itself, so that the whole tangled mass of undisciplined growth seems like nothing more than a trifling layer of casual accretions. Birds and animals nest in the trees. He watches a speckled yellow serpent writhe in a proprietorial way along the friezes. Enough. He will go in. He advances to the steps.

Cobwebs, of course, hang across the entrance. When he slaps at them to sweep them away, they pull free with a faint whispering chiming clang, like fine strands of metal rubbing one against another. He goes in, breathing mustiness. He enters a vestibule, narrow, dark, and deep, with clammy onyx walls. A high doorway confronts him. The door is of pink alabaster, warmly glowing, engraved with linear symbols that flow and bend and mingle in disturbing patterns of metamorphosis. He puts forth a finger and hesitantly touches the door; instantly it pivots inward, admitting him to a courtyard that seems to occupy the entire central section of the building. A shaft of mote-flecked sunlight thrusts diagonally downward from an immense wound, invisible from outside, in the ceiling. The atmosphere in here is dank and coldly humid, like that of some vast subterranean cistern. His eyes slowly acclimate themselves to the dimness that prevails everywhere but at the place where that column of brightness strikes. He sees eroded statuary in careless corners, piled over with mud. Mud carpets the floor; by his third step inward he is ankle-deep in chilly ooze, and thinking twice about continuing. There is an unpleasant acrid odor, as of a sea of walrus urine. He feels the closeness of animal life. He senses metabolizing mass. And, belatedly, he becomes aware of the quintet of gigantic creatures, motionless and awesome, on the courtyard's farther side.

They could almost be dinosaurs. Certainly they have the proper dimensions, and more. The two in the middle must be more than a hundred feet long; the two that flank them are nearly as huge, and the small one on the left end is larger than the largest elephant. What he can see of their skin is reptilian: shining, scaly, armored, dark. They sit in a curiously human posture, uncomfortable and incongruous, heads upright, arms dangling, spine bent to form a base, tails curled underneath, legs jutting out in front. The bodies that they arrange in this fashion are elongated saurian ones, with thick short limbs and long tapering tails. Folds of flesh descend in multiple wrinkles over their bellies and chests. The shapes of their heads vary: one has a tremendously protuberant snout, thrusting forward forty or fifty feet, and one is a spherical horned dome, and one is tiny, at the end of a serpentine neck, and one is neckless and immense, and one is toothy, like an Eater's, but incredibly larger. All five creatures are embedded in thick black mud, which nearly covers one to the shoulders, barely soils another, and mires the rest to intermediate degrees. There seems no way for these monsters to have entered the ruined building through any of its openings; was it, then, erected around them, as a shrine? There they sit, side by side, infinitely patient, emitting stinks and inner rumbles, studying him with dim interest like a row of bored judges who have passed into the weariness that transcends all fatigues. They look familiar to him: Ninameen, once, in a moment of panic, flashed him a vision of them. Clay realizes that they are the Interceders, the ultimate hierarchs of mankind, to whose authority all seem to defer. He is frightened. Of all the varieties of humanity he has encountered, these mud-dwellers within the wrecked stone temple are the least comprehensible. They are at once imperial and loathsome. The silence remains unbroken, but he seems to hear the ringing of noiseless trumpets and the crack of trombones; next will come the mighty roar of the chorus. Shall he kneel? Shall he smear himself with mud in ritual abasement? He dares not go closer. Those five great heads move slowly to and fro, rubbing in the sticky mud, and he knows it would take no strenuous effort for one of them to lean forward a bit and snap him up. A tender morsel, bearing the archaic genes. How did this happen? How did you come forth from my loins? He trembles. He is devastated by fear. In his terror he regards his own skeleton as an alien intruder within his flesh. The Interceders snort and mumble. One of them, the long-snouted one, pushes up a furrow of muck with the curve of its chin and delivers a deep, slow roar that brings a slab of stone down into the courtyard. 'My name is Clay,' he says timidly. Has he ever spoken to such implausibilities before? 'I am of the human race. I was brought here by the time-flux long ago, and have had – many experiences – have – had – I was brought here—' He cannot remain standing. He crouches, squats, dips forward, knees in the cold slippery mud. The Interceders have taken no notice of him. 'Will you – help – me? I have six friends who have chosen to die.' His rigid fingers slide into the mud. A stream of hot urine runs down his right thigh. His teeth chatter. The biggest of the Interceders lifts its head and swings it slowly from side to side above him; Clay looks up doubtfully, expecting to be seized. The head withdraws. A sluggish tail coils and loosens. 'Go anywhere,' Clay murmurs. 'Do anything. Die in their place, if necessary. To change their decision. How? What? If?' Can he reach the Interceders' minds? He gropes toward them, but touches nothing; the Interceders have not deigned to open to him. Do they have minds? Are they in fact human, as human is now defined? His fear of them evaporates. 'Nothing but stupid mountains of meat,' he says. 'Buried alive, rotting neck-deep in mud. Ugly! Inflated! Empty!' The Interceders now bellow in unison; the ponderous walls of the building shake; another slab falls. He shrinks from them, throwing one hand across his forehead. They keep up their roaring. 'No!' he tells them. 'I didn't mean – I only wanted to – please – my friends, my friends, my poor friends—' He can barely stand the thin, cutting smell of their rage, and he thinks the cries of the Interceders will bring the ruined museum to its final calamity. But he forces himself to remain. 'I submit to your will,' he declares, and waits. They grow calm. They return to their earlier aloofness, ignoring him, rooting in the mud with tongues and teeth. He smiles uncertainly. He kneels again. He prostrates himself fully. 'Why must the Skimmers die?' he asks. 'To prevent. To persuade. To sacrifice on behalf of.' He hears the rolling of distant drums, a noble and in-spiring sound – or is it thunder, or are the Interceders releasing monstrous farts? Without rising, he wriggles towards the door, feet first. What to do? What to do? He finds the answer in his mind, and, since it could not have been there a few minutes ago, the Interceders must have placed it there. He is to go to the Well of First Things; he is to yield; he is to accept everything. There is no other way. He rises and thanks the Interceders. They snarl and growl. Their dim eyes look elsewhere. He is dismissed. He stumbles out of the building, into a dismal dusk.

33

The little animals help him when morning dances down. In twos and threes they come to his side. 'This way,' they tell him softly, and, 'This way,' and again, 'This way,' and he follows them, trustingly, blithely, happy to be out of the hands of apparitions for a while. His guides are simple beasts; birds, bats, lizards, toads, serpents, furry creatures of various sorts. None is of a species he can remember from the old days, but there are correspondences, each seems to fill an equivalent evolutionary notch: this might be a rabbit, this a badger, this an iguana, this a sparrow, this a tanager, this a chipmunk. But all changed and made wondrous. The toad has a crescent of many jeweled eyes; the bat has luminous wings that precede themselves with a delicate violet glow; the rabbit, though cuddly, carries a spiked tail, just in case. And they speak his language, or he theirs. 'Follow us, follow us, follow us! This way! To the Well! To the Well!' He follows.

A sweet journey, but a long one. He puts his back to the grim Interceders and walks till noon, through a land that grows even more tender – pliable trees, frilly leaves, fuzzy flowers, balmy perfumes, pastel hues, the tinkle of airy music on the horizon. Unreal, a playland. Up and down gentle hills, soft as breasts. Wading through warm shallow ponds in which no monsters lurk. 'This way! This way!' Even resting is lyrical: he sits under a vertical sun at the entrance to a grand valley that spreads for manicured leagues toward a probable river. When he chooses to continue, the animals sing him onward. In the valley the grass is close-knit and thick, each stem having a plastic firmness of texture; as he puts a foot down, the blades lean away from it, and hold their angle for ten minutes or more, so that he can trace his track across the meadow by looking back at the slowly closing gaps in the green carpet.

The sun climbs. This is the warmest day yet, though the heat is tempered by the softness of the air. 'Swim here,' an amphibious twelve-legger tells him. 'Climb this rock for the view,' insists a fragrant conical animal. 'Don't overlook these flowers,' says a purple mole, lifting a flat stone with its long nose to reveal a miniature garden of exquisite rosettes. Kindly beasts. A delight to travel with them. 'Is it far to the Well?' he asks, halting for the night. 'There is only one route,' a prickly salamander says, wriggling into a tiny cave.

He decides that he is traveling southeast, though he has forgotten which continent this is or where he may be in relation to the place of his awakening. On the fourth day the landscape begins to lose its coy, sugary tone. The sweetness bleeds from it rapidly, and the character of the route undergoes a complete change in a single hour. The yellow toadstools, the grinning squirrels, the talk pink caterpillars, the trees with golden gumdrops, are seen no more: he enters into a vast and stark savanna patrolled by immense herds of big game.

To the limits of his vision sprawl flat fields of knee-high

coppery grass on which bulky beasts graze. In the foreground are stocky quadrupeds, like short-faced horses, whose hides are dappled with shifting patterns of red and gold; they look like ten thousand sunsets at large in the plain. Pausing in their munching, they give him cold eyes. He discovers that his little guides have faded from sight. 'I seek the Well of First Things,' he explains, and the red-and-gold munchers snort and toss their hooves and glare toward the horizon. So he goes on. In a glade of spiky gray trees he finds a troop of long-necked browsers at least forty feet high. They fill the ecological niche of giraffes, he realizes, but these fellows must have been brought forth in one of evolution's moments of indigestion, for they are as graceless as a giraffe is noble: absurdly, they have only three legs, arranged in an isosceles way as props for a sack of a body out of which, in the center, erupts the endless neck. The legs are rigid and angular, with three sets of equidistant knees between gaskin and fetlock, but the neck is serpentinely flexible, and the contrast between the knobbiness below and the ropiness above is an unnatural vulgarity of design. The heads of these animals are little more than gigantic mouths, topped with dim uneasy eyes. Diligently they rip greasy leaves from the towering trees on which they feed, and as they pass on, new leaves spring forth with indecent swiftness. The animals take no heed of Clay. In a fit of abstract curiosity he tries to panic them with shouts, merely to see how a three-legged beast would manage to run, but the titans continue with their meal. 'Run!' Clay yells. 'Run!' One of the biggest lifts its head, peers at him a moment, and – unmistakably – laughs. Clay decides to continue. He passes a squat tank-shaped thing like a double rhinoceros, with an armored hide; he sees, in the pocket of the grassland beyond a gentle rise, a herd of tens of thousands of broad-nosed animals that might be pigs with antelopes' legs; he wonders where the lions are, and finds them at the far side of the herd, three slim, tawny carnivores with harsh wedge-shaped heads, fierce forearms, and powerful kangaroo-like hind legs. They lie growling and bloody-mouthed in a heap of gnawed ribs. A mother and two cubs: they lift their heads and show Clay bright eyes like red stars, with odd twitching antennae just above them, but they show no desire to attack him. He circles warily wide. Keeping the afternoon's light on his shoulders, he plods diligently through a succession of fauna, and, dulled by the surfeit of strangeness, he hardly tries to analyze what he sees, but calls this great pile of meat an elephant, and those frisky blurs gazelles, and this streaking bolt of toothiness a cheetah, and that comic perambulation of lumps a warthog, though conscience tells him the parallels are inexact. When darkness comes he camps at the foot of a dwarf mountain, a ship-sized pile of rock perhaps eighty feet high that rises precipitously from the plain, and sits impatiently through the night, trying to outstare the glistening eyes that peer at him.

The next day he leaves the savanna behind. The terrain becomes more apocalyptic. This is a zone of thermal disturbances; geysers spout, warm springs bubble, and much of the ground is scalded into moist brown bareness. He examines chalky terraces, like clustered bathtubs, that hold algae-corrupted sheets of water, red and green and blue and mixtures thereof. He pauses to watch black steam spout hundreds of feet from a purse-shaped fumarole. He crosses a dead plateau of glassy sediments, zig-zagging to avoid the vents that release foul rotting gases. Here, again, he acquires small guides: 'Is this the path to the Well of First Things?' he asks an owlish thing hooked to a limb of a withered tree, and it tells him to keep going. A many-legged rosy slitherer conducts him graciously through an intricate array of thermal pools that gurgle and heave and moan and seem about to deluge him with boiling fluids. The sky here is gray-blue with smoke even at midday. The air has a chemical reek. His skin is quickly covered with dark exhalations; when he runs his fingernails across his chest, he leaves tracks. 'Can I bathe here?' he asks a friendly hopping thing, pointing with his toes at a pond from which no vapors rise. 'Not wise,' the hopper says. 'Not wise, not wise, not wise!' and the pond instantly flushes a dangerous scarlet as if acid has come flooding into it from a trapdoor in its belly. He remains coated.

A shelf of blunt rock closes in this place of geysers at its farther end, stretching off to north and south. Scaling it calls for some skill, for it rises almost vertically and there are many loose boulders, but he manages to clamber up, preferring that to the endless-looking detour around its sides. He is relieved to see that the slope is much more gentle on the cliff's other face. As he descends, he looks outward into the zone ahead, and beholds a sight so extraordinary that he knows he has reached his destination. By a deep light, as though from a filtered sun, he views a completely naked flatland: not a bush, not a tree, not a rock, only a level span of land running from the extreme left to the extreme right, and curving away from him over the belly of the world. The soil, so Martianly barren, is brick-red. Straight ahead, at least several days' march into the plain, there is a column of light that bursts from the ground and rises with perfect straightness, like a great marble pillar, losing its upper end in the lofty atmosphere. This column must be half a mile in width, Clay guesses. It has the sheen of polished stone, yet he is certain that it is no material substance but rather an upwelling of sheer energy. Motion is evident within its depths; huge sectors of it swirl, clash, tangle, blend. Colors shift randomly, now red predominating, now blue, now green, now brown. Some areas of the column appear more dense in texture than others. Sparks often detach themselves and flutter off to perish. Above, the uncertain summit of the column blends with the clouds, darkening and staining them. He can hear a hissing, crackling sound, as of an electric discharge. That single mighty rod of brilliance in the midst of this forlorn plain overwhelms him. It is a scepter of power; it is a focus of change and creation; it is an axis of might on which the entire planet could spin. He narrows his eyes to screen some of the splendor. 'The Well of First Things?' he asks. But he has no guide, and must answer himself, with 'Yes,' and 'Yes,' and 'Yes' again. This is the place. He stumbles forward. He yields. He accepts everything. He will give himself to the Well.

He stands on the Well's lip. A broad calcified rim, bone-white, porcelain-smooth; a few yards in front of him the column of light surges upward from an abyss beyond measure. This close, he is surprised not to feel more of an effect. There is warmth, and a certain electrical dryness in the air, and maybe the snap of ozone; but for all that rushing force blasting out of the ground he expects prodigies of sensation, and does not get them. The column seems intangible, like the beam of a colossal search-light. He takes another step toward it. He is moving slowly, but not out of fear or hesitation, for his path now is resolved; before he goes in, he wants to understand as much as is possible. The rim slopes away from him, heading down. He is still on the flat part, but as he shuffles forward his big toes touch the beginning of the curve. Nothing more than a trifling shift in his weight will send him toppling in. He is willing. I am the sacrifice. I am the scapegoat. I am the tool of redemption. He will go. He begins to lean. He spreads his arms wide; he opens his hands, palms toward the light. The skin of the column seems silvery, mirror-bright: he sees his own approaching face, eyes dark and dark-ringed, lips tightly pressed. The tip of his nose touches the column. He sinks through it; he falls; he is weight-less; he is ecstatic. His descent ceases within moments. Like a speck of cinder caught in an updraft, he is whirled toward the top of the column, drifting freely, tossed about, soaring beyond all control. His physical body is dissolving. What remains is a mere net of electrical pulses. He no longer knows whether he is rising or falling. He is within the column, passing from zones of great density to zones of lightness, changing levels at the whim of the force that holds him, and he knows only that he spins and swirls and shuttles in the blazing effluent of the Well of First Things.

There are shapes within the column.

Some are strange. Many are familiar. These are the templates of creation. He discerns the outlines of cats, dogs, seals, snakes, deer, cattle, pigs, sheep, raccoons, otters, bison, bears, camels, and other creatures of the remote past. They have had their chance; they are gone; they remain here only in essence, in residue. Then he sees the figures of the beasts of this era, all those he had encountered on the savanna, and scores of others that he has met in his journey. Mixed with them are misty replicas of bizarre new things. They flutter by him madly and vanish, leaving him with a mouth full of sandy questions. Are they life-forms yet to come? Are they animals that have come and gone between his era and this? Are they the lumpy fauna of the Miocene and the Oligocene and the Eocene, forgotten even in his own day? He is tossed in a phantasmagoric bestiary, hurled past hooves and horns and gaping jaws. Here is the fount of invention. Here is the spring of life. How does one tell the dream from the undream? What are these chimeras, sphinxes, gorgons, basilisks, gryphons, krakens, hippogriffs, bandersnatches, jabberwocks, orcs, this whole horde of desperate marvels? Of time past? Of time yet unarrived? The turbulent dreams, nothing more, of the Fountain of Life?

'Mankind,' Clay whispers. 'What of mankind here?'

He sees all. Out of the mists come dark figures, firehaloed, creation's puppets. Is this brown ape the owner of the Java skullcap? Are these capering clowns the australopithecines? What are you, massive giant: the man of Heidelberg? He wishes he had studied more. Something with a flat crested head nears him; he meets its gaze, and finds only feeble kinship. Then, fair-haired and shaggy, comes an unmistakable Neanderthal, and seizes him and peers eye to eye, and gives off so terrible an aura of intelligence and thwarted striving that Clay becomes a burst of flaming tears strung across the abyss. Who are these others? The unknown simian forebears. The painters in the caves. The gnawers of bones above Peking. The primordial lemurs. The patient scuffers of the fertile Palestinian soil. The builders of walls. The wielders of handaxes. The chippers of flint. The hunters of mastodons. The gibbering sorcerers, painted yellow and red. The scribes. The pharaohs. The astronomers. The abyss spews humanity faster than he can assimilate what he sees. Every species, every false trail, every dangler from the crowded tree. 'I am mankind,' says the Neanderthal, and 'I am mankind,' the Pithecanthropus insists, and the fur-clad artist of the caves cries, 'I am mankind,' and the lithe Australopithecus calls, 'I am mankind,' and the king from his throne says, 'I am mankind,' and the priest in his temple says, 'I am mankind,' and the astronaut in his capsule says, 'I am mankind,' and they hurtle past Clay and are lost in the shaft of brilliant light, and he whispers, 'I am mankind' to their backs.

And what are these things that come now?

Spheroids in cages, and turd-spattered goat-men, and things with gills, and beings that are all eye, and many more, and they are mankind too. He calls out. He roasts and bakes amid the history of the race. 'We are the changed ones,' they tell him. 'We are the ones who devised our own destinies. Who bears witness for us? Who assumes the responsibility?'

'I bear witness,' he replies. 'I assume responsibility.'

They pour forth inexhaustibly, a million million forms, all of them claiming humanity. What can he do? He weeps. He stretches forth his hands. He blesses them. How was such prodigality of design ever permitted to a single race? Why were these transformations tolerated? 'Will you forgive us our metamorphoses?' they call out to him, and he forgives them, and the legion of the changed ones goes past.

'And we are the sons of man,' proclaim those who next emerge.

Breathers. Eaters. Destroyers. Awaiters. Interceders. Skimmers. All the denizens of this present age. Clay looks close at the Skimmers, hoping to recognize one of his, but they are unfamiliar to him, and drift by. A monstrous Interceder passes him, lost in dreams of mud. A phalanx of Destroyers. Three unmoving Awaiters. Clay senses, as he has never before sensed, the full span of time through which he has passed; for now he is caught in a sea of shapes, prehuman and human and posthuman, coming and going, smothering him, demanding comfort from him, seeking redemption, chattering, laughing, weeping—

'Hanmer?' he calls. 'Serifice? Ti? Brill? Angelon? Ninameen?'

He sees them. They lurk near the root of the column, deep in the ground. He cannot reach them. They are swathed in faded colors, and their figures are indistinct. He struggles downward, but again and again is buoyed up. After a time they vanish. Are they dead? Can they be saved? He understands what he must do. He will experience the whole history of his race. He will take all the world's anguish into himself. He will give himself up so that his Skimmers will not die. He floats freely through the column, passing without hindrance from era to era, now confronting a tormented Neanderthal, now a smug Destroyer, now a spheroid, now a goat. 'Give me your sorrows,' he whispers. 'Give me your failures and your errors and your fears. Give me your boredom. Give me your loneliness.' They give. He writhes. He has never known such pain. His soul is a white sheet of agony. Yet there is a core of strength within it that he had not known was there. He drains the sufferings of the millennia; he dispenses redemption in crimson spurts. Working his way downward, offering himself freely to men of all species, he reaches the barrier that separates him from the six Skimmers, and gently presses against it, rebounding, returning, rebounding, returning, finally penetrating. Snowflake-light he descends to them. 'Look at me,' he murmurs. 'How imperfect I am, eh? How coarse. How vile. But consider the potential. You realize that I am you, don't you? Just as these chinless apes are me. And the Interceders, the Neanderthals, the spheroids, the Destroyers – all one, all streams of the same river. Why deny it? Why turn away? Look at me. Look at me. I am Clay. I am love.' He takes their hands. They smile. They come nearer to him. He perceives their true forms, neither female nor male; he sees the glow within them. 'We traveled a long way together,' he says. 'But your journey doesn't end here.' He points upward into the shaft of cold fire, showing them the unborn shapes that hover, the sons of the sons of man. 'Give me your fear. Give me your hate. Give me your doubt. And go. And return to your world. And go. And go.' He embraces them. 'I am Clay. I am love.' The pain is rising within him; he feels a white pinpoint of anguish in the middle of his skull. 'I am Hanmer,' they say to him. 'I am Ninameen.' 'I am Ti.' 'I am Bril.' 'I am Angelon.' 'I am Serifice.' And he says, 'Do you need death? What can you learn from it? Let me. Let me. My time is over; yours is still beginning.' He reaches into them and sees that they throb with pity and love. Good. Good. He gestures; they rise; high above him, they turn, dance in the blazing light, blow him kisses. Farewell. Farewell. We love you. 'Dreams end,' Ti once told him. Ending now. Going out on a tide of love. The Skimmers will not die. About him, colors wheel and spiral, and he sees the fiery nebulae, he sees the colliding galaxies, he sees the golden arch of mankind curving out of time past and disappearing, agleam, in time yet to come. And all of the men and sons of man are walking it now, Eaters, Destroyers, spheroids, goats, Hanmer, Ninameen, Ti, Interceders, Neanderthals, Bril, Serifice, Angelon, everyone, the delegates of the eons, heading toward that shimmering spectrum which he after all will not reach. Not now. Not ever. Dreams end. He bears their burdens. He floats up through the abyss, coming now to the rim of the Well. There he pauses, looking back at the splendor of creation's might, seeing a vision of what will one day emerge, to which this is mere prologue. The pain is gone from him now. He carries himself well. He is man, and he is Son of Man, and the dream is over. He climbs from the pit. He walks slowly outward on the porcelain rim. The beasts have assembled in that barren plain. So, too, have all his friends. He smiles. He lies down. At last he sleeps. At last. He sleeps.

Take ye heed, watch and pray: for ye know not when the time is.

For the Son of man is as a man taking a far journey, who left his house, and gave authority to his servants, and to every man his work, and commanded the porter to watch.

Watch ye therefore: for ye know not when the master of the house cometh, at even, or at midnight, or at the cock-crowing, or in the morning:

Lest coming suddenly he find you sleeping.

And what I say unto you I say unto all, Watch.

– Mark 13:33–37